The Fourth Prophecy...

Needle's mind boggled. He groped vainly at comprehension. He held the ancient prophecy in his trembling hands, standing stock still and silent as his thoughts raced and the fury of thunder raged in his ears. Brynn and Mallet flanked him, craning their necks as they stared. The two friends trying to cope with the impossible words.

"This... this can't be," Brynn mumbled, breaking the sound of the water lapping against the side of the boat. "How old is this?"

PROPHECIES OF OLD
Cult of Yex Saga: Part II

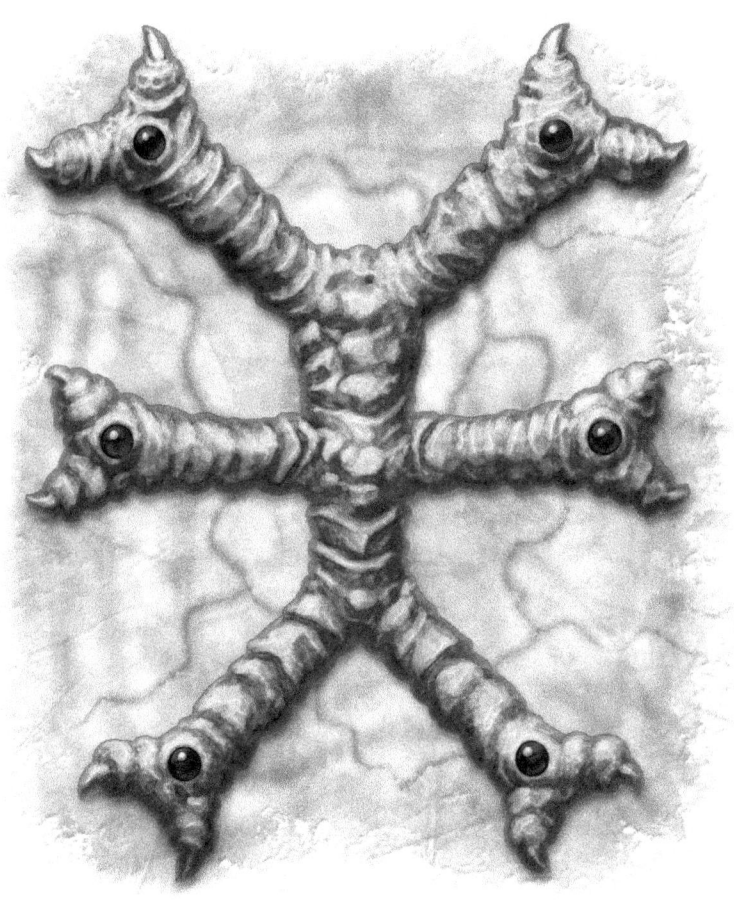

Jason F. Smith & C. Parker Garlitz
www.cultofyex.com

We dedicate this book to all our gaming groups over the years, for all the roll and role playing.

Prophecies of Old is the second book of the Cult of Yex Saga. It is the continuation of the story that began in the first book, Second Cataclysm. If you have not read the first book in the series, we recommend you read it first before moving on to this one.

TABLE OF CONTENTS

PROLOGUE

"It is said that one man saved the world in ancient times. During the darkest hours when it seemed certain that the Cult of Yex would emerge victorious, Adirak, Wizard of Taglyon, stood strong. His unflinching leadership crushed the Cult and his cunning tactics imprisoned the great demon himself in the astral realm.

Adirak was crowned King of Taglyon. He spent his reign vanquishing remnants of the cult and establishing safeguards to ensure that its pernicious evil could never rise again. Despite his efforts, Adirak feared that a residue had somehow managed to elude him, awaiting a time of rebirth. But nary was a whisper heard from the Cult for thousands of years. But for the occasional rambling prophecies of madmen, the Cult was almost forgotten and the few who feared resurgence grew complacent.

If Adirak had lived a thousand lifetimes, he never could have predicted the manner in which the Cult had hidden itself. In his most fevered dreams he could not have imagined the demonic arcana that abetted them, nor their patient scheme to rise again and unleash their demon master."

-Prologue to the as yet unwritten Return of the Cult of Yex, by Caed the Chronicler

CHAPTER ONE
The King of the Bystle Vale

"The Bystle Vale shall endure as long as the Guardian Kings shall rule righteously."

- Codex of Bystle Quatrains

2nd Day of Summer - 1:30 AM – Tharchelon's Court – 13 Days to the Full Moon

"Letharchenel..." King Tharchelon whispered to himself in sing-song voice. "Have you killed the four wretched little thieves yet?"

"M'lord?" A young Rothkin Halfling named Rathenel asked, looking over at Tharchelon. Rathenel was his adjutant. He had short-cropped brown hair, chiseled face and was dressed in the same black official state-robes that Tharchelon wore. The green and golden seal of the Bystle Vale was emblazoned over the left breast.

"I didn't catch what you asked," Rathenel said.

"Just thinking aloud," Tharchelon smiled, or at least he hoped it was a smile. He looked away from Rathenel and continued thinking: *Just wondering if those outlanders have been dealt with... Has Letharchenel succeeded? Are they dead now?*

Tharchelon swallowed and surveyed the throng gathered in his court to hear his judgements. The air suddenly smelled stale and dusty. He closed his eyes. Something momentous was occurring. Somehow, by intuition or imagination, he saw Letharchenel, his assassin, standing in a dark place... in trouble.

Tharchelon imagined he saw a hand, a blade, and then he saw red...

Tharchelon opened his eyes. He smelled blood.

While of course he couldn't know the answer for sure unless Letharchenel returned with his report, somehow he knew that his trusted assassin would never come back. Even if Letharchenel had succeeded, and some deep worry told Tharchelon that he had not, he must proceed... he must strategize as if the four interlopers were still coming.

Damn Hells! You failed me, Letharchenel, you worthless bastard... the four are still alive... and... they are coming for my moss...

"You look weary," said Rathenel. "Why don't you sit, my king?"

Rathenel motioned to the wooden throne of interwoven brown branches growing straight up from the floor of the throne room. "It's well past midnight and many affairs of the vale still await your wisdom before we can retire."

Tharchelon smiled down at his adjutant, trying desperately to put on an unconcerned face. Late nights didn't concern him. What concerned him was the imminent arrival of four coming to steal his moss. *His* moss! From the dreams that were the exclusive right of kings, Tharchelon had recently been told to prepare the moss to give to the four outsiders who were coming.

Give the moss away? *His* moss away?

Not going to happen.

At that moment, the light in the throne room flickered off. Tharchelon stopped breathing, balled his fists, and dug his nails into the heels of his hands. Then to his immense relief, the lights turned back on.

He madly scanned the warm yellowish glow of the Bystle fruits hanging from the inward growing branches on the ceiling of his throne room. His stomach clenched in a moment of near-overwhelming anxiety.

"That seems to be happening more and more lately," mused Rathenel with mild curiosity on his face.

Tharchelon expelled the breath he had been holding, hoping that concern did not show on his face. Rathenel couldn't comprehend the degree of danger to Tharchelon, nor of course the danger to the entire vale, if the light of the Bystle Fruit ever failed completely.

"Will you sit?" Rathenel said to his King with a look of concern. "You don't look well."

Out of nowhere, Tharchelon felt a peculiar sensation, as if the floor upon which he stood was suddenly unstable. The branches, laden with the glowing Bystle Fruits, began to sway. A single fruit was shaken off its branch, falling to the floor. His people murmured and looked around in confusion. It was as if some giant was outside shaking the tree. But as soon as it began it was over. The whispering of his people soon subsided. *Peculiar.*

"I'll stand," Tharchelon said, returning his attention to his adjutant. His tone was soft but commanding. The throne was no longer comfortable. A bump at the very base of his spine had appeared last month and it was growing larger. Just thinking about it, he almost reached back to rub it. The bump was sore and tender. Sitting only aggravated it. It reminded him of the small nubs that had appeared at the same time, just above the hairline on his forehead. They were sore too. He adjusted his woven crown of small Bystle Tree leaves, making sure it hid the budding little kernels.

If I were crazy, he thought, *I might believe I was sprouting horns and a tail.*

Tharchelon reached out and put a comforting hand on Rathenel's shoulder and spoke in a light tone: "I'm right as rain, Rathenel." He adopted what he hoped was a comforting fatherly smile. "Never felt better and eager to keep working." As he said this, his eyes scanned the Bystle Fruits hanging in his massive throne room inside the hollowed out trunk of the great Bystle Tree, the ancestral home of his people.

The tree was the central feature of the vale. It was massive, well over three hundred feet tall with a trunk over eighty feet in diameter. It had been here as long as anyone could remember.

Rothkin druids had used their magic to manipulate the wood inside the tree to shape it to their will. From before the recorded history of the vale, the druids had shaped chambers and passageways inside the wood of the tree, turning the interior into an enormous palace.

My palace, Tharchelon thought, *where generations of my fathers have ruled.*

Tharchelon scanned the oblong throne room whose rounded vault rose more than fifteen feet. The throne and all the furniture were seamlessly fused into the golden brown wood of the floor as if it had grown that way. His druids who shaped the tree were masters of crafting the Bystle Wood with their magic. The wood was bright and polished, and the deep grains in the curvaceous patterns of the ancient tree were easily seen by the light of the plump Bystle Fruits. Fruits hung from short leafy branches that grew intermittently throughout the ceiling and walls of not just the throne room but indeed all halls and rooms.

Tharchelon was one of the few who truly understood the source of magic that the Rothkin druids wielded. Their magic came from the glowing light of the Bystle Fruits that infused the entire vale with their power, but where did the light of the Bystle Fruits come from?

That was the secret.

The true power of the Rothkin Kingdom of Bystle Vale was the long, red, stringy Bystle Moss which grew in only one place: The Sacred Moss Garden, sole province of the king.

He shuddered just thinking about the moss. How long had it been since he had been in the garden?

Tharchelon had often considered the three-way symbiosis in which he played a critical part as the keeper of the moss. The Bystle Tree and the glowing fruits it bore thrived on the magic exuded by the moss, which in turn, grew by light emitted by the plentiful glowing Bystle Fruits. The druids of the vale harnessed the magic of the Bystle Fruit, which grew only because he himself tended to the moss.

The Bystle Moss was the life bringer and the giver of magic for the entire vale. And it wasn't just the power source for the light and nourishment of the Bystle Fruits, it was the basis for their entire way of life. Without it...

Tharchelon shuddered. *What would I do without the moss? What would my people do?*

Tharchelon's people and their entire culture would be devastated--changed forever. They would be consigned to a life to misery and toil. Without the moss, they would be left as a babe against the ravenous wolves.

And what would become of me? Tharchelon thought.

He had already sent his best assassin, but he knew in his heart they were still coming, and worse--worse than anything--eager traitors, here in his own vale, his own people, were ready to help them. He was certain of it.

"M'lord!" Rathenel said.

Tharchelon jerked out of his reverie. If only he could run up to the garden... just for a moment... see the moss, just look at it... just one look...

"Your subjects!" Rathenel said. Standing before his throne, Tharchelon looked at the throng of his people gathered before him: guards, advisors, advocates, petitioners, defendants and even a few observers.

"M'Lord," said Rathenel in consternation, pulling gently on the sleeve of Tharchelon's black robe. "There are still a few that have waited long for an audience with you and the hour has grown exceedingly late."

Tharchelon glanced at the fruits in anticipation; they did not flicker again. At least that was good news. He tried another smile for Rathenel. "Of course, I am right as rain Rathenel, feeling just fine. You eager to get home to your new wife, are you?"

Rathenel just looked at him.

"Well then," said Tharchelon. "Let's get on with it, shall we?"

He needed to hurry... to quell his insatiable need. Soon he would lose the carefully feigned pretense of self-control... but he couldn't just leave now. He needed to appear calm and normal.

Just a little longer. I must appear in command...powerful.

He looked down at his hands. Were they shaking? He stuffed them into the folds of his robe. "Well?" he said to Rathenel. "Are we going to proceed?"

Rathenel slowly nodded. "Yes, yes." He looked down at a scroll in his hands and spoke loudly, reading from it to the assemblage: "Come before the court of the wise King Tharchelon we have Ockler, shepherd of Narch Ostenath."

Tharchelon looked down at the small crowd of his people in

the throne room. Which ones were traitors? Which ones might collude with the outsiders to surrender his moss to them and render the entire Bystle Vale powerless?

His eyes fell on Ockler and a moment of fear grappled him. He wasn't accustomed to such strain and anxiety. His own father had said so to him when he was much younger. He could hear his voice in the echoes of his memory: "One day you will be Guardian and King of the Vale; fearless and strong! Your will must stand like the mighty Bystle Tree against the winter winds, firm and unmovable. I sometimes fear that a mere breeze may topple you."

Thanks father, Tharchelon thought. *But you were wrong.*

Then he thought of the moss. *Or were you?*

"My king," said Ockler the shepherd with a sly smile.

Tharchelon swallowed hard. He remembered Ockler. Oh he remembered him.

When they were children, being the same age, they had played together. Ockler had been large for his age and he used this advantage against other children. Tharchelon, by contrast, had been smaller than average for his age. Tharchelon, being of royal blood, had been a favorite target of the bully. Ockler had once made him eat dirt and had, on more than one occasion, hurled him into the pig sties.

The memory of the many humiliations Ockler had inflicted on him stung Tharchelon as he looked down at his old tormentor. The echoes of memory spoke again, this time in Ockler's voice: *"Look at the prince! Covered in filth. Prince of the pig sty!"*

Tharchelon's father had never defended him from such attacks, saying he needed to learn to defend himself if he was ever going to make a good king. "Respect," he always said. "Is earned, not given."

I'm not weak anymore, Tharchelon realized with a strangely calm resolve coming over him. *Respect is not earned but taken! And it is time to prove it... and right an old wrong at the same time.*

"What did this damn fool do?" Tharchelon asked, looking down at Ockler with self-assurance. Ockler was dressed in his brown shepherd's robes, holding a tall gnarled staff with both hands. His carved face, worn by the wind and the sun, turned up at him.

Ockler's eyes were dark, but Tharchelon saw an unsettling twinkle in them.

"Nothing, my king," Ockler said with a slight bow. "I only sought audience so that I might ask of thee a boon."

"He seeks permission to leave the vale," said Rathenel. "So he can retrieve some lambs that have wandered up into the western forest toward the great river canyon."

Tharchelon suppressed a wry smile. He carefully allowed shock to grow on his face. Not that it should have been a surprise that Ockler was conspiring against him... but for him to confess it so easily was indeed a pleasant turn of events!

He looked at Ockler with a disapproving sneer.

"Do you not recall that last month I decreed it a crime to leave the vale?" Tharchelon said. "You know this but yet you ask. Enemies are abroad in the land that would destroy us; all they need is but an ally inside the vale to abet them."

"But... I...I seek only to retrieve my sheep," Ockler stammered.

"Why were you grazing them so close to the western edge of the vale?" Tharchelon demanded. "That ground is rocky, not as fit as the pastures in the east."

"I graze my flock where it seems best to me. The pastures in the east have been overgrazed and needed a rest," Ockler said, his voice slightly lower.

"Your request to leave the vale is denied," Tharchelon said. He felt suddenly sick inside, as if a part of him didn't think he could do what he had to do. But that part was wrong; he could do it. *Respect is taken!*

"Furthermore," he said, then paused. Oh, this was a delicious moment. He waited. Everyone looked at him. What was he going to say? He smiled slyly. One last thing to do, and then he was going to go check on his moss. "Furthermore, you treacherous lying bastard... you are sentenced to death!"

Ockler's eyes widened in surprise. Tharchelon heard Rathenel gasp. The crowd in the room was murmuring amongst themselves.

"You trying to be funny, Prince?" Ockler sneered.

Tharchelon felt the sting of childhood humiliation.

"Guards! Arrest this traitor. Take him to the new prison near Narch Ecklon and throw him in a barrier enclosure to await his execution."

Two of his royal guards, dressed in their sharp green tunics with sheathed blades on their belts, stepped forward immediately but then hesitated slightly as they realized what they were being ordered to do. Ockler waved the guards off with a look of disgust on his face, his robes swirled as he spun to go.

"Guards!" Tharchelon snapped in a commanding tone and this time they did not hesitate. They went to either side of Ockler. One took his staff and the other took his arm.

Ockler yanked his arm loose and reached for his staff, cursing loudly.

Two more guards in their green tunics came up to him, and one of them pulled out his narrow sword, which hissed from its sheath.

"What is this, Tharchelon?" Ockler asked. "You can't kill me for losing sheep!"

"Your crime is treason!"

"What in the hells are you talking about?"

"Take him away!"

"I demand an explanation of this outrageous injustice!"

"Take him away!" Tharchelon's voice rose into a screech and he felt suddenly out of control. He tried to take a deep breath; he couldn't lose it in front of his people. They needed to see him calm and in control.

The guards, properly motivated by the indignation of their king, grabbed Ockler and dragged him through the eastern archway in a flurry of robes and obscenities.

"My king?" Rathenel's stammering voice bordered on a whine.

Tharchelon shook his head. He just couldn't take hearing Rathenel's voice right now. The Moss Garden was where he wanted to be; where he *needed* to be.

"My king!" Rathenel said, his voice rising in desperation.

"Dismiss the assemblage," Tharchelon said. "Done for the night. Go home."

He spun and walked around the throne to the door behind

it. The door anticipated his approach and magically parted before him. Behind him as he left, Tharchelon heard the bewildered murmurs of his subjects.

I did the right thing, he thought. *It will serve as a necessary example for the rest.* But a small and fading part of his conscience doubted.

As Tharchelon made his way through the wooden halls of his Bystle Tree palace, up numerous flights of stairs toward the highest room in the tree, another childhood memory came to him. He had been only six years old, right before his mother had died from a terrible fever. She had said to him: "Tharchelon, you are my precious boy. You will always be my boy and I will always be watching you. You must always be kind and gentle. I will love you always. You will make a great king, if you always remember to be kind and gentle."

Tharchelon had promised his mother that he would be a kind and gentle king. Today he felt like he had betrayed his dead mother, but what could he do? His mother had made him promise in a time of peace. Things had changed. Enemies crept about and conspired both without and within the vale.

They want my moss...

The sacred trust of over a hundred generations of Guardian Kings was upon him. This was what the line of kings was for! They were anointed to protect the vale and to preserve above all things, the Bystle Moss for themselves.

And nothing... *nothing...* was going to prevent him from doing his sacred duty. Not even the memory of a long ago promise given to his mother.

Suddenly, the soft glow of Bystle Fruit in the hallway flickered again. Tharchelon stopped and braced himself against the edge of the tunnel. He breathed deeply to try to calm himself. The deep rich smell of the Bystle wood filled his nostrils.

What if the four thieves were already here?

A surge of energy filled him as this new panic gripped him.

He pushed himself from the polished wall and began to hurry through the winding tunnel toward the stairway that led up to the holy Moss Garden. Tharchelon's hands trembled as he sped down the rounded wooden hallways of his tree palace as fast as he could go without running. How long had it been since he had last tasted his secret shame? Five hours? Six? It felt like an age.

Tharchelon turned a corner and all but collided with Nelcherath, one of his many druid advisors. The impact mussed the little druid's pitch black hair. What was he doing here? Tharchelon had recently developed suspicions about Nelcherath. He was a whisperer. He couldn't be trusted.

"My Lord, I..."

"Not now, Nelcherath. I haven't the time for your trivialities," said Tharchelon as he strode past.

"But my lord, my dreams of late..."

Of all the things Nelcherath might have said, mention of dreams was the only thing that could have stopped Tharchelon in his tracks as he raced toward his vice. He whirled.

"What of your dreams?" Tharchelon fumed, his eyes flashing with fury.

Nelcherath expected an odd reaction from Tharchelon, but this was even more aggressive than he anticipated. "M...m...M' Lord?"

Like most of the palace staff, he had become concerned with the increasingly erratic behavior of the king. It had started over a year ago. Tharchelon had transformed slowly from a stern but fair monarch to an increasingly cruel and unpredictable despot. While Nelcherath knew he was taking an awful risk by even putting himself in the center of Tharchelon's attentions, his loyalty to his people demanded it. He was prepared for a quixotic response from Tharchelon, but this sudden flash of anger caught him by surprise. What possible reason could Tharchelon have to be so angry at the mention of dreams?

Nelcherath, being a Rothkin of unpretentious character, decided that given the disturbing nature of his dreams, straightforwardness was the best approach. "My Lord... an apparition has visited me in my dreams each night for the last three nights." Tharchelon's eyes grew wide as Nelcherath spoke. Anger changed to concern.

"And?"

"The first two nights I felt disturbed and worried when I woke, but I could not recall what the apparition had said to me... until last night."

Tharchelon braced himself for the worst. Things were indeed spiraling out of control.

"...I do remember," said Nelcherath. "That it warned of a threat to the kingdom, and I was to assist you with the performance of your most sacred duties in tending the moss."

Tharchelon knew what was coming next. His mind raced. How could this be? The visitor in dreams had appeared to *Nelcherath the Whisperer?!* It was the exclusive right of kings to be advised by the apparition! It had always been so. This had all gone too far! Now even the visitor in his dreams was conspiring against him!

"The apparition told me that four would come soon in search of..."

Tharchelon bolted.

"...our sacred moss." Nelcherath trailed off, as Tharchelon raced down the hallway toward the stairs leading to the sacred Moss Garden.

CHAPTER TWO
Of Rat & Man

"Out from Demon's Bluff, the Great Desert stretches for nearly a hundred leagues in every direction. Only the verdant flood plains of the Demon River are a stark contrast to the harsh landscape round about. Despite the inhospitable terrain, the Agrabi seemed able not only to survive, but to thrive out in the deep desert. Few Buerdeleise could hope to manage so well. The notable exceptions are the desert rangers, who pass the secrets of desert living from master to apprentice. Legend has it that their skills were first learned from the Agrabi themselves. Mostly solitary types, the rangers prefer the loneliness of the desert to crowded city life. Often they hire themselves out as guides when some Buerdeleise has the notion to wander off the established trade roads or away from the safety of the Demon River itself."

-Excerpted from The Great Desert by Puppus Chugg, Taglyon Loremaster of Flora & Fauna

2nd Day of Summer - 3:05 AM – On the River - 13 Days 'til the Full Moon

Danilus heard a thump. He was unfurling the sail as he watched the broken rat-faced man skulking crookedly back up the pier. He looked down and saw that the big boy had just fallen to the deck, passed out cold. This had to be Mallet, according to Boxxaway's descriptions.

"Cael!" Danilus called. "Grab yonder wheel and get us out of here."

"There are a hundred boats out here!" said Cael. "It's as if the whole city is trying to leave at once."

"Just get to it!" said Danilus as he knelt at Mallet's side. "And don't wreck my boat!"

He knelt by the side of Mallet. The girl, must be Brynn, joined him. The wounds looked bad--real bad.

"He's going to follow us," the little Agrabi boy yelled. "He can't be killed. We got to get away."

"Will you shut up?" Cael yelled from the wheel as the sail caught the full force of the southwesterly wind. "There are too many boats out here. Oh no!" Cael swerved, barely avoiding a collision with another boat. "Damn! That was close!"

"This one is messed up," Danilus said, peeling away Mallet's bloody clothes.

"It was Wheizer, that man on the dock who chased us," said Brynn, biting her lip and pulling at her hair. "I've never seen so much blood."

Mallet had been torn up something fierce. The flesh of his chest was clawed to ribbons, and there was a series of deep puncture wounds on both the front and back of his shoulder. The largest was an unmistakable bucktooth wound that looked like it could have been caused by a giant rat.

"He's bad off," Danilus admitted. In fact... he didn't want to say it out loud, but this kid wasn't going to make it. The girl, his sister, if he recalled what Boxxaway told him correctly, was apt to take that news hard.

"He's a wererat," she continued.

"Wererat?" Danilus said. "You sure?"

"Look at those bites," said Brynn. "I saw him change into a big half-rat half-man thing."

A wererat! Danilus knew well the lore of such creatures; twisted by a powerful arcane disease with a fancy name: Lycan-something-or-some-such-nonsense. He reckoned the word 'wererat' did the job well enough. A poor soul so afflicted would transform under a full moon into a murderous half-rat, half-man creature of immense strength. Legend held that some wererats eventually gained control of their changes and could shape-shift at will. If that was the case, Danilus reckoned that the children had encountered just such a creature, as the full moon was still two weeks away. Danilus would have struggled to believe such a tale from these youngsters were it not for Mallet's wounds.

But these wounds told the tale: a wererat bite. No doubt, the boy was now infected with the poison. And that changed everything.

"Watch out!" Needle screamed from the front where he stood with Cael.

"You want to steer?" Cael yelled back at him.

"He isn't going to make it, is he?" Brynn asked, as Danilus peeled back a strip of shredded flesh on Mallet's chest.

"No need to worry, reckon," said Danilus. "None at all. I know what I'm doing."

"You a wizard?"

"Here, hand me that there box," said Danilus. "Got my herbs in it, and no, I ain't no wizard, and no, I ain't no leech monger like in the streets of Demon's Bluff, with their camel-dung poultices or boar-bile enemas. I'm a desert ranger, and I know my herbs."

Brynn grabbed the wooden healer box with the oak leaf carved on the lid from where it sat against the side of the boat. She shoved it over to him. She seemed keenly interested in the herbs. "What you got in there? You think it will save him?"

Danilus nodded. "They'll save him," he said, but that was a lie. Truth was, Mallet wouldn't need healing, not the type herbs provided anyway. If he was infected... well, he had his own healing now. The wererat disease was no normal sickness. It was arcane in nature, and Danilus knew something about the disease that not many others understood. Wounds from a wererat always stayed clean of the types of infections that any other similar wound would suffer. The malady of the wererat itself fought off all other infections and sickness. It was as if the disease eliminated all competition to ensure the survival of its host. Yes, Mallet would likely survive... but the truth was, and he didn't want to tell Brynn this, the big boy would probably end up wishing he had died. Few fates were worse than becoming a rampaging beast every full moon. Danilus heard tales of wererats butchering their own kin, unable to stop themselves.

"Some skullcap and willow bark will ease his pain," said Danilus, showing Brynn the herbs. "And some valerian and mandrake will help him sleep."

He stirred several large pinches of each powdered herb into a tin cup.

"Hand me that jug of rum," he told Brynn. She got it for him.

"There is so much blood," she said. "How can he survive this?"

"Rum cures almost anything," Danilus joked. He filled the tin cup with the rum and with Brynn's help, he held Mallet's head as they poured it down his throat.

"Now I got to stitch him up," Danilus said.

It took a while for him to stitch Mallet up, but Brynn helped, and seemed unfazed by the blood or sight of the needle and thread zipping in and out of the torn flesh. Together they finished binding the big boy's wounds, then dragged him into the boat's only cabin and helped him into one of the several hammocks.

"No way I'm going to lift him," said Danilus. "Let's just let him lie on the floor."

"He's going to live?" Brynn asked hopefully.

"Yeah," Danilus grunted.

The kids wanted answers; Danilus gave them none. Boxxaway had entrusted him to watch over the four of them, particularly Cael, and one look at their exhausted, soot-stained faces told him all he needed to know.

Them kids needed rest.

They argued, particularly the Agrabi boy, Needle.

"I want to know where we are going," he demanded.

"Just get some rest," said Danilus. "I reckon you need it."

"I don't need rest, I need answers."

"You'll get your answers," Danilus said, raising his voice. To his way of thinking, kids didn't take that kind of tone with their elders.

"He's right," Cael said, letting Danilus take the wheel. "We need rest, Needle."

The little Agrabi set his lips in a frown, but didn't say another word. He walked to the bow and curled up into a ball under a tarp.

Danilus took the wheel. Cael always was smart, that was for sure. And from the look on his filthy face, his blue eyes flashing in the yellow light from the burning city, he had more on his mind than where they were going next.

"You done good getting us through that traffic," Danilus said, pointing back down river where hundreds of boats still milled around in a pack at the edge of the burning city. "Now get some sleep."

Cael nodded, and took Brynn by the arm, leading her to the cabin.

Danilus took a deep breath. He listened carefully and thought he could hear sobbing. It was the Agrabi boy, Needle. Something awful must have happened to him. The way he had blathered about Wheizer coming after them, for sure his encounter with the wererat and the destruction of the city had affected him more than the others.

Danilus turned his head and took a long look at the wreckage of Demon's Bluff. He really didn't have a home town anymore, but if he had to pick a place, Demon's Bluff was it. Seeing the town destroyed made him feel melancholy for his own childhood home.

Danilus was the seventh out of eleven children, born to hardworking farmers in the Hamlet of Dorwabi, northwest of Demon's Bluff. The land there was of a higher altitude and did not benefit from the yearly floods of the Demon River. As rain was scarce, the family depended on well water for irrigation. The labor was hard, and the fruits were few. Danilus spent his childhood clearing irrigation ditches and shouldering a double-bucket yoke to carry water to the family's meager crops. He hated it and wished every single day he could leave. At the age of 14, inspired by a passing bard who told tales of adventure, Danilus left to make his fortune.

Unfortunately, he knew only of farming and found himself ill-equipped to be an adventurer. His luck ran poorly, and after a couple of years he returned in desperation to his family farm, only to find that the well had run dry and his family had disappeared. All that their old Agrabi neighbors could tell him was that they 'headed east'. He tried in vain to find them but his situation only grew worse.

Alone, hungry and feeling as if he had abandoned his family in their time of need, salvation came during the most recent flare up in the interminable war between Balankov and Taglyon. He enlisted as a mercenary for Taglyon. It was that or starve.

He'd had some great adventures in the army, and he had eaten better than he had ever eaten in his life. It made him tough and taught him how to fight and survive, but army life wasn't really for him. When the inevitable fragile treaty was declared, Taglyon, with all its troubles, decided to spare its treasury and dismissed half the army, him included. It was soon after that he met Boxxaway, who recommended him to old Hamalcar, a desert ranger who was willing to take him on as an apprentice. At long last, Danilus felt as if he had found his true calling. He learned much from old Hamalcar... until the night Danilus woke to find the old ranger had died during the night. Danilus would never forget the haunted, open-eyed, panicky look on his face.

After the death of his master, Danilus stayed in touch with Boxxaway. The old man always needed errands run, or had a line on an odd job now and then when Danilus had need for hard coin. They helped each other out, and right now, Boxxaway needed him to look after Cael and the other kids on their way north to the great northern dam. It was a stone dam, built by dwarves in ancient times. It spanned the Demon River near the headwaters high in the Bystle Plateau, creating a vast reservoir.

Over the years, Danilus had grown quite fond of Boxxaway, and even fonder of Cael. The two were alike in so many ways, despite the vast difference in their ages. He and Cael got along so well that Cael had even started to call him Uncle Danilus, though they were no relation. For Danilus, Boxxaway and his grandson were like a substitute family. He and Cael had spent a lot of time together, mostly on the river fishing, and even once on Lake Balankov. There wasn't anything Danilus liked more than fishing with Cael. The boy was dear to his heart, for sure. Nothing mattered more to him right now than protecting Cael. And to hear Boxxaway tell it, tough times were ahead. Cael and his friends needed protection.

With the kids settled and dawn still a few hours away, Danilus stood at the tiller of the old, single-mast, flat-bottomed boat (an inheritance from old Hamalcar). His old master had called the boat *Riparian Scout*, a name he stuck with despite not knowing its meaning. The boat barged northward upstream through the calm waters of the Demon River, past the last hints of smoke. Looking back, the fire of Demon's bluff could no longer be seen directly, but it lit the southern sky in a hellish glow.

He used the *Riparian Scout* for fishing and as an occasional home. He could have used the boat to start a business and there was certainly no shortage of trade goods in need of ferrying up and down the Demon. But what sort of life would that be? Hadn't he gone off on his own to escape that sort of drudgery in the first place? Fishing with Cael had been a much more welcome use of the old boat. He felt a sense of contentment as he surveyed the small craft. He loved every knot and splintery plank on the old girl.

The main cabin, a squarish hut which he affectionately called his bedroom, was on the deck toward the stern of the boat and contained a few hammocks. The mast rose right through the center and roof of his cabin, where one tan-colored square canvas sail stood taut against the southwest wind.

Fore of the cabin, the main deck was guarded by a waist high railing. The worn wooden pegs of the tiller wheel stood to the fore of his cabin where he could steer with a commanding view to fore, starboard and port.

Mounted to the top of the column that held the tiller wheel was Tajaa, his little statuette to the old Agrabi river god, which he rubbed frequently for good luck. The idol had been painstakingly carved from a large hippopotamus tusk. The idol's ivory head was rubbed smooth from his constant ministrations. At its base, an inscription was written in Agrabi script: *I carried off their women and smote their bulls.*

Early on the previous morning before the earthquake, Boxxaway had given him a pouch of silver coins with instructions to equip for a long journey. The *Riparian Scout* had never been so well-provisioned. Among a number of wooden crates on the deck, some of which doubled as stools, were a few woven reed baskets and dozens of wooden barrels. All were filled with supplies and foodstuffs.

At the top of his priorities had been two large barrels of dark bitter ale (his favorite). He'd thrown in a half a dozen jugs of wine and rum, and a few ox horns filled with fermented goat milk (another favorite). Other barrels held dozens of loaves of flatbread, chickpeas, lentils, black beans, onions, dried fish wrapped in eucalyptus leaves, a few wheels of wax-encased hard cheese, several cured hams, bushels of figs and dates, cornmeal in earthen jars, and finally as a special treat, a small amphora of honey. His kitchen kit, a large wooden chest with a hinged lid, lay up against the wall of the cabin on the starboard side, stocked with spices, flour, salt and more. Next to it was another chest with implements to repair the boat: ox hides, a hammer, saw, nail, leather strips and the like.

Of course, there were the special barrels under the tarp at the bow, and a few crates with supplies and weapons that Boxxaway specifically instructed to gather for the kids.

His bow, unstrung at the moment, hung on the outside of the cabin wall behind where he stood at the tiller. Next to it hung his old Taglyon army long sword snugly sheathed in its scabbard.

Fishing poles lay along the port side near the anchor, which rested upon a coil of hemp rope. Fishing nets hung above them on the port wall of the cabin.

In short, he had everything necessary for a long and possibly perilous journey upriver to the dam. He just needed to keep the kids safe and deliver them as Boxxaway had instructed.

As morning dawned, a chill settled upon Danilus, despite the gentle warmth of the desert morning. At his feet, Dheke, Boxxaway's grey mastiff, lay sleeping with his head cradled on his front paws, his snores gently rhyming with the gurgle of the water as it flowed under the boat.

Danilus alternately kept an eye ahead and an eye to the south, monitoring the smoky glow rising from Demon's Bluff. There, the red star, Soutep the Evanescent, would soon be rising. Hamalcar had taught him that the few moments between the rise of the star above the horizon and the time it disappeared, obscured by the light of the sun, was a magical time. To see Soutep in these few moments brought good fortune for the day. But Soutep was not visible, for an ominous mass of black clouds had risen from the south, menacing the entire horizon.

He had been through some crazy adventures in his life, but never had he witnessed anything to compare to the devastation wrought by last night's earthquake and fires... to say nothing of the sinkhole. He needed to collect himself before the kids woke. He didn't want to let on how badly last night's events had shaken him. Truth was, he hadn't believed much *could* shake him. But he had been wrong.

He reached out and rubbed Tajaa again.

2nd Day of Summer - 8:00 AM – The Riparian Scout - 13 Days to the Full Moon

"Wake up! Cael! Wake up!"

Cael jerked awake at the sound of the hissed whisper. His hammock was swinging back and forth until Danilus reached out and settled him. They were in the small cabin aboard the *Riparian Scout*. It was a narrow claustrophobic room, with four hammocks. Cael saw Brynn sleeping in another hammock, her auburn hair plastered to her sweaty forehead. Below, on the floor, Mallet slept fitfully. A dark red stain had seeped through the bandage Danilus had wrapped around his shoulder. Needle had slept on deck, and was not in the cabin.

"Hurry up!" Danilus whispered, his eyes wide.

"What's happening?" Cael whispered back, swinging his feet from the hammock to the floor, though this took some dexterity as Mallet lay below him. His bare feet landed with a soft thud on the wooden floor of the cabin.

Danilus said nothing. He just beckoned as he turned, with his head bent, and shuffled toward the open door where a peculiar muted daylight streamed into the cabin.

Cael heard a strange light tapping sound, like the knock of a thrush, then heavier and more insistent. What in the hells?

He stumbled from the cabin up onto the deck into... *rain.* Cool, wet, susurrus rain. It fell on him gently, a cold wet sensation of tapping splatters on his upturned face. He closed his eyes and felt the water drip over his eyelids. Rivulets ran into his mouth and he marveled at how sweet and pure the water tasted.

Next he was struck by the smell. Everything was amplified, the wood odor of the ship, the smell of the cloth sail, and the strong smell of wet dog as Dheke frolicked in the rain. He felt a lifting of his spirit, and a strange calm come over him.

When was the last time he had seen rain? He had certainly never seen rain like *this* before. Demon's Bluff simply didn't get much rain. He looked down at his black robes, the ones Madam Dunkley had improvised for him so he could sneak into the library. They were getting soaked and starting to cling to his body. He relocated the parchments he had taken from the Academy Library from the pocket of his robes to the pocket of his trousers underneath, where they would be safe and dry. Strings of his hair clung to his forehead while runnels of water dripped across his cheeks and dribbled off his chin. He whipped his head back, flinging the hair off his face and sending an arc of water behind him.

He turned and looked to Danilus, who had his face turned toward the rain. His red hair was plastered to his head and his freckled face was split with a wide grin. The big red-headed man reached out a hand, taking Cael by the shoulder. Cael smelled his uncle's scent, an aroma of herbs and fish and desert dust that elicited memories of his childhood spent on the river.

They both smiled and turned their faces back up to the sky. The clouds unleashed a torrent of rain, and they stood out in the open letting it soak them through and through.

To either side of the river, farmers dressed in white and tan linens worked in grain fields that stretched as far as the eye could see. Flood season was fast approaching, where the Demon River would swell its banks, depositing rich silt over these fields, insuring a bounteous harvest. Most of the grain had been shorn from the earth and stacked in sheaves until the wagons could come. The farmers paid no attention to them in their boat. Of much more interest was the rain falling from the sky, and the column of smoke that could barely be seen through the storm, rising from Demon's Bluff to the south.

Cael fixed his attention on the smoke.

"How can this be? I ain't never seen nothing like this!" Danilus crowed to the rain.

The rain continued to fall, tapping on the wood of the ship and smacking loudly in gusts against the sail. The river itself was a sheet of raindrop ripples, and the black clouds above completely obliterated the sun.

Cael considered Danilus' question for a moment before he realized he felt something in the rain. Something unnatural. It was sorcery. *Something had conjured this rain.*

"It had to be the wizards," Cael said in a sudden flash of realization. "There is a thread of energy in this rain. It feels like a spell." And indeed it did. Now that he focused on it, the residue of the *Arcanus Navitas* in the storm was evident.

The *Arcanus Navitas* was an unseen magical energy whose effusive flow was detectable only by wizards trained to sense it. Cael could feel the magic, sometimes dense and fast flowing, other times thin. Wizards drew in the magic to power their spells. Cael was sure of one thing: the residue of the *Arcanus Navitas* in the storm was unmistakable.

Danilus gave him a look. "What? You sure?"

"Pretty sure," Cael said, "I bet they figured it was their only option to put out the fires that burned in Demon's Bluff. Besides, the wind is blowing from the south. It never blows from the south. It only ever blows from the west or southwest."

"Well, ain't that smart?" Danilus said, "For sure, you got a fire, you summon a rain. Why didn't they do that before though, during times of drought?"

"It must have taken dozens of wizards to do this, all working together. No single wizard would dare pay such a heavy cost." Cael considered it further. It had to be a large group of wizards from the cliff, as the energy it took to do this must have been massive. It gave Cael a thrill to think of it; everyone acting together, their energy perfectly in sync. He wished he could have been part of it.

Danilus shrugged. Not the ways of a wizard were his.

They stood in contemplative silence for several moments, enjoying the rain and watching the mostly-harvested grain fields drift by as the storm wind pushed them further up river.

"I reckon I ought to check on Mallet and then I aim to get me some sleep," said Danilus. "I been up all night. You take the tiller, give Tajaa a rub, and if it ever stops raining, fix us up some breakfast."

Cael shook his head: "But where are we going? Boxxaway just said to come to your boat, and you would tell us what to do next."

"For sure," Danilus said, a crafty smile on his face. "But let's wait till everyone has woke up. We'll have us a palaver."

Cael frowned at his uncle. The man was maddeningly slow and deliberate about some things, and irritatingly patient. He used to love to tell stories about his adventures in the war, but he often broke them up into pieces, and would leave Cael hanging, sometimes making him wait for days until the story resumed.

"That Agrabi boy had a rough night I reckon," said Danilus as he gazed off at nothing in particular on the eastern shore. "He curled up and fell asleep in the front of the ship last night.

Thought I heard him sobbing a time or two. When the rain started he just laid in it for a while, then pushed him a little cubby between some barrels under that there tarp." Danilus pointed toward the bow with his chin. "Ain't heard a peep since."

Cael considered this as Danilus headed off for a rest. He and Needle had occasion to be together from time to time, but he never really considered him a friend. Cael was a little annoyed that they would have to be companions. He had never before felt the need to work at a friendship with the Agrabi boy, and Needle hadn't tried much either. But now that would all have to change. At some point he would have to reach out to Needle, despite his recalcitrant manner. He thought about it and decided to let him sleep a while longer. He didn't want to complicate things by getting Needle angry from being woken before he was ready.

Cael took the pegs of the tiller in his hands, and felt the smooth wet wood under his palm. He reached out and touched Tajaa, rubbing the idol's head. Of all the places Cael would want to be besides his home, this was the most comfortable for him.

And now, it was suddenly dear to him in a way it never could have been before. His normal sanctuary from the world, his home with Boxxaway, the place where he had grown up, where he had eaten and played and studied and read, was now gone. Indeed, just yesterday he had learned that it was the place where he had been born. Now it was all rubble at the bottom of that great, gaping sinkhole.

All his books, all the rocks he collected, all the pictures his Grandfather had painted, his collection of rattlesnake rattles, his favorite wooden mug, the wall he had climbed, the yard he had run around in... and... Madam Dunkley. Gone. *All gone.*

He thought of the kitchen in his grandfather's now destroyed home, and suddenly realized how hungry he was. He hadn't eaten since yesterday morning and he was famished. He secured the tiller with a looped hemp rope Danilus kept nearby for just that purpose, and headed over to one of the barrels on the deck. Prying the lid off and finding it filled with figs, he made a carrying fold in his robes and threw in about a dozen of them.

Cael looked away to the south again as he bit into a large fig. Cael had never been a huge fan, but hells! These were the most delicious figs he'd ever eaten. He placed the stem between his thumb and middle finger and flicked it into the river.

The distant column of smoke from Demon's Bluff was thick and white, like the smoke that surged when a bucket of water was poured over a campfire. How many had died last night? What would become of his town?

He turned his gaze northward up the rippling river as he bit into another fig. What lay ahead? Whatever his future held, he had to believe it couldn't be any worse than the hellish night he had just survived.

This boat was the last familiar place for him left in the entire world. He thought of his grandfather. Who knew if the old man could survive this kind of activity much longer? Cael could soon find himself totally alone in the world, and the feeling gave him a shiver.

At least he had Danilus now, and Dheke. The great grey mastiff hound was curled up under a bench.

He sighed and peered through the rain, guiding the ship up the Demon River, steering clear of the banks, tree limbs and other debris that the rising river was starting to pick up and carry with it.

The rain continued more than an hour, then trailed off into an intermittent drizzle. Cael could feel the magic residue in the storm ebb as the rain dissipated. The Storm must have blown northward after the wizards released it, dousing the fires in Demon's Bluff.

A nice cool wind blew from the south, filling the white sail and pushing them northward up the wide, slow river. It seemed like every creature in the valley had come out to witness the rain. He scanned the banks of the river. A host of animals emerged from amidst the verdant bounty of trees and shrubs shadowing the edge of the muddy river: eucalyptus, acacia, cedar, cypress, mesquite, date palms and fig trees laden with fruit.

A pair of chattering monkeys, unsettled by the uncommon rainstorm, swung from the low hanging limbs on the east bank. Their gibbering high-pitched voices put Cael on edge. He gritted his teeth at the unmistakable wake of a river asp slithering through the water. Just off the western bank, a crocodile lay atop a matted clump of reeds, waiting for the sun to return.

The smell of agapanthus blooms filled the air and made Cael sneeze as the boat sailed along past the cacophonous primates. A mist of water blew into the air ahead and he knew he was nearing a bloat of hippopotamuses. Cael carefully steered the boat around the beasts. He had heard more than one story of people being killed when they got too close to the unpredictable river cows.

Rounding a slight bend in the river, the trees thinned out and Cael could see the fields here had been completely harvested and were fallow, in preparation for the summer floods that should begin soon. Would the floods come early or late this year? Would the flooding be deep and long, or shallow and short?

Boxxaway had often told Cael that the heavens favored Demons' Bluff with the gift of the Demon River. Some years the inundation was tremendous, and the water level rose as high as five feet across those fields. Other years it was much less. A low flood meant a smaller wheat and barley harvest. Boxxaway said in other places the farmers toiled ceaselessly to scratch a living from the earth, but in the farmland around Demon's Bluff the fields were fertilized by the annual floods of the Demon River. The farmers simply scattered their seed onto the muddy plains after the floods receded, and drove in their pigs or oxen to trample the seed. The fields in the river valley produced not just one, but two bounteous harvests each year; so much in fact, that they had excess to brew into a vast assortment of beers, ales and meads. Surplus grain and ales were sent down river to Balankov and Taglyon in trade for many other goods, including wood, gold, spices, salt and wine. Even caravans bearing the surplus headed out on The Road to the distant cities in the east.

Cael spotted a small village ahead past the bend. It was built atop a long flat knoll where it would be safe above the waterline even in the deepest of flood years. A number of small skiffs from the village were out, with fishermen casting their nets. Aside from the fishermen, Cael noticed that right now most people didn't seem to be working. Instead, they were gathered in what struck him as conspiratorial knots, taking in the rain and whispering about the ominous smoke rising southward from Demon's Bluff. Cael was suddenly reminded of the Cult of Yex. Maybe he was just being paranoid, but there was no way to know where the cult might have spies. If just one of those people in the village was a spy for the cult, then their whereabouts might be betrayed. Cael suddenly felt very vulnerable.

Three shepherds stood near the eastern bank, watering their flocks, watching the southern horizon more than they tended to their animals, casting furtive glances over to Cael. He waved nonchalantly but inside, his guts churned.

Don't be stupid, he thought. *These villagers don't know me from Adirak. They are just curious because of the smoke from the south. I might bear news.*

Just a bit further from the shore, field workers dressed in their loose linens stood in a small huddle, their heads bent together as they whispered among themselves, pointing south. One pointed to him, but Cael just pretended not to notice.

At the shore nearer the village, a group of brick makers were excavating mud from the river bank and mixing it with straw to stuff into molds. Soon the summer heat would return to bake them into bricks. As Cael neared them, someone called out to him. Next to the brick makers, a boy was pounding out papyrus reed stalks into sticky sheets and laying them between boards to flatten and dry. It was he who had shouted to Cael.

Cael waved feebly back. He was sure they wanted news, but he wasn't about to pull the *Riparian Scout* over to the bank to talk to anyone. He sailed on by.

Suddenly a crowd in the village reacted with excitement as they spied a chariot pulled by two black horses rushing from the south up the road that paralleled the eastern bank of the river. News was coming at last.

At least they aren't paying attention to him anymore. He gave Tajaa a rub and turned the tiller to give the village docks ahead a wide berth. He wondered how these villagers would react to news of the destruction. Likely they would ascribe it to an unfortunate natural disaster.

Natural disaster? *Unnatural* was the sobering truth of it.

He remembered the words of the Fourth Prophecy. The feeling of bewilderment and dread he'd experienced when he found it in the Library of Mirrors back in Demon's Bluff, came flooding back to him. The hapless fools on the shore had no idea that the greatest evil the world had ever known, just announced its triumphant return by wreaking devastation on his hometown. Hells, the thought scared him! He alone knew the truth of what they faced, and he was just a kid. Even his companions didn't yet know the gravity of it. How and when was he to tell them?

The stiff wind propelled the boat past the village and northward toward a stretch of river where there were no people to be seen. Cael's companions would wake soon. There were a great many things that needed to be talked about, not the least of which were his discoveries in the library the night before. What would they say when the saw the prophecies for themselves?

Cael looked back toward the south. The smoke had been thinning, but the column of white on the horizon was still there to see. He considered the nightmare it must be back in the city: the refugees, the wounded, the dead. A visceral emotion of near panic welled up in him as he replayed the events of last night... and their underlying true meaning.

He turned his gaze back to the north, where the lazy flow of the Demon stretched on forever. What lay ahead for them? Whatever it was... it wasn't going to be easy. How much longer could everyone sleep? They needed to talk. All of them.

He clenched his fist, feeling his nails dig into his palm. He wanted to release the fist he had made, but his knuckles, white with exertion, did not relax

CHAPTER THREE
Breaking Bones

"For as long as I live, I will never forget the feeling of dread that swept over me as the demon stepped through the Cult's infernal gate. The earth seemed to tremble and I could see raging flames behind him. The acrid smell of noxious fumes effused my nostrils as he passed into our world from the very Abyss itself. I cannot say from whence came the courage that propelled me to action as his contorted form rose up to its full height and towered above me."

- Excerpt from the lost Journal of King Adirak of Taglyon

2nd Day of Summer - 5:30 AM – Dagorn's Estate - 13 Days to the Full Moon

Duke Bygrave's heart felt as if it would pound its way out of his chest. Frantic, he searched through rubble-strewn darkness for his missing children. He could hear their faint voices calling out to him in desperation. As he pushed his way through unfamiliar smoky streets, he seemed to be getting closer to the voices. Suddenly he was digging toward the voice through a large debris pile, but he couldn't seem to make any progress as smoke stung his eyes.

Dagorn.

Mallet and Brynn's voices called out to him in unison... growing louder... closer.

Dagorn.

Suddenly it wasn't the voices of his children. It had become a single voice and it had taken on a disturbing edge... sinister. Had he been chasing the voice? It had been a trick! The voice had been luring him, and he had succumbed to its seductive call.

Dagorn.

The voice was tinged with a decidedly demonic tone: high-pitched and nefarious. Panic overtook him. He tried desperately to breathe, but no air came. His heart raced, and he could feel a cold bead of sweat dribble down his forehead.

Dagorn.

The demon had found his children before he could save them. And now the demon had come for him. The twisted and bent shadowy figure stood over him menacingly. He tried desperately to breathe as he braced himself for the inevitable end. He had never expected to die this way.

Dagorn.

Air rushed suddenly into his lungs and blood surged into his head in a painful and dizzying rush. It felt as if he had grit under his eyelids and he could not focus. Standing before him at the foot of his bed, silhouetted in a hellish light, was the shadowy horror of his dream! An inhuman twisted demon, hunched over, limbs bent at impossible angles, calling his name again in a nasally voice. Terror overwhelmed him.

Before he started to wake Dagorn, Wheizer had paused for a moment to look out at the smoke and haze that still hung thick in the air over Demon's Bluff. Dagorn's bedroom had the best view of any room in the manor, it being on the top floor of the southeast tower. There was a clear view between the cedar and mesquite trees that bordered the estate. The devastation was incredible. A rare and merciful thunderstorm had helped bring the fires under control in the pre-dawn hours, sparing the town even more suffering. The sky was overcast and the rain had subsided to a drizzle. Wheizer paused to savor the rare sight for a few moments.

Turning his attention to Dagorn, Wheizer had gazed disapprovingly at the disarray in which Dagorn lived. Clearly the servants tidied the room each day, but Dagorn's clothes from last night were strewn about the room. A chair was overturned, and wine from a spilled goblet was soaked into the thick dark carpet. Dagorn himself lay splayed on his bed, his silken sheets wrapped helter-skelter around his form. Sweat poured off him as he slept fitfully. His muscles were tensing as if he were reacting to some troubling dream. The stench of his sweat and his stale alcohol breath hung in the stagnant air.

Wheizer had called his name several times, but Dagorn struggled in persistent sleep.

"Dagorn. Wake up. You're dreaming."

Dagorn's fists gripped at his sheets as his entire body tensed. His eyes shot open and then squinted in reaction to the light silhouetting Wheizer's form. A look of horror erupted on Dagorn's face as he scrambled backward on his bed away from Wheizer.

"It's me. Wheizer."

Lucidity returned suddenly as Dagorn sat up blinking in his soaked silken sheets.

"Wheizer?" Dagorn breathed with a rush of relief in his voice. "I thought for a moment..." Dagorn squinted at Wheizer for several seconds. "What in the hells happened to you?"

"Let's just say I've had a rough night. But I kept your children safe."

"You look a fright. What happened?" Dagorn slid his legs over the edge of his bed and reached for the silk robe draped over the bedpost. The fright Dagorn showed in his troubled dreams had promptly been replaced with a demeanor of prescience and control. This was the Dagorn that Wheizer respected.

Wheizer imagined he indeed did look a fright. His shoulder was still dislocated. Dried blood covered his face and tunic and he knew his head was perched oddly on his neck. The grinding sound he heard when he moved his head wasn't as bad as it had been last night: that was something. His broken limbs had re-knitted at horrifying angles.

"As you feared, Brynn has learned too much about her

mother. She went last night to the mausoleum, and I'm sorry to say, Mallet followed her. It's a good thing I was there or things might've gotten out of hand."

"What happened?" Dagorn asked as he rubbed his eyes with the heels of his hands. Wheizer knew the man had drunk far too much wine the night before and was paying the price this morning. Dagorn reached for the crystal decanter at the bedside. The first ray of sunlight from the eastern window glinted off the onyx ring he perpetually wore on his right hand.

"I don't know how she did it, but Brynn actually summoned the bitch from the grave. Elowynn was about to tell them everything, but I stuck her ghostly form and sent her back to the hells she came from." Wheizer's hand moved absently to the hilt of his rapier hanging at his waist, his bent and broken fingers wrapping awkwardly around it.

"Good," Dagorn said, then took a long draw of stale wine. "And how did you come to be in this condition?"

"They fled for the lifts with two other boys from town. One was Kemano's whelp. The other was a scrawny Buerdeleise boy I have never seen before."

"What do you make of that?"

"They know something... but how much I couldn't say. Not enough I'll wager. Else why would they have gone to the mausoleum?"

"Kemano's boy, eh?" Dagorn said as he rose to his feet. He arched his back and Wheizer could hear the crack. "He came to see me last night you know. Trying to sell me some of his father's old artifacts. Maybe he followed Brynn up there after he left?"

"Maybe."

"No. They must know something," Dagorn mused. "How else do you explain those two together?"

Wheizer shrugged. He had concluded as much yesterday from following Brynn to Needle's hovel.

Dagorn pressed on. "I mean, really... what are the odds? So where are they now?"

"Your boy knocked me out of the lift."

Dagorn's eyebrows rose in surprise. He took three gulps of wine. It poured from both corners of his mouth, and dripped from his salt and pepper goatee.

"Damn near broke every bone I got."

"You can hardly notice," Dagorn said dryly, wiping his mouth with the sleeve of his robe.

"You always this funny in the morning?"

Dagorn just smiled. "You never said where they are."

"I tracked them through the flames and rubble. They went straight for a boat at the granary dock. I caught up with them just as they were unfurling their sails and heading up the river.

"What in the hells?" Dagorn said in a mere whisper.

"A redheaded man was with them. I've seen him around town once or twice, but I don't know him."

Wheizer knew Dagorn was ruminating on the questions he had already considered. Where were Mallet and Brynn going... and why? Why with Kemano's runt? Who were the Buerdeleise boy and the red headed man? How much did they know? If they did know... how did they find out? But any answer was purely speculative. Their bizarre actions were no more surprising than anything else that had happened yesterday.

"You sure she didn't tell them anything?"

"Positive."

"This stinks of her meddling."

"I was there. I'm positive."

"Well I think you'd better find out where they're headed."

"I'm on it. I won't have any trouble catching up with them. I'll get a gryphon and maybe get upriver of them, but I'm in no condition for that at the moment."

"You came to me for help then," Dagorn said flatly, holding his back with his hands as he slowly creaked up out of bed.

"Who else would I go to?"

"What am I supposed to--"

Wheizer cut him off. "Get a hammer."

Dagorn replaced the decanter on the bedside table and strode toward the window. "A what?"

"A hammer. A big one."

"For what?"

"Look at me. What do you think?"

A horrified look crept onto Dagorn's face as the realization of what Wheizer was asking him to do dawned on him...

CHAPTER FOUR
Palaver

The Inn Corporeal in the fabled City of Taslaar on the Astral Plane is a renowned lyceum where the greatest debaters of the multiverse endlessly argue their philosophies. Most denizens of this peculiar tavern have projected themselves into the astral from whatever worlds they inhabit. Free of body, they have no need for food, drink nor sleep. The currency of this place is talk.

-Gazetteer of the Known Planes of Existence

2nd Day of Summer - 10:00 AM – The Demon River - 13 Days to the Full Moon

"Some night last night, eh?" said Danilus emerging from the cabin.

You got no idea, Cael thought. Only a few hours had passed since Danilus had turned in, and it was mid-morning. The sky was still overcast, but the rain had abated. A stifling humid heat had arisen, and Cael's brow was beaded with sweat. Swarms of gnats and mosquitoes, a usual staple on the river, returned with a vengeance. The rain had kept them at bay for the morning, and they seemed eager to make up for lost time.

"You didn't sleep long," Cael said, though privately he was glad his tall red-headed, freckle-faced friend was up. "I don't like being out here all by myself."

"Me?" Danilus said, coming and taking the tiller in his large calloused hands, "I don't need much sleep, for sure. Them other two is still sound asleep though. I suppose they need it, considering what y'all went through last night."

"What about Mallet, how's he doing?"

"Sleeping all fitful," said Danilus, chin pointing at the fishing poles. "We're stocked up alright, but I reckon some fresh fish would taste good for breakfast. I done changed his bandages, and gave him some more of my rum medicine to help him rest. I tell you what Cael, that ol' boy is tougher'n a boot."

"You should have seen him last night... running through the city all bloody," Cael said, running his hand through his damp hair as he kneeled by the long cane poles. He untangled a fishing pole and held it reverently. Fishing was big business on the Demon River. The Buerdeleise for the most part fished with nets, while the Agrabi fished the bottom with hooks baited with worms or mussels dug from the muddy shore.

But Danilus had a different way of fishing, having learned from Hamalcar, who learned in turn from his master. Cael was quite taken with it.

Danilus made light thin line braided from crocodile gut. Danilus had never taught Cael how to make it. He seemed to guard the lore of rangers jealously, and somehow Cael felt mildly offended by that, as Cael had told Danilus about magic quite often. For bait Danilus used colorful bits of string to tie heron and parrot feathers to a hook, creating a passable facsimile of an insect. The feathered hook floated on top of the water and attracted the surface-feeders like moon fish, bonebacks, and silver-sides.

The growing heat made him grateful he still had on his usual clothing, white tunic and pants, under the blasted black robes Madam Dunkley had given him.

"I thought Mallet was going to collapse a dozen times last night," he said to his uncle, as he stripped off the black robes. "Wheizer tore into him up on the plateau, in the graveyard, and he made it all the way down to the dock on his own. He ran a good bit of the way too."

Danilus raised his bushy red eyebrows.

"Will he be okay?" Cael asked.

"Oh, I reckon so. I'm just a bit worried about that wererat bite."

Me too, Cael thought. Facing Wheizer had been terrifying. It hadn't been so bad in the mausoleum, because he had been a fair distance away. But on the lift... with Wheizer in close and reaching for him... that was something entirely different. He could feel his heart start to pound at the thought of it.

Cael finished tying on a colorful lure that looked like a scarlet locust, and stared at it in his hands for several moments. He imagined having to face Mallet as a mad rat creature, and a sense of dread crept over him. But there were other things to worry about for the moment, so he pushed the troubling thought out of his mind.

Speaking of troubling... Needle was still camped out under the tarp. Cael had been grateful the Agrabi boy had stayed asleep so long, but he needed to talk to him... alone... before the others got up. Maybe try to get off to a fresh start with him.

Cael mulled it over as he leaned on the port railing. Finally, he sighed and set his fishing pole down and headed to the bow. A number of iron banded wooden barrels had been covered with a tan colored tarp that made a popping sound as a gust of wind caught it.

Cael bent down to his knees and crawled under the tarp. Needle lay curled in a fetal ball in a space between several barrels, his back to Cael. His bony spine was visible through the holes in his linen tunic.

"Needle?" he whispered.

"You got anything to eat?" Needle asked quietly, though he didn't move. Cael sat down cross-legged, his head bent as the tarp pressed down upon the top of his unkempt hair. It was hotter than hells under the tarp and he could feel perspiration beginning to sprout on his forehead. He could smell the peculiar odor of musty tarpaulin.

"Sorry. You want me to grab you something? Danilus has some provisions. I'm gonna catch us some fish, too."

"Ain't hungry."

"Then why did you ask?"

Needle didn't say anything.

"Danilus said you had a rough night," said Cael. "He said you were crying." He paused, not entirely sure how to approach the subject. Cael recalled again why he never really liked Needle. The Agrabi boy sure made it difficult. But that didn't really matter. Boxxaway had said Needle was needed, and after seeing the Fourth Prophecy, it was impossible to disagree. Their lot was cast together, and they might as well get along.

"Ain't crying," Needle said quietly.

"Danilus said--"

"Like *you* never cried in your life?"

"What happened?"

Needle didn't say anything.

Cael had a sudden inspiration. Needle's great devotion had always been his parents. "Is your mother okay?"

Needle made a choking sound.

Cael sucked in his breath. He should have guessed. She had been killed in the earthquake. "Did she get sucked down that sinkhole?"

Needle didn't move.

"I'm sorry, Needle," Cael said. He felt it was important to make a connection here, and so he reached out and touched Needle's shoulder. "I'm really sorry."

Needle didn't say anything.

"Do you want to talk about it?"

"I killed her," Needle said finally, his voice a hoary whisper. Cael felt a chill go up his spine as if beetles were crawling over his back, and his face flushed uncomfortably.

"You...you what?" he asked lamely, pulling his hand away.

"You don't know what it's like to lose a mother."

The confirmation from Needle was not surprising, but the impact of the words struck Cael suddenly in a very personal way. He *did* know. By the hells, he *knew*! It had been only yesterday that he had cast that ill-fated divination, and had witnessed the murder of his own mother and father. Worse, had he not seen the vision through the eyes of the assassin? And had it not been as if he had plunged that blade into his parents himself? The freshness of the memory stung him anew.

"You may not believe this Needle," Cael said, and now it was his turn to go hoarse, his voice crackled like there was sand in his throat. "But I do understand how you feel."

"You have no idea!" Needle hissed, "I don't even know why I'm here. And as soon as I can, I'm going back home."

The intensity of Needle's anger caught him off guard, and he had to think about what he was saying. Go back home? He needed the Agrabi boy, but telling him outright that he had to stay wasn't going to work.

"What do you mean, 'you killed her'?"

"I should never have come. This is ridiculous," Needle said.

"But you have nowhere to go."

"Least of all with you! You? Of all people? I must have been insane to listen to your lying old bastard of a grandfather."

"Needle," Cael began, and he changed his mind and decided it was time to be honest. "We need you. I got something to tell you, later when Mallet and Brynn wake up. Something... something that will change your mind."

"Yeah. Well, good luck with that. Let me know how it turns out if you get back to Demon's Bluff alive."

If I keep talking, Cael thought, it will only get worse. He'll just dig in even further. If he's going to stay, it's going to have to be *his* idea. Not mine.

Needle just lay there, unmoving.

What could he do or say to get Needle to want to stay? Cael's hopes were pinned on the Fourth Prophecy, but that was problematic on so many levels. It could backfire.

He had to think on it some more, so he quietly backed out from under the tarp. But at the last moment he turned and blurted out without thinking: "I watched my mother and father die yesterday, Needle."

Needle did not move. Cael pressed on. "I... I was in my grandfather's house yesterday morning... in a back room. I used a magical artifact that let me see into the past. I saw them murdered on the day I was born. I probably shouldn't have tried it. And I know how it probably sounds to you Needle, but for me it was real, and it's as fresh as if it had happened yesterday... 'cause for me it did."

Needle said nothing.

"We need you, Needle. I... I need you." He almost stopped then, but a last thought occurred to him, a thought that was surprising to him because it wasn't a manipulation, but the truth.

"Needle, I'm glad you are here with me."

Needle just lay there in quiet defiance.

Cael suddenly worried that he had pushed it too far. Maybe it had been a dumb thing to say. But there was actually a small part of him that found it hard to dislike Needle despite his faults.

Cael returned and picked up his fishing pole. With a practiced flick of his wrist, he flipped the feathered hook off the port side. He watched the colorful fly drift along on the eddies, as the *Riparian Scout* continued slowly northward upriver. The moonies must have been hungry because they were biting like crazy. In short order he had pulled in over half a dozen. He strung them on a line and dangled them over the edge in the water to keep them fresh.

There wasn't much that relaxed him like fishing. He hitched up his leggings and sat on the edge of the boat. The cool water beckoned his feet, but he didn't dare. You never knew what could be lurking down in the dark depths.

He'd spent a lot of time on this old ship with Danilus. Looking back on it, they all seemed like such happy, carefree times. Now he felt the weight of the world on his shoulders, and even fishing couldn't shake the worry from his mind. As he fished, he slowly became aware of a commotion coming from inside the cabin.

Brynn and Mallet were arguing, the volume and intensity of their voices increasing steadily. Cael strained to hear, but the words were too muffled.

The door to the cabin burst open and Mallet stumbled out. Brynn was almost hanging off of him... struggling to stop him, her eyes squinting against the increased light. Mallet held Brynn's satchel just out of her reach. He was deathly pale and sweating. It looked to Cael as if he would collapse at any moment.

"You didn't see her!" He bellowed, turning his back to block her desperate grabs. He started rooting through her pack. "You couldn't know what she had done to herself!" Blood was already seeping through his fresh bandages.

"I did see her!" screamed Brynn, "When her ghost came back!"

"You didn't see her die!"

"Mallet, you don't understand!"

"Oh I understand! I won't let you end up like mother!"

"Just let me explain!"

"Don't bother. I already know. I know what she was!" He jerked his fist out of Brynn's satchel. Cael saw two glass vials filled with pale blue liquid in Mallet's meaty hand. Fast as you please, he tossed them over the side. Cael sat frozen as he watched them arc through the air and plop into the muddy water. Mallet jammed his fist back into the satchel for another go.

"What in the infected bowels of the infinite hells is this?" Mallet bellowed as he pulled out a thin book with a wooden cover of a curious golden-hued wood, and bound by a dark cord woven through the spine. "I don't think so!"

The look of anger on Brynn's face morphed into abject panic. She reached desperately for the book but her brother was far too tall. He started to toss the book overboard, when out of desperation Brynn grabbed the only thing she could get hold of... the bandages on his shoulder. She jerked down and disrupted his throw. Cael could see the pain erupt on Mallet's face as the big boy, already woozy, toppled over sideways, taking Brynn down with him.

The book sailed short and clattered on the deck, sliding toward the gap between the rails. It came to rest balancing on the edge of the deck, rocking as if it would tip into the river at any moment.

Brynn, despite having her massive brother collapse on top of her, struggled in complete desperation to save the imperiled tome.

All Cael could do was sit dumbfounded as he watched the improbable scene unfold. A gust of wind caught the sails and rocked the boat. Brynn cried out as the book began to tip beyond the point of balance, into the river.

Suddenly, a dark flash slid across the still damp deck toward the edge. To Cael's utter amazement Needle had appeared out of nowhere and dived across the deck. In an astounding display of reflexes and athleticism that Cael would not have thought possible from the underfed Agrabi boy, Needle snatched Brynn's book from its watery fate.

"So what's this then?" he said rolling over toward Brynn, holding the dry book in his hand.

2nd Day of Summer - 11:00 AM – The Demon River - 13 days to the Full Moon

Mallet had overexerted himself. It had taken three of them to drag the big brute back into the cabin while Brynn gingerly held the tiller wheel. Her other arm clutched the rescued book to her chest. Mallet mumbled incoherently as Danilus changed his bloody bandages. Danlius held his head up and helped him drink half a mug of rum that he had spiked with several pinches of powdered herbs from his little wooden box.

Danilus finished with Mallet and came back and took the tiller, giving Tajaa a rub. Cael and Needle and Brynn now sat on crates on the foredeck. Brynn had a concerned look on her face and Cael knew she was fretting over her brother. Her face was glistening from sweat and some of her auburn hair was stuck to her face which was still smeared with soot from the night before. She was wearing the brown coarse robe he had first seen her in, which seemed odd considering she was supposed to be a duke's daughter. The robe looked more like servants attire than a noble's.

The first time he had seen her last night, he noticed how pretty she was. The events of last night hadn't given him much time to consider it, but he experienced the same feeling again this morning despite her soot-stained face and disheveled hair.

"Do you think he'll be okay?" she asked to no one in particular.

"I reckon you ain't got nothing to worry about," Danilus called from the tiller. "But I wouldn't go jerking on his bandages no more."

"That's not proper grammar," Brynn corrected.

Danilus cocked his head at her as if trying to understand what she was saying. Then he smiled. "Well... I reckon I ain't got no problem with it."

She ignored his grin. "It rained?" she asked.

"You missed it, them clouds ain't nothin'," Danilus said

looking up, with an impish smirk on his face.

"That's not correct. 'These clouds are not anything'," said Brynn in exasperation. "And even then, you wouldn't say it that way."

Cael saw Danilus just chuckle as he turned his full attention back to piloting upriver.

"I think the wizards on the cliff summoned the rain to put out the fires," said Cael. "You slept through most of it. It was pretty amazing."

"It was all real, wasn't it?" she said. "It seems like a dream now, what happened last night."

"I wish," Cael said.

"So, you never answered the question," Needle said to Brynn flatly.

She just gave him a quizzical look.

"That book you're clutching there, like it was your baby."

Brynn looked down at the book she held tightly wrapped in her arms. "You're welcome, by the way," Needle said.

Brynn sighed. "You're right Needle. Thank you for saving it. It means everything to me. My mother left it for me to find after she died."

"And?" Needle prompted.

Brynn sighed resignedly. "It's a book of sigils."

"Sigils?" Cael asked.

"Son of Abyss!" Needle exclaimed. "I knew it. The light on the floor in the mausoleum... Wheizer was right about you. And those blue bottles Mallet tossed overboard. That was your tattoo ink wasn't it?"

Brynn looked like a cornered cat for just a moment, but then a resolved look came upon her. "And why not? It's nothing I'm ashamed of!"

"I don't know," Needle said. "Your brother sure seemed concerned."

"You're a witch?" Cael asked, not quite following the speed at which this was all moving.

"Well... not yet... I mean... I hope to be."

"Let's see your tats then..." Needle said, with the intensity of an interrogator.

"Well... I don't have any yet. I was waiting for the right

time..."

"But Mallet threw all your ink into the river."

"I can make more. My mother taught me. Mostly."

"And that book was your mother's?"

"Wait just a damn minute!" Cael interjected. "That's a book of witch tattoos?"

"Sigil is the preferred term, Cael. And yes, but they aren't all for tattooing."

"And they're magical? How can a tattoo be magical? It doesn't make any sense."

"They wouldn't make any sense to a wizard. For example, some sigils confer certain protections and abjurations."

"But where does the power come from? How do they gather in magic?"

"They don't gather magic as you think of it, Cael. There are certain patterns and truths that underlie all of creation. The patterns have a power all of their own. Different from the magic you understand. There are patterns found all around us, but most people don't notice them, because they exist under the surface of what most people perceive. It takes careful training to be able to see them... to release their power."

"But that's impossible," Cael said with an edge of doubt in his voice. "Magic doesn't work that way."

"*Your* magic doesn't. Witch sigils are completely different. If all your magic vanished from the world... sigils would still have their power."

"What's their power source? For wizards it is the *Arcanus Navitas*."

"There can be no other power than the one you know?" Brynn asked. "There are more mysteries of the multiverse, don't you think?"

"What kind of abjurations?" asked Cael.

"I only know of a few so far," Brynn said. "I still have much to learn. But some sigils protect against certain hexes and curses; others against the elements and others still against certain illnesses and different types of magic."

Cael just shook his head. It seemed foreign to him. His wizardry couldn't do those things. Indeed his training didn't even consider the possibility.

"Would you like to see?" Brynn asked with a smirk, holding the golden-hued book out toward him.

Cael carefully opened the cover of the book, curiosity overtaking him. On the first page was a large and complicated pattern. He flipped through ancient, yellowed pages that contained no words, only symbol after symbol. He settled on a page and stared at the pattern before him. It was big and filled the page. It seemed to have no starting point and no ending point, but it had a bizarre and compelling symmetry. He tilted his head to try to comprehend it. The pattern seemed to turn to meet his new angle of view. The center defied him, and the edges seemed to wrap back upon themselves to the middle. He tried to imagine drawing such a pattern, but the starting point eluded him. He searched for it desperately, turning the book sideways to get a new perspective. A rushing sound like a chime in a windstorm rose up in his ears as the pattern seemed to draw him in. He suddenly felt unwell, but he couldn't look away. The pattern seemed to twist as it tormented him, accelerating into a spinning vortex. Light seemed to dim and he could feel his eyes roll back up in his head as his stomach heaved and he vomited to the side violently.

Brynn snatched the book from his limp fingers with a grin.

"What in the--?" Needle asked. "Where did he get figs?"

Cael tasted spiced wine. Needle held his head up as Brynn held a wineskin to his lips. His head was pounding. He focused his eyes in the searing light. Danilus was splashing water from a bucket to rinse off the deck.

"What happened?" Cael asked weakly.

"You puked your guts out and fainted," Needle said with a smirk.

"How long?" Cael asked as he sat up. He felt dizzy and detached.

"No more than a minute," Brynn said, helping him back up onto his crate. "Are you okay?" She sat back down.

"That was... strange," was all Cael could muster.

"It's like my mother always warned," said Needle. "Witches dance the ballet of the insane. They play with madness and their wicked symbols eventually drive them to lunacy."

"That's not true!" Brynn exclaimed. "Your mother doesn't understand."

"Well how do you explain what just happened, then?"

"Maybe it's that Cael hasn't been trained. I guess you have to be conditioned to comprehend the sigils. Some of the more powerful ones still have an unsettling effect even on me. I still have much to learn so I can progress in reading and using the elder sigils."

"So you knew?" Cael asked.

Brynn gave him an innocent look. Then she grinned. "I have felt dizzy when I've tried to look at the more complex sigils, but all the ones in that book are simple."

"Simple?" Cael exclaimed.

"I'm sorry Cael. I should have warned you."

"You should have seen yourself," said Needle with a grin. "You went down like a limp sack of turnips."

"Just one thing I don't understand though," Cael asked, rubbing his temples with thumb and middle finger. "You said you can read the symbols... are they words? Some crazy language?"

Brynn whistled her approval. "Good question. The patterns aren't words, per se. At least not like we understand words. The first time I looked at the book of sigils, I was baffled as to why there were no words that described sigils or explained what they did. It took me a while to understand that the patterns themselves communicated everything I needed to know about what they were and what they did. Once I comprehend a pattern, it communicates directly to my mind, but not in words. More in pictures... and..."

"And what?" Needle asked, intrigued. He sat back down on his crate.

"And... I know this will sound silly, but... music. Each pattern has its own melody, and once I study the pattern enough to discern the melody, I also somehow understand what it does. It's hard to explain, but I just know. I can see it in my mind. I could translate it into words, but words would be inadequate. It's like the patterns are pure communication. I can't escape the feeling that I'm only touching the surface of their true meaning; that somehow, there is much more to them that I can comprehend. I think the patterns are ancient. I think they might be the language of creation itself."

"So... you're okay with being a witch, then?" Needle asked.

"I'm just following in the footsteps of my mother, and my mother's mother."

"Well your brother doesn't seem too happy about it."

Brynn didn't answer for a few moments as she contemplated Needle's words. "I should check on him," she said as she slid her sigil book into her satchel and headed for the cabin.

Needle watched her go. When she was safely inside the cabin, he leaned in closer toward Cael. "Are you going to take care of your little problem, or do you want me to take care of it for you?" Needle said in a low voice.

Cael frowned and cradled his head in his hands with his elbows on his knees for a moment. A splash sounded on the west bank. Cael looked up to see a croc swimming away from an isthmus of matted reeds. He stared out at the river bank waiting for Needle's question to find a framework in his mind.

"Do what now?" he finally said.

"Mallet!" Needle hissed, his eyes wide with intensity. He nodded toward the cabin. "She won't be in there forever and something's got to be done. We should make a plan."

Cael could only give the Agrabi boy a baffled look.

"He's infected! If he rats out there will be no stopping him. He's got to be killed. It's the only way." Needle produced his silver dagger from the ragged folds of his shabby clothes. His small hand held the dagger steadily. Dried blood could be seen on the blade. Wheizer's blood. "It should be done soon... before his strength returns."

Cael was completely taken aback.

"Are you insane?" he hissed, frowning. "Besides, I thought you were leaving."

"I'm going to grab something to eat and go. But you're right. It's your problem, not mine." Needle shrugged. "I'm just offering to help."

"Talk sensible Needle!" Cael leaned forward and lowered his voice further. "Yes. I'm worried about it too, but there has to be another solution."

"Well, you think about it all you want. He's infected and if you wait too long he's gonna shift and tear you all to shreds. Surely you see that? I, for one, don't plan on being around when that happens. Where did you get those figs from?"

"We have plenty of time still," Cael said contemplatively, pointing to the fig barrel. "I need to think about it."

Needle shook his head as he stood up and headed over to the barrel. "Whatever. I'm just telling it like it is."

"I appreciate your concern Needle, but just let me think about it."

"Think about what?" It was Brynn emerging from the cabin.

Needle hastily hid the dagger in the folds of his shirt, dropping a few figs in the process. He cursed under his breath.

"Oh, nothing," Cael said hastily. "I caught us a mess of fish this morning before you two woke up. What say we get some breakfast going?"

"I don't suppose you caught any armored cats or whiptails?" Needle asked, taking a bite out of a large fig.

"Catfish?" Brynn asked shaking her head. "But they're bottom feeders."

Cael winced. He knew that comment would anger Needle. Catfish were an Agrabi favorite, but disdained by Buerdeleise in general.

"No more so than your average Buerdeleise noble," Needle shot back.

Brynn's green eyes flashed as she took a step back with a horrified look on her face. Her cheeks were flushed. She opened her mouth to say something, but snapped it shut.

"No catfish, Needle," Cael interjected quickly. "But I got us some moonies. If that doesn't suit you, there is plenty more to eat aboard."

"Naw. Moonies are fine by me," Needle said with a smug look on his face. "But you see what I'm talking about? I don't belong here."

"Speaking of belonging here, what are we all doing here?" Brynn asked. "I mean getting on this boat seemed to make sense in the chaos of the earthquake last night, but where are we going? When are we going home?"

"North," Danilus spat over the starboard railing. "Upriver."

Brynn looked at Danilus with irritation. "Yes, I know that," she finally said. "But why? What is the plan?"

Danilus flashed Cael an amused look. "It's a fair question I reckon Brynn, but it's a big one. Give your brother some more time to rest. Don't make no sense saying everything twice."

"Don't make no..." Brynn trailed off with a look of exasperation. "Can you at least tell me where we are going?"

"Them moonies ain't gonna cook themselves," Danilus said with a wry grin. "I bet the smell o' breakfast will get your brother up. Sides... I reckon he ought to stay good and fed."

2nd Day of Summer - 11:30 AM – The Demon River - 13 Days to the Full Moon

In short order they had the brazier going and Brynn took over the cooking. Cael had filleted the moon fish while Needle pushed a few large crates to the middle of the deck for a makeshift table, and smaller ones for chairs. He piled the table with cheese, bread, dates and more figs. He seemed to eat as much food as he put on the table, gleefully stuffing his face. He filled several frothy mugs with Danilus' dark ale. Cael tossed the fish scraps to Dheke who wolfed them down appreciatively.

Danilus had shown Brynn his trunk of cooking gear, and she exclaimed in delight when she found a box filled with small spice jars.

"Can I use these?" Brynn had asked. Danilus told her that she was welcome to use them, but to go easy as they were scarce and he saved them for special occasions. They had been a gift from a spice merchant whose caravan he had guided on a journey east a few years back.

Cael had to admit the smell of Brynn's cooking made his mouth water. His appetite had returned in full force after the nauseating feeling of looking at Brynn's sigil. He wondered how hungry Needle was, the way he was stuffing food down his gullet. The Agrabi boy's ratty linens hung loosely off his frame. It looked like he hadn't eaten a meal like this in quite some time.

Danilus secured the tiller and joined them. The fish was hot and colored with Brynn's selection of spices. Cael shoveled the food into his mouth. He had never tasted fish that delicious. Needle tried to maintain a pretense of composure, but it was clear to Cael that he had never tasted anything so delicious either.

"By the hells, girl!" Danilus exclaimed. "You're gonna have to learn me what combination of spices you done used!"

Brynn opened her mouth to say something, but then thought better of it.

Danilus got up and resumed his position at the tiller, humming to himself and tapping his finger on Tajaa's head.

Needle got up from his crate and started to clear the table. "So Brynn, there's something I've been wondering. How is it that the man who works for your father turns out to be, let's see... a leader in the thieves' guild and a filthy wererat?"

"He's not saying you had anything to do with it," Cael interjected quickly. The tension between these two was already high and he didn't need another fight. He already knew that Mallet and Needle were going to be a problem; he hoped it wouldn't spread to Brynn.

"Did I say she had anything to do with it?" Needle asked Cael.

Cael sighed. Between Needle's threat to leave them, and the trouble he seemed bent on causing, Cael wondered if it might be just as easy to shove him overboard and send him on his way.

"He tried to kill us, too," Brynn said. "And what in the world do you mean by implying he's a leader in the thieves' guild?"

"You know," Danilus said from the tiller. "Why don't you kids pull up a crate over here and sit and tell me about this Wheizer fellow. I'd like to hear about him, for sure."

"Yeah," Needle said with mock sincerity. "Me too."

Needle remained standing, but Cael pulled over a crate and sat down with Brynn next to him.

"Wheizer has been working for my father as long as I can recall," Brynn started. "I've never really liked him, but I've never really *not* liked him either. My mother didn't like him, I remember that for sure. She was always wary of him, but he never gave me cause. My father depended on him and he was loyal to my family, and very hard working. I don't think he ever failed to get something done that my father assigned him."

"Get this," Needle said, "She's defending him!"

"I am telling you what I know of him. An enemy should be known and understood, do you not agree? Wheizer has always been glib and sarcastic. Often, I would decipher his meaning only after the conversation was over, and had time to contemplate his words. He's intelligent, is what I'm trying to say. Very smart. Now, it's *your* turn to tell me what *you* know. What do mean he's a member of the thieves' guild?"

"The bigger question is, how is it possible you don't know that? I bet your father knows it. Even Mallet probably knows it. Come to think of it, you didn't even know until yesterday your father collected artifacts. I went and saw him last night to sell some to him to get money for that damn lift. Can you guess which ones were the only ones he wanted?"

"What are you talking about?" Brynn asked. "And what does it matter?"

"Let's see, he was buying... let me try and remember. Oh yeah, I got it, it was Cult of Yex artifacts. Your father is in the cult! Hells, he's probably the leader!"

"That would mean," said Cael. "That your father and my grandfather have been selling the leader of the cult artifacts for pretty much our whole lives. Are you saying Kemano was doing that, Needle?"

Needle took a seat, considering that in silence.

"I've been meaning to ask," Brynn said. "Why did you come back last night, to the docks?"

Needle's face became a mask. He looked away for several seconds as if contemplating his answer, but when he turned back he wiped his eye with his sleeve. He revealed a silver dagger from the folds of his shabby clothing: "I didn't come for you. My mother said this dagger would kill him... that silver would kill him. So I came back."

"So you came back because your mother gave you a weapon against Wheizer?" Brynn continued. "You saved our lives. I hadn't really thought of it that way. I suppose I'm indebted to you."

Needle laughed, wiping another tear from his eye, "Like I said, I didn't do it for you."

"What made you think he would be there at the dock? I mean, as far as anyone knew, he should have been dead. And even if he wasn't dead, how could he possibly have known we were going to the docks?"

Needle's face was blank. At first Cael didn't think he would say anything, and then the little Agrabi kid spoke, his voice soft and papery: "He just kept coming. The fall from the lift should have killed him, but he kept coming." He turned and stared straight at Cael for several seconds. He opened his mouth to say something, but then snapped it shut. He slumped over and dropped his silver dagger onto the deck. His chest heaved as he held his head in his hands and cried.

Cael looked to Brynn, whose face was etched with concern for the sobbing Agrabi boy. He looked to Danilus, who just shrugged.

"What happened, Needle?" Brynn asked, kneeling down and putting her hand on his shoulder. "Tell us."

"He killed my mother," he sobbed. "I went home to see her, to make sure she was okay from the earthquake. She was okay, but then Wheizer broke the door open and came in."

"That's impossible," Brynn said. "Did he follow you?"

"No," Needle said. "He followed *you*."

"What are you talking about?"

"He learned where I lived because he was spying on you earlier the same day. Remember when you said you felt like someone was following you?"

A stunned look spread across Brynn's face.

Needle broke down again in a series of sobs before he finally regained his composure. "So after the earthquake, he figured I'd go home to take care of my mother. And like an idiot I went home and told my mother about everything, and about you going to the north docks. He must have been just outside. He heard *everything*. He came in, laughing at us. He was half-man, half-rat, all broken and bent from his fall. I froze up and couldn't move as I watched him kill my mom. I couldn't do anything, I had the dagger in my hand, but I couldn't move, I couldn't talk, I couldn't scream. Then he gave me a look like he was going to come back for me, and he left laughing. I knew he was going to find you first. I knew he was going to the granary docks. Something in my head snapped, and I knew I had to kill him or die trying. I got to the gate and saw him standing there threatening you, and this time, by the abyss, I didn't hesitate."

He reached down and grabbed the hilt of the dagger and squeezed it until his brown knuckles turned white.

Brynn wrapped her arms around him. Cael considered the story he had just heard. Wheizer was clever, and someone to fear. He was alive and Cael suddenly had a new concern. When they returned to Demon's Bluff... if they returned... what would become of their situation with Wheizer? Would the wererat forget? Not likely.

Brynn stood up and moved back to her crate and began talking to herself: "He followed me *yesterday*? He overheard everything I said to Needle? He knows about my Mother? *That's* why he was at the mausoleum last night!"

"If I hadn't gone home last night, she'd still be alive," Needle sobbed.

"I thought silver killed wererats." Cael said.

"He followed me," Brynn said, shaking her head.

Needle reached out, grabbed a fig and took a bite.

"No really, how is it possible that the silver dagger didn't kill him last night?" Cael asked.

"It's a good question, I reckon," said Danilus. "All the lore I ever heard says wererats are more susceptible to wounds from silvered weapons, but it don't mean they automatically die from them."

"I'm going to find him and finish the job," The olive skinned Agrabi boy said squeezing the hilt of his dagger again.

"I'll help you." It was Mallet's voice. "I could smell fish cooking. I hope you saved some for me." He supported his frame by hanging on the open door of the cabin, though some of his color had returned. "I'm starving."

"How you feeling?" Danilus asked.

"I'll feel better once I eat."

Mallet limped over and took one of the crates, the wood creaking under the strain of his weight. Cael thought it might collapse.

"Your bandages are soaking through," Needle said.

"Ale," Mallet said. He ran a hand over his bald dome which was already covered in dark stubble.

Cael got him a mug of dark ale while Danilus changed his bandages.

Cael marveled at Mallet's resilience. The big boy sat upon his crate drinking his ale as Danilus once again cleaned his wounds and changed his bandages. Some places on Mallet's chest the skin hung in ribbons. Several of the stitches had torn from when Brynn had jerked on his bandages. Apparently Danilus had just put Mallet back down to bed without re-stitching them. Danilus re-stitched the mess with a needle and thread as the boy gritted his teeth against the pain. Cael almost vomited again at the sight of the injuries. He couldn't understand how Mallet had survived such wounds. Cael was certain that if he had been the recipient of those wounds, he would have died. And even if he had survived, he would be in no state to be eating...or even sitting up, for that matter.

When Danilus was finished, Mallet smiled. "What's left to eat?"

Cael sat with Mallet on his left and Brynn on his right at the makeshift table. Needle sat across from him, and Danilus stood at the tiller. They had re-stocked the table, including a dried ham for Mallet, who was focused on devouring his breakfast. He now seemed to be an eating machine. He consumed what remained of the fish, a slab of cured ham, a large wedge of cheese, several loaves of bread, dozens of dates and figs, and by Cael's estimate, almost a gallon of ale. Needle had remarked only once as Mallet ate, noting: "Like that cheese, do ya?"

The south wind, which had been cool before, now blew hot

and humid. Cael eyed the water, thinking of splashing the back of his neck. Brynn produced oil from her satchel, which had a pungent fruity aroma, and dabbed it on herself.

"Holy hells," said Needle as he watched her. "What other useless stuff you got in that bag?"

"Well, I have a comb and ivory gold clasps to help keep my hair back out of my face," said Brynn missing Needle's sarcasm. "I keep a few ointments and crocodile fat as a base to soften the skin. And a few bottles of flower oil so I smell nice. I have ox tallow candles scented with myrrh, and quite a few other items. Do you want me to dig them out and show you?"

Cael just shook his head.

They were passing the northern reaches of the irrigated grain fields that marked the border of the lands of Demon's Bluff. This far north, all the fields had been shorn and the grain put on barges for transport down river.

"Well, now that we are all together, it's about time we had us a talk," said Cael, the Fourth Prophecy weighing heavily on his mind. So many questions remained unanswered. Not the least of which was where they were going.

"How you feelin' then?" Needle looked at Mallet warily.

"Huh?" The big boy looked up as he sucked the marrow out of a ham bone. His eyes narrowed as he looked at Needle. "What's it to you? And don't think I haven't noticed you eyeballin' me."

"I have no idea what you're talking about." Needle allowed a grin to sneak onto his face. "I'm just worried about you, that's all."

"That's what I'm talking about," Mallet said. "Don't go thinking I'm deaf to your tone."

"What are you trying to say, Mallet?" Needle said, flashing a glance to Cael.

"You know damn well what I'm trying to say," Mallet said.

"Do I?"

"I know exactly what you're thinking you little Agrabi scrub. You're thinking it's just a matter of time before I turn into a rat and murder everyone on this boat. You're *afraid.*"

"No," Needle smiled. "I damn near killed Wheizer myself. I don't think you'll be as big a problem."

Mallet put down his ham bone. "You *are* afraid. I can see it in your eyes."

"So, brother," said Brynn, "Did you know Father collected Cult of Yex artifacts?"

"You're the one that should be afraid!" Needle shot back.

Mallet stood up ominously, his body swaying with the motion of the boat as the sails caught a gust of wind.

"Cult of Yex, where are we going, prophecies, earthquakes... hello!" said Cael. "We got bigger questions to answer. Hells... we're *all* afraid."

"Convince me you aren't afraid!" Needle said to Mallet as he stood up facing the much bigger boy. "It doesn't matter to me, because I'm leaving. But don't tell me you haven't thought your predicament through... You're infected with lycanthropy and come the next full moon, maybe sooner if you keep getting angry, you'll shift and kill everyone around you in an uncontrollable rage. And by everyone, I specifically mean your precious little sister, whom I suspect you actually care about, even if you don't care about anyone else. So the question is; why are *you* still here? Have you considered the noble way out? But without silver, no blade you fall upon will ultimately do the job. If you need a loan, consider me a willing lender." Needle drew the blood stained dagger from his tunic and held it out to Mallet, hilt first. "I'll gladly provide the means by which you pass into the next life with your honor intact!"

Cael was amazed. It was quite a speech from the Agrabi boy. Mallet, on the other hand, was not so easily impressed.

"I really don't like you," he growled.

"You're breaking my heart," said Needle. "But that's beside the point. What's it going to be?"

Mallet's face fell and he started to advance around the makeshift table on Needle, who almost fell over the crate he had been sitting on as he quickly backed away. He deftly flipped the blade over to grasp it by the hilt as he held the blade forth menacingly.

"Or... there is *this* option," said Needle. "It's an exciting choice, if nothing else."

Mallet moved faster than anyone anticipated, and with his height, his reach was enormous. He deftly slapped the dagger from Needle's hand. It clattered to the deck. With his other hand he reached out and grabbed the boy by the front of his tunic and lifted him, feet dangling a foot off the deck. Mallet pulled Needle in, holding him so that their faces were an inch apart.

Needle's face flashed with fear, but he grinned through it, "Wooh! Your breath is terrible. I think that ham you were sucking on may have turned."

"Mallet," Brynn said quietly, moving toward her brother. Danilus leaned back against the cabin wall behind him, watching intently, but not saying a word. Dheke lay nearby sleeping with his head on a coil of rope.

Mallet ignored his sister and continued to hold Needle aloft. His face was red with anger but he said nothing.

"Needle might have a point," Cael said.

Mallet turned and looked at Cael.

"You know," Cael said, "If you *do* turn into a wererat and are about to kill your sister, Needle and his dagger might save her life. He'll be doing you a favor."

Mallet grimaced and looked back at the scrawny Agrabi boy he held. He put Needle down and released the grip on his ragged tunic.

"That's it? No kiss?" Needle said.

Cael smiled in relief. "This is the Needle I remember growing up with."

"How long have you known him?" Brynn asked.

"We spent a lot of time together in the desert when we were younger," Cael said. "He's clever and useful. You'll come to see that." In point of fact, Needle had just made himself very useful by forcing a delicate issue out into the open. It wasn't the way Cael would have preferred, but it had worked. Cael was also surprised by Needle's bravery. Injured or not, Mallet could probably still take most men in a fight, much less a scrawny boy like Needle. He didn't back down. Like Needle or not, that had to be respected.

"Oh, I can see that already," said Brynn, "But if he gets himself killed by Mallet, how useful will he be then?"

Mallet sat down again, and picked up his mug of ale.

Cael considered Needle's concerns. Mallet had just displayed a hint of how formidable he could be. Cael could only imagine that as a superhuman rampaging wererat, he'd be nigh unstoppable.

"How do you suppose Father and our home fared last night in the earthquake?" Brynn asked Mallet, coming to sit next to him. Her eyes were fixed downriver toward the south.

Cael looked in that direction, and there was only the faintest hint of smoke on the horizon.

"After what he did to me last night, I don't care."

"What?" Brynn asked. "Wheizer you mean."

"Wheizer is just a tool... just my father's tool." Mallet hung his head. "Father betrayed me last night, Brynn," He looked up at her with a tear in his eye. "What happened at the mausoleum last night was *nothing*," Mallet continued.

"What do you mean, 'nothing'?" Needle said. "Your mother's ghost appeared, and was about to tell us what the holy hells is going on, and Wheizer killed her. You were bitten by a wererat and are probably infected!"

"Oh I'm infected all right," said Mallet. "But I was infected *before* Wheizer bit me last night."

"What in the nine hells are you talking about?" Needle asked.

Mallet took a deep breath and then expelled it. He responded, not to Needle, but to Brynn. "Yesterday morning, I discovered something about father... about his business... about our family's business, Brynn." Mallet paused for a moment, as Brynn looked on expectantly. "Father runs slaves down to Balankov."

Brynn's face was stone. Cael saw the strangest look come over Needle's face as Mallet continued. "I think it has been going on for years."

"No." Brynn said.

"I saw it yesterday," said Mallet. "With my own eyes. I was at the warehouse but the deliveries were late. I decided to head to the docks to help them unload, and Captain Vosc was acting strange. He tried to get me to leave. I know now that he was trying to keep me from learning the truth. His men were taking on crates of slaves for transport to market in Balankov. I...I got in a fight with Vosc."

"And?" Brynn asked.

"Then I went home to talk to Father about it. I thought he would say it was Vosc, but he admitted he was the one behind it. He told me everything. Wheizer runs the slaving operation for Father... and who knows what else? I guess they'd been waiting for the right time to tell me. I don't think last night was the night they planned for, but when I discovered what was going on... I think it forced their hand. They expected me to just go along with it. Father said it was my family duty. He and Wheizer took me into a secret chamber off Father's study. It's where he keeps his collection of ancient artifacts emblazoned with evil symbols."

"I bet there's a fortune in that room," Needle said.

"No," Brynn repeated.

"I told father what I had discovered," Mallet continued, "Thinking that I had done right and protected the family. But Father wasn't happy. I'm pretty sure that Wheizer already knew everything and told Father before I confessed."

"And then?" Brynn asked.

"Father said it was time I helped carry the burdens of the family. He said Wheizer had been running the... um... dangerous parts of the family business for years, and it was time for me to help." Mallet's voice was low. "I could see he wasn't sure what I would do. He needed some way to control me. Some way for Wheizer to control me."

"So Wheizer bit you then? And infected you?" Needle interjected. Cael could still see the intensity in his eyes.

Mallet continued as if he hadn't heard. "He asked me to swear an oath to him... to the family."

"Did you?" Brynn asked.

"What choice did I have? I've always put the family first. Mother taught us that."

"No, she taught us to put principles first."

"And family is the number one principle."

"I don't think you understood her correctly."

"Either way, I thought if I didn't swear the oath, Wheizer would kill me then and there."

"Oh Mallet..." Brynn said.

"Then father said it wasn't enough. He said I had to seal the oath in blood. By drinking blood... by—"

"You drank the wererat's blood!" Needle said. "They wanted to make you into a wererat. Son of abyss. You got to be kidding me."

"I didn't understand at the time what was happening," Mallet sighed, ignoring Needle's editorial. "I didn't know he was a wererat. He just peeled open a vein... and I had to drink."

"There's no mistaking it now," Needle said in amazement.

"You saw Wheizer change in the mausoleum," Brynn finished. "But you had already been infected."

Mallet's shoulders slumped. He looked up at Needle after a moment. "I'm sorry about your mother, Needle. I heard you tell everyone while I was down in the cabin. Like I promised... if your silver dagger didn't kill Wheizer... I'll help you finish the job. I want him dead too."

"Um... Mallet. What happens now?" asked Cael, clearing his throat.

Mallet just looked at him quizzically. A gust of wind made the sail pop.

"You know. You're infected. What's going to happen? As much as I would like to depend on Needle and his dagger to protect us from you, something tells me the odds aren't in our favor."

"The hells they aren't," Needle said.

Mallet just shrugged. "I don't know. Needle might be right. Last night before Needle showed up and stabbed the bastard, Wheizer told me that I will change at the next full moon."

Cael looked up into the sky. No one said anything for an uncomfortable eternity. Needle looked up at Cael, as if to say "I told you so."

"So... anyone going to eat that last piece of dried ham?" Mallet finally asked.

"Where are we going?" asked Needle. "And where is your grandfather? I thought he was coming with us."

"He's not coming with us," Cael said. "He said he was going to Taglyon."

"Taglyon?" Needle asked. "Why?"

"He flew off on a flying carpet," said Brynn.

"What in the holy hells?" asked Needle. "Where did that old ember get a flying carpet?"

"Yeah. I thought old wizards couldn't cast spells anymore," said Brynn.

"It doesn't work that way with magical devices like that carpet," Cael explained. "Boxxaway could use it without casting a spell. With a little practice I could learn to use it and I wouldn't age at all. Just like the embers operating the lifts."

"So what makes it magical?" asked Mallet, a handful of figs paused halfway between his hand and his mouth.

"Well. It was created... infused with magic. It takes a group of wizards working together to forge a magical item. They bind the magic into the device. The lifts in Demon's Bluff are the same kind of idea. Magic was bound into the lifts by a group of wizards from the Academy. The wizards spend their age when they create it, but afterwards it works like any tool."

"Why does it have to be a group of wizards? One wizard couldn't make a magical device?" Brynn asked.

"Well, yes... but it's complicated," Cael responded. "A wizard could make a magical device himself, but none would want to if they could help it. When a wizard uses magic, that magic takes a piece of him with it. It ages him a little bit, whether he is casting a spell or infusing magic into an item. Some magical devices require so much magic to make, that no wizard wants to pay the whole cost. If a whole group of wizards join together, each pays only a small price."

"Is that why Boxxaway is so old?" asked Mallet. "He made the carpet himself?"

"Well, no... I don't know. I don't think so," Cael said. "That carpet has been in our hallway my whole life. It looks really old... but I'm guessing it's much older than it looks; probably much older than my grandfather. That's common with magical items. The magic in them preserves them through the ages."

"What does it feel like?" Mallet asked, taking another swig from his mug.

Cael looked at him quizzically.

"You know... casting a spell. Does it hurt? When you age?"

"A little. It feels nice and hurts at the same time. It's hard to explain. Some wizards like it too much. They use too much magic and grow old before their time."

"Embers," Needle said flatly. "How old *is* your grandfather, then?"

Cael scrunched his nose. "I'm not sure. He has never told me, but I know that he looks older than he really is. He has told me that much, at least. I think he might be ashamed about how much magic he spent in his youth. He warns me constantly about being careful. Not using magic for stupid or simple things. Saving it. You know."

"What would happen if he did cast spells?" Mallet asked.

"It's hard to say. But every spell ages a wizard. Some spells only a few minutes. Powerful spells could age a wizard days or even months. I've heard of spells that can take a year or more from a wizard... but no one would be foolish enough to do that. At Boxxaway's age... it's dangerous. He has only cast a few minor spells since I can remember. He just doesn't take the risk any more. Except for the last few days... he said he's cast a few divinations."

"Imagine," Mallet exclaimed. "What sorts of spells could be that powerful to age someone *years*?"

"I don't know," Cael said. "My grandfather would never tell me. He says such spells are best left unknown. Only the wicked or insane would dare pay the price."

"One thing I don't understand..." said Brynn. "Can only a wizard use a magical device? I thought anyone could. The soothsayers in the market district sell talismans for luck and protection."

Cael was surprised by the insight of her question. She had picked up on a subtlety most people would miss. "Those talismans aren't really magical. If they were, they would cost more. No wizard would spend himself so cheaply."

"I knew it," said Mallet. "I always thought they were lying."

"You're not the sharpest wheel of cheese in the shop are

you?" said Needle, shaking his head. Mallet looked confused for a moment before comprehension dawned on him. He flashed Needle a dirty look.

Cael continued. "Most magical items anyone can use. Like an enchanted sword or ring. But some things... only a wizard can use."

"Like the lifts!" Brynn said. "That's why a wizard operates them. It's not just to collect the money is it?"

"Right," Cael said. "It just depends. In the case of the lifts, they assign old burned out wizards to operate them because they don't have to spend any of their life force, but it takes the skill of wizards to make them work. They just sort of... plug into the magic bound into it."

"So nobody answered my question," Needle said. Cael saw Brynn and Mallet looking at him in confusion. Cael didn't understand either.

"Where in the abyss are we going?" Needle said with a hint of exasperation.

Danilus' voice rang out from the distance where he stood at the tiller. "I reckon it's time for Boxxaway to tell you himself. I've something for you, Cael... all of you, really. Come and fetch these things from your grandfather."

Danilus produced a rolled piece of parchment from a trunk on the port side of the boat and tucked it in a pocket near the breast of his tunic. "Ol' Boxxaway sent fresh clothing for all of you and some things to protect yourselves with."

He produced a glaive from behind the trunk and handed it to Mallet. The big boy spun the shaft in his hands and examined the blade appreciatively. Danilus gave Brynn a dagger with belt and scabbard. She took them and set them down next to her with a distasteful look on her face. Next, Danilus handed Needle another dagger with belt and scabbard.

The Agrabi boy pulled the blade from its sheath and examined it. "My blade is better," Needle said with a furtive glance at Mallet. "But I could use the scabbard and belt." He handed the dagger back to Danilus, who laid it back in the trunk with a shrug. Needle slid his own silver blade into the sheath and continued to fiddle with it.

"And for Cael..." Danilus said with a flourish. "Boxxaway

has something for you, my boy, but the time ain't yet. But don't you worry none. Time will be right soon."

Danilus took the rolled up parchment from his breast pocket and handed it to Cael.

Cael sat down with the parchment, breaking the wax seal with his fingers. He reached out and hooked one of the crates with his foot, pulling it under him as he sat down. The rest sat down, heads leaning toward Cael as he unrolled the long papyrus. Boxxaway's tight scrawl was unmistakable. Cael read aloud.

My Dearest Grandson Cael,

I expect you and your companions have many questions. This letter will answer some of them, but some answers will have to wait until we meet again, as I don't have much time to write. Agents of the newly-risen cult are surely about, and I also think it unwise to reveal too much of our plans in writing.

I have known this day would come since the day you were born Cael, but despite signs and portents that grew ever clearer I foolishly allowed myself to hope that this day was still years into the future. It was only in the last week that I began to fully realize that the return of the Cult of Yex was indeed at hand. You and your companions are still so young, and I have had but scant days in which to make final preparations.

I should start by telling you a truth I have kept hidden in order to protect you. On the night that your parents were murdered, I was able to defeat the assassin that the Cult sent to kill your parents. My daughter (your mother) died without another word, but your father lived on for a few minutes before he succumbed to his wounds.

In his final breaths he told a tale that seemed to me outlandish at the time. But in the years since, I have come to know the awful truth of it. Thousands of years ago, after King Adirak had vanquished the Cult of Yex, he established a secret organization that would endure through the ages in vigilance, lest the Cult of Yex try to reemerge. The league of Watchers that Adirak formed was called "The Society of Eyes" and your father confided in me that he was a member, as was his father, and his father before him.

Your father's dying wish was that I raise you up and prepare you to don the mantle as a Watcher. He told me the other Watchers would seek you out when you were ready to take your rightful place amongst the few of them that remained. Before he died, he made me swear an oath to protect and prepare you for that time.

I fear the Cult of Yex killed whatever Watchers remained, as they killed your parents. I believe many secrets of the Society of Eyes may have perished with them, leaving us at an even greater disadvantage. But I have discovered the existence of three other children who are tied to the Society of Eyes. These are your companions, Needle, Mallet, and Brynn.

In the years that followed your parent's murder, I researched the Cult of Yex and came to my own realization that not only was your father's tale true, but the time that the Society of Eyes had always feared was very close. I prayed it was far enough into the future that you would have grown into manhood and could bear that responsibility on your own, and I could spend my last years in peace and rest. Sadly, I let hope cloud my judgment and we find ourselves in our current predicament; underprepared and underequipped. I am afraid we are alone in this and it falls to us. There will be no rest for an old man.

I have spent the past days puzzling out what to do, and I believe I have hit on a plan that constitutes our best hope. As you are now certainly aware, the Cult of Yex has indeed returned, just as their prophecies have foretold.

I believe they seek even now to kill you and your companions... for you are the only ones who can stop them from regaining power and calling their demon master to this world.

My plan is not yet complete, but for now I know that we must do two things. The first is that we protect you and your companions, for without you all hope is lost. Next, we must prepare ourselves to face the Cult before they grow too strong.

To these ends, I am sending you north up the river with Danilus as your guide. This will remove you from the immediate vicinity of Demon's Bluff for a time, and while you are there you must retrieve something of critical importance to our cause.

Many day's journey to the north, past the Foetid Swamp and up the canyon of the Bystle Plateau there is a great dam that spans the waters of the Demon River. Danilus will see you safely to that point. There on the eastern shore you will find a concealed path that leads to the top of the canyon. Due east from there is a small hidden kingdom of Rothkin in a place called Bystle Vale.

A King named Tharchelon rules there. He is guardian of a dangerous but powerful herb called Bystle Moss. The newly-emerged Cult of Yex is bound to seek it out eventually to augment their sorceries as they did in ancient times. Getting to it first and stealing it will deprive them of a powerful asset. Additionally, we have an important task (that I will explain later because I don't want to say too much here) that can only be accomplished with the power of the moss. Fortunately, I found a safe way to use it without eating it as the cult's sorcerers did in ancient times. Whatever you do, do not eat the moss.

After you were born, I spent years researching and largely spent myself using divinations to prepare. Among other things, I learned the location of this herb.

Before the ancient Cult of Yex fell those many thousands of years ago, their agents fled to the far corners of the world and hid themselves. One of their agents fled to the Bystle Vale, taking with them the moss to hide from the world, waiting for the time that the cult should return.

King Tharchelon is descended from those first agents and now keeps the Bystle Moss. Fortunately, the passing generations have erased memories of their origins.

As guardian of the moss, King Tharchelon was instructed by his father, who was instructed by his father all the way back to the beginning, that he should only give the moss to one who presents him with the proper tokens, though I'm sure he knows not why. After the fall of the Cult of Yex, these tokens were left as beacons to guide surviving Rothkin to the vale.

Cael, it is up to you to find these tokens. Danilus will take you to a certain place, and there he will give you further instructions on what to do to get the tokens.

You must find and present these tokens to King Tharchelon. He will then give you the moss in return. Bring it back to me in Demon's Bluff where we will plan our next moves. All of you take great care to avoid attention when you return. There are likely active cult spies in Demon's Bluff looking for you.

You should destroy this letter after you have read it, and be wary and watchful for agents of the Cult of Yex.

I have left some provisions with Danilus for you, Brynn, Mallet & Needle.

May the blessing of the heavens accompany you,
Boxxaway Hotheway

"Well, I like a good conspiracy as much as the next fellow," said Needle. "But let's keep this in the realm of reality, shall we?

"Um... when did he write that letter?" Brynn asked.

"I... I... don't know." Cael hesitated, understanding what Brynn was really asking. Cael already knew some of the things in the letter, but he had to admit it seemed surreal.

"He gave it to me yesterday afternoon," Danilus said. "He met me at the docks. He had hired a wagon so I could bring supplies from the market. He left Dheke with me, gave me that letter and some other stuff. He said I was to take a load of supplies down to Needle's mother, food, money and whatnot, which I did that evening, and then return and wait at the granary dock until you four showed up. No matter how long I had to wait."

At the mention of his name, Dheke looked up from where he was lying on the deck. He woofed softly, and put his head back down and closed his eyes.

"But that's just not possible," Brynn said. "How could he have written that letter *before* we met last night at the Mausoleum? How could he know we'd all be there? How could he possibly know we'd all be here now?"

"He said he cast divinations in the letter," Cael said.

"So then he knew everything?" Brynn asked.

"No, divinations are expensive, Brynn... especially at my grandfather's age. I'm actually shocked that he would dare. He must have felt he had no other choice."

"Expensive?" Needle wrinkled his nose.

"I mean in terms of how much of your life you have to spend to divine the future," Cael said. "It gets harder and harder to see the future the farther ahead you look. Looking ahead by an hour might age you an hour or two. Looking ahead a day might age you a few days. Looking a whole year ahead might age you several years. The cost is just too high. Besides that, the divinations aren't completely reliable anyway. The farther ahead in time you look, the less certain the outcome is."

"So he could have aged himself to death just to find out where we would be?" Brynn asked.

Cael nodded solemnly.

"Then that would mean he knew about the earthquake." Mallet exclaimed. "He knew it was going to happen."

"Maybe, but divinations are just not clear, like I said." Cael interjected. "Or he wouldn't have had us meet him at his cottage. He knew *something* was going to happen... something big, and bad. It's possible he didn't know exactly what or exactly when. Just that it was close. Why else would he be caught running out of it when it happened?"

"How could you possibly know that?" shot Needle. "You saw him on the great stair waving us back just before the sinkhole opened up. It looked to me like he knew."

"But just barely. He almost got caught in it himself!"

Cael's thoughts raced again to the Fourth Prophecy and to his discussion with Boxxaway at the edge of the sinkhole. How much should he tell his companions? And when? Something in him urged caution. He would save the details until later. As frustrated as he was at Boxxaway for withholding such things from him, he suddenly understood the need to go slow with his companions. They needed to be eased into this.

"Surely he told you something," Needle said.

"He... he really didn't tell me any details. He's just been acting strangely the last few days. He has told me about the Cult of Yex since I was a child, and that they promised to one day return. I never paid any attention to it."

"So?" Needle prompted. "Surely he told you something about his divinations."

Cael didn't like the pressure he was feeling; especially from Needle. He was suddenly remembering his conflicted feelings about the Agrabi boy. Even from their first meeting at Ganger's tomb. Needle seemed angry, and that was understandable given the circumstances, but it was hard to know where his anger was directed. "Yesterday morning, he told me that something important was about to happen," Cael said. "He told me I needed to go to the Bygrave Mausoleum. It didn't make sense to me at the time. It still doesn't, really."

"What in the name of all the hells?" Needle breathed. "The old bastard told me the same thing yesterday after he... at the river district. I bumped into him on the way back from fishing. He told me I needed to go there too and even gave me some artifacts to... um... sell to pay the passage on the lifts. He made me promise I would go."

"When was this?" Brynn demanded. "Were those the artifacts that were on your table?"

"Before. Just before. I had gotten home just a few minutes before you showed up."

"Why did you not tell me that? Did it not seem important? I tried for an hour to convince you to come up to the Mausoleum with me, and you already knew about it, and just neglected to tell me about it?"

"Well... yeah. But I still hadn't made up mind to go. It all seemed so foolish. You Buerdeleise just don't understand!"

A defensive edge was creeping into Needle's voice. Cael could sense the anger that percolated just under the surface.

Needle pressed on. "I'm sure the expense of riding those lifts is nothing to you. But it is a fortune to me and my mother." Needle's voice quieted as he spoke of his mother.

"But..." said Mallet. "I thought you said the old wizard gave you artifacts to sell to get the money?"

"That money could have saved us from poverty!" Needle said. "It was foolishness then and its foolishness now!"

"I don't think so, Needle," Brynn said. "Don't you see that something big is happening? Something evil?"

"The only evil is that old bastard Boxxaway. Our home town was destroyed and he sends us away? Where? For what? To find some moss? To fight an imaginary cult that has been gone for thousands of years?" Needle's olive face was getting a tinge of red. "Don't you all see how crazy this is?"

"How can you say that, Needle?" Brynn stood up, showing a flash of irritation. "You saw the letter I showed you earlier! You said yourself it was your father's own handwriting! Your father believed the Cult of Yex had already returned. It was clear that he feared them."

Needle had risen to his feet and seemed poised to unleash, but he had no response to that. His mouth opened, but no words came.

Cael could see that Needle's mind was racing. Brynn's revelation about a letter from Needle's father had his mind racing too.

Mallet beat him to it. "What letter?"

Needle sat down. He was still angry, but ceded to Brynn.

Brynn was silent for several moments. She took a deep breath. "I found some of Mother's things. I think she left them for me to find, actually. I think she knew she was in danger. There was a letter to her from Needle's father. I think it was written just before they were both murdered. I brought it with me."

Brynn started digging in her satchel.

"I'm gonna need to rest pretty soon," Mallet said with an odd tenor in his voice. "I'm not feeling well all of a sudden." Mallet leaned back on his crate, hands holding his head as he looked into the blue sky. All the clouds had dissipated, and the weather was getting back to normal.

Brynn handed Mallet the letter. He took a long time to read it. Cael assumed he was reading it twice. He wondered if he should ask to read it, but Mallet spared him the awkward question by handing it to him.

"I don't understand, Brynn. What does this mean?" Mallet asked.

Cael read the note quickly and instantly understood its significance. Did Brynn? Her response told Cael that she did.

"It means that Mother was a Watcher in this Society of Eyes, just like Cael's father. It means Needle's father was a Watcher too. It means the Cult of Yex is real. It means what Cael's grandfather told us is true. And I for one intend to help."

"Oh, I ain't believin' this!" Needle said as he threw his arms in the air. "This is wrong. It's all wrong. We should be home helping people recover from that earthquake. We are running away like cowards on a foolish errand for a foolish old man. Can't you see that? You are desperate for a reason for the bad things that happened last night. You are so desperate that you see connections between us that aren't there. Well, all I know is that you are Buerdeleise and I am Agrabi. There is no reason for it all and there are no connections. We should turn around and go home."

Cael considered Needle's words. You would have to be truly obtuse not to see the connections. Needle wasn't dumb; he was just emotionally wrought. He had been bitter since the disappearance of his father, and now he had witnessed the murder of his mother and blamed himself for it. For a time, as they ate breakfast, it seemed like Needle was coming around, but the letter from Boxxaway had riled him. Now he was being contrary just for the sake of being contrary. The question was how to deal with him? What to say?

"I don't think you really believe that," Cael challenged him.

"Needle, how can you say that?" Brynn added. "Have you already forgotten what happened last night in the Mausoleum? You saw it with your own eyes!"

But Needle was proving to be exceptionally stubborn. "All I know is I spent a fortune in the hope of learning about my father. And I didn't learn anything! The ghost we saw there said that my father wasn't in her vision. She didn't know anything!" Needle was almost shouting now. "That rat bastard was there and I led him home to kill my mother! I shouldn't have gone last night and I shouldn't be here. If I had just listened to my better judgment I'd be home right now and my mother would still be alive!"

"The hells," Cael retorted. "Your instincts told you to go, not stay." Cael wasn't sure how he knew this, but he did. Needle shot him a look of such vehement anger that Cael was forced to grit his teeth and clench his fists to stop himself from responding.

"Needle, I'm sorry for your loss," Brynn said. "I truly am. I wish it could have been another way, but why can't you see that something is going on? Can't you see the pattern? Evil forces are afoot, Needle, and they are working against *us*! My mother had something important to tell us last night and she *would have* told us! Do you think it's an accident that Wheizer was there? My mother was about to warn us about someone. Haven't you thought about that? Can't you see the connection?"

"Oh for hells' sake, Brynn!" Needle said in exasperation. "There is no connection there! You're grasping!"

"Listen to me, Needle," Brynn said. "This is simple. Your father and my mother were members of the Society of Eyes. Just like Cael's father was. They knew the Cult of Yex was returning. Your father sent my mother a letter because he had discovered something. I think he had discovered a member of the Cult of Yex! He wanted to talk to my mother about it. He told her and it got her killed. Last night at the Mausoleum, she was going to tell us what she knew. What your father had told her."

Needle hesitated for a moment and the anger seemed to leave him. But it returned quickly as he started speaking again. "Fine, Brynn. Assume all that is true. Assume the Cult of Yex is real and has returned. Assume that Wheizer is a member—"

Brynn tried to interject but Needle pressed on. "Because that's what you're driving at. And by extension, so is Duke Dagorn Bygrave."

Mallet jerked at this assertion, but Needle continued. "Oh, don't tell me you haven't thought it! You connected all those imaginary dots but forgot to connect the most important one? *Please*! None of you had to ask who I sold those artifacts to!"

Cael feared where this might lead. Mallet's face was turning red and his fists were clenched. But Needle was Needle; if he sensed Mallet's ire, he pressed on in spite of it.

"Assume it's all true! So what? Why is that my problem? What am I supposed to do about it? You need *me* to stop the return of the most evil cult in history? Hells, we are just kids!

I don't know if you noticed, but *I'm* just an Agrabi kid. I'm not needed here, and furthermore... I don't really belong anyway. Despite what you say, there is nothing but an old man's fevered scheme that connects us."

"You're wrong, Needle." Cael said. "We *are* connected. All of us are. We have been connected since birth, whether we knew it or not."

"Brynn went through this already, Cael," Needle said.

"We're all orphans, Needle." Cael continued calmly. "Our parents were all killed by the Cult of Yex. My parents were killed by the cult on the day I was born. They tried to kill me too, but my Grandfather saved me. They killed Brynn and Mallet's mother. And they killed your father, Needle... *and* your mother. We are connected because our parents were murdered for daring to fight against them. Like it or not, the four of us have inherited our parents' legacy. If nothing else, we are bound by a desire for revenge. At least I am, and I know you want Wheizer dead. By your own logic, Wheizer must be a member of the Cult. You know it won't take him long to connect the dots on his end either... if he hasn't already. He'll figure out you are dangerous and you'll be on his list with the rest of us. Do you think it matters to them if you have decided not to fight? That they won't kill you anyway?"

"They won't stop," Mallet agreed wearily, slumping back down on his crate. "My father won't stop. You are right about that."

A river heron cried in the distance. Dheke woofed without looking up.

Needle hesitated again as he weighed Cael's words. "That's just a theory. A theory you can't prove. I can throw out theories just as easy as you. How's this for a theory? Boxxaway is an old fool who has finally gone crazy. He has had it in for me and my father ever since you stole our dig back at Ganger's tomb. My father was a fool for trusting him then, and I was a fool for trusting him yesterday. Well, I won't be a fool today. My mother was right about him. She has been right about everything."

Needle walked over to the gap in the barrels and crates where he had slept through the night and snatched up his pack. "Forget this... I'm going home!" Needle headed for the port rail. "Thanks for breakfast."

Danilus watched intently, but said nothing as he gave Tajaa a rub.

Cael felt a sense of panic. Needle *couldn't* leave. He just couldn't. The chilling words of the Fourth Prophecy raced through his mind again. He fingered the folded parchment that was still in his pocket. Cael had to convince him. Needle had to come with them. But Needle's intention was clear; a swim of a hundred yards or so to the western shore, and a couple day's walk and he would be back home in Demon's Bluff. Boxxaway had seemed so certain Needle would return and accompany them last night. And then to Cael's utter amazement... Needle had indeed returned. Something deep inside Cael told him that they needed Needle. Needle was a Watcher, a member of the Society of Eyes, and as such had power against the Cult of Yex; even if Needle didn't understand it himself. Hells, Cael himself didn't understand it. But one thing was for sure... the cult understood, and feared them.

Needle was about to straddle the rail and dive off the boat when Cael realized that he had no choice. "Wait, Needle. There is something I have to show you before you leave." Cael pulled the parchments with all four prophecies from his pocket. "Please look at it. Then... if you still want to go... I won't stop you."

Needle looked annoyed but stopped short of diving into the river.

"I'll show you this, Needle, but give me a minute to tell you how I came to find it, will you?"

Needle sat on the rail with his arms folded and looked at Cael impatiently.

"Yesterday morning I got up early because I couldn't sleep. I don't know what led me to it, but I had been thinking about my parents a lot recently. They died on the day I was born and I never knew them. My grandfather raised me from the time I was a baby. I went into the back room of our cottage and... well the details of how aren't important now... but I had a vision of the past." Cael absently rubbed the bandaged wound on his wrist. "I saw the moment of my birth. I was born right there in that room. I saw my mother... she was beautiful. I... I never knew what she looked like until then. I saw an assassin rush into the room and attack her as she held me. The assassin stabbed her with a long dagger. It was emblazoned with the Cult of Yex symbol. My father tried to stop him, but he stabbed my father, too. That's when my vision ended. Boxxaway was angry with me for having done it, but he told me that what I had seen was true. I never knew before yesterday that the Cult of Yex killed my parents. It is as fresh in my mind as if it had happened yesterday, because for me... it did. It was then that Boxxaway told me I should stay home and rest and then go to the Bygrave Mausoleum at night. Then he left. He must have written that letter sometime yesterday after I had that vision. Then he delivered it to Danilus, and prepared the way for us."

"And he came to find me, too," Needle mumbled.

"I was supposed to rest, but after what I had learned," Cael said. "I couldn't just sit there. I couldn't help myself, and I went to the academy library to learn more about the cult that killed my parents. As I left, a Rothkin snuck into our house. He held a small crossbow, and carried a dagger. I'm sure he didn't see me, but I saw him and his intentions were clear."

"What are you saying, he was from the Cult?" Needle asked incredulously. "An assassin sent to kill you? This keeps getting better. Why are we hearing of this for the first time now?"

"Let him speak, Needle," Brynn said. "When was he supposed to tell us? In the middle of the earthquake? He hasn't had much opportunity until now."

Needle strode back over to them from the edge of the boat. But the look on his face was still angry skepticism.

Cael pressed on. "I spent the day at the library, researching the Cult of Yex. I didn't learn much I didn't already know... until I found these late last night." He held up the parchments. Was it a mistake to show them? What would they say? He was about to find out, because he didn't know what else to do to convince Needle to stay with them.

"It was in a very old book of prophecies that looked like it hadn't been opened for years. I tore out the prophecies and went to the mausoleum like Boxxaway instructed me. I'll show it to you Needle, but know this: Your father was a member of the Society of Eyes, and you are his son. He was a Watcher from birth, and so are you. You have a sacred responsibility to carry on his legacy. Everything we have been through testifies of this. Think back, Needle. Did you ever wonder how your father knew the way to open Ganger's Tomb? It was warded by the symbol of the Society of Eyes, and he opened it! In the letter your father wrote to Brynn's mother he says he is a Watcher, and says it was too early for replacements. Who do you think he was talking about, Needle? He was talking about you. Our parents were all hunted down and killed. The cult is trying even now to kill us, too. They fear us, Needle. They fear you."

Needle's face was unreadable, but he extended his hand. The hot sun beat down upon them, and the humid air oppressed their lungs. The sour aftertaste of Danilus' bitter ale was strong in Cael's mouth. Everything smelled like mildew. He swallowed, picked out the right parchment, and handed it to Needle: *The Fourth Prophecy.* Brynn and Mallet huddled in close to read:

How shall Yex return unto the world?

It shall come to pass, that in the end times, the four Children of the Watchers will stand vigilant.

Revealed are the names of destiny!

Cael the Apprentice
Brynn the Witch
Raju the Desert Prince
Bannon the Warrior

Their vigilance is in vain!

The trembling of the earth is the trump which foretells the triumphant return of the Demon Yex. The earth shall split asunder and the great and terrible epoch of the Demon Lord will be close at hand.

The Apprentice will stand at the precipice of the abyss and evil will beckon unto him. The voice of the first disciple shall cry from the dust unto him, and he will fulfill his destiny and will answer the clarion of evil.

He shall turn to evil, and with his companions, usher in the reign of Yex upon this world.

CHAPTER FIVE
Dreams of My Fathers

"The counsel of the visitor in dreams has always been the most valuable asset to the Guardian Kings of the Bystle Vale. His advice has never led us astray."

> - Archenel, Forty-Eighth Guardian King of the Bystle Vale

2nd Day of Summer - 2:00 AM – The Moss Garden - 13 Days to the Full Moon

Tharchelon raced down the hallway toward the base of the stairs that ascended to the holy Moss Garden of the Bystle Tree. He knew it was undignified for the King of the Vale to be sprinting through the halls of the Bystle Tree but he had panicked. The visitor in dreams had been telling him for months now that the outsiders were coming for the moss and he was to be its final guardian. It was he who was to fulfill the purpose of the line of Guardian Kings and bequeath the sacred moss to the four visitors. There was only one problem with that...

Tharchelon knew that he should slow to a walk before he turned the corner and came into view of the guard, but he could not help himself. He continued running as he rounded the bend and came in sight of a very startled guard.

With a new wave of panic, Tharchelon saw that Thock was on duty. Damn hells! Why couldn't it have been Sergeant Deth on duty? Thock was a corporal in his personal guard and he was part of the rotation for guarding the stairway up to the sacred garden. Tharchelon did not doubt his loyalty, but Thock was not the brightest Bystle Fruit on the branch…

"If Nelcherath approaches," gasped Tharchelon as he ran through the open door, "arrest him!"

He raced down the hall and up the stairs. The glowing Bystle Fruits grew much more thickly here as Tharchelon arrived at the top of the steps. He entered the well-lit Moss Garden, a sanctum that by tradition, only he and his ancestor kings could enter. It was the exclusive right and responsibility of the Guardian Kings to cultivate the moss that grew only here. He looked over the garden with a pang of guilt; the garden was a shadow of its former glory.

When Tharchelon's father had first shown him the garden, the moss was plentiful. It grew from an altar of Bystle wood that protruded seamlessly from the floor in the center of the round room. Back then, the moss grew lushly in long bushy strands of blood-red. The garden itself was brightly lit with Bystle Fruits that grew from branches that generations of kings had carefully pruned, trained and grafted to produce large quantities of fruit. His father had instructed him in the watering, nourishment and care of the slow-growing sacred moss, which included a stern admonition to never touch it. To touch it, his father had told him, would have dangerous consequences. Like his ancestors before him, Tharchelon had become an expert in the care of the moss, which radiated intense eldritch magic. The magic exuded by the moss had become the symbiotic foundation of the Rothkin culture.

Tharchelon's father also told him of the apparition that visited the Guardian Kings by night. The visitor had come in dreams to each and every King of the Vale from eons back. The visitor had always been a trusted counselor to the line of kings; one known only to the kings themselves. This dream-bound apparition had always advised on matters that had kept the Rothkin safe from outside intrusion, stable politically, and more than anything else, had insured the continued health of the Bystle Moss, which supported their entire way of life. The visitor had first appeared to Tharchelon as he slept on the night of his coronation, just as his father said it would.

The moss, however, was no longer as healthy as it was on the day of his coronation. The mere sight of the moss in its current state wracked Tharchelon with guilt. Once bushy and healthy, the moss now looked sickly and drooping. Where large tufts of moss had once grown long and thick, now only nubs of it remained, clinging pitifully to the Bystle Wood altar upon which it grew. Less than a tenth of the original quantity of moss now remained, compared to the lush garden that grew here a year ago.

This was Tharchelon's horrible secret. He remembered the day it began. He had been taken with shakes and chills. It had been a sleepless night followed by a particularly hard day for him. He had barely worked up the energy to even go to the Moss Garden and perform his regular duties. As he entered the garden that day he suddenly felt buoyed by the magical aura of the moss. Without even thinking he had reached down and done the unthinkable. He had pinched off a small bit of the moss, and quickly placed it on his tongue. It had been a fateful mistake. Exhilaration such as he had never felt in his life had coursed through him instantly. That first taste of the moss had been harsh and bitter, but now he craved it as the sweetest taste in all the world.

He knew he was trembling noticeably as he stood over the sickly remnants of the Bystle Moss. Even the overpowering guilt and shame he felt was not enough to constrain him. As if by its own will, his trembling hand reached out and pinched off a bit of moss. His ears were ringing from want as he closed his eyes to savor the moss as he placed a pinch of it on his tongue.

Relief washed over him almost instantly as the power of the moss surged directly into his being. His anxiousness washed away and his extremities ceased to tremble. He felt calm and in control. As his senses sharpened, Tharchelon suddenly became aware that he was not alone.

He opened his eyes and turned slowly to find Nelcherath standing stock still in the entry way to the garden, his jaw hanging slack in disbelief. Tharchelon knew instantly that in the ravages of his need, he did not hear Nelcherath approach, but now Nelcherath's breathing was loud to Tharchelon's razor-sharp hearing. Tharchelon did not need to ask.

He knew that Nelcherath had seen.

CHAPTER SIX
Prophecies of Old

"The multiverse is governed by a host of opposing powers: fire and ice, good and evil, the heavens and the hells, justice and mercy. Of the many, the opposition between choice and destiny is the most troublesome. Philosophers and dreamers through the ages have championed one or the other, arguing that one must ultimately emerge triumphant. But only the wisest truly comprehend; the clash between these two immovable forces is unimaginably strange."

-Excerpted from Enigmatica by Haerrus the Mad

2nd Day of Summer - 1:30 PM – The Demon River - 13 Days to the Full Moon

Needle's mind boggled. He groped vainly at comprehension. He held the ancient prophecy in his trembling hands, standing stock still and silent as his thoughts raced and the fury of thunder raged in his ears. Brynn and Mallet flanked him, craning their necks as they stared; themselves trying to cope with the impossible words.

"This... this can't be," Brynn mumbled, breaking the sound of the water lapping against the side of the boat. "How old is this?"

Needle knew the answer. His father had often carried ancient documents and maps as they scoured the desert wastes for Cult of Yex artifacts. The parchment he held was old... *impossibly old.* Based on the yellowing of the papyrus and the fading ink, it had to be hundreds of years old at the very least.

And there, in the middle of an ancient prophecy from a long dead cult... Needle's own name screamed out at him from the distant past. The meaning of this impossible anachronism was sinking in much more quickly than he was prepared to handle. He was being forced to acknowledge that indeed everything Cael and Boxxaway had said was true. All of it. On some level he logically understood the truth of it, but on a much deeper, emotional level, he *felt* the truth of it.

The fact of the matter was that he had been way too angry to acquiesce, even though deep down inside he knew it was all true. Deep down he'd known it since his improbable encounter with Boxxaway at the river yesterday. Deep down Needle wasn't surprised at all when Brynn had delivered the letter written by his father's own hand. Deep down he'd understood that the earthquake was no random event, but that it was connected to the sinister past. Deep down he'd believed that something portentous was happening. He could *feel* it. Though he had tried to deny it, he had felt it since his father had gone miss-ing. Everything that had happened to him in the last few days testified of it.

However, the shock of this prophecy was prematurely forc-ing him to confront a reality that he had deliberately shoved aside. It was so much easier to be angry. It was easy to blame Boxxaway. It was easy to blame the Buerdeleise. It was easy to blame Cael. And didn't he have the right? After all he had been through?

The truth was, he'd been behaving like an ass. He had re-sponded with anger and mistrust when these Buerdeleise had shown him nothing but patience and treated him as an equal. Needle suddenly felt ashamed when he considered what his father would think if he'd known how his son had acted.

Needle knew he would have eventually come around to deal with the unpleasant reality... but he hadn't been ready yet. But his name... his own name... appearing in the prophecy along with the names of these three Buerdeleise kids had forced the issue. This was all real. He, Raju 'Needle' Graji, was indeed a *Watcher*, just as his father had been. From this moment, he would put aside his anger. He would make his father proud. It was his duty to fight against an ancient evil he had believed was long dead. The title of 'desert prince' in the prophecy was intriguing but he mentally put it aside for consideration later. There was just too much to process at once.

"How old?" Brynn repeated.

"I don't know, Brynn," said Cael. "And it's probably older than it looks, as I am pretty sure it has been recopied by scribes through the ages."

"There can be no doubt," said Needle. "I've seen old documents like this before. I couldn't say how old it is, but by the look of the parchment and the fading ink, I'd say it was written generations before we were even born."

"But..." was all Brynn could say.

"And Cael is probably right," Needle went on somberly. "It is entirely possible that this is a copy of a copy of a copy."

They stared at each other in silence for several moments.

"But that would mean..." Brynn trailed off.

Needle finished for her. "That the prophecy itself was probably given thousands of years ago."

"It means the Cult of Yex prophesied our birth and our lives," said Cael. "They've been expecting us for generations."

"Then why didn't they just kill us?" Mallet asked. "I mean... if they knew about us before we were even born, why didn't they even try?"

"You seem certain that they didn't," Cael responded. "An assassin from the cult tried to kill me the moment I was born. He... he killed my parents."

"And don't forget the Rothkin assassin this morning!" exclaimed Needle, his mind still racing.

"But what about the rest of us?" Mallet continued. "Nobody has ever tried to kill me."

"You mean besides Wheizer?" Needle said sarcastically.

Mallet flashed an angry glance.

"I was going to ask how you could be certain, but then Needle has answered it," Cael added.

"Maybe they haven't had resources until recently," Needle added. "They are supposed to be hidden, right? Maybe their attempt on Cael's life was the only thing they were willing to risk before they re-emerged. Or maybe they didn't know where to look for the rest of us. I got the feeling from the letter my father wrote to Elowynn that the *Watchers* were hiding from the cult. Maybe they were hiding us. Think about it; two of us aren't even called by our real names."

"It was even more than that," Brynn said with conviction. "I think our parents gave their lives to keep us hidden from the cult. We have a duty to them now. They did their duty to ensure we would live to carry on the *Society of Eyes*."

That sobering thought quieted everyone for a moment.

"But they never even told us about all this," said Needle. "I mean, how are we supposed to carry on a legacy we know nothing about?"

"I think that was part of their strategy to keep us safe, Needle," said Cael. "We can barely handle knowing now. Imagine if they had told all this to us when we were younger."

"I think they *did* tell us," said Brynn. "Or... at least my mother was telling me. She never said anything specific, but in the last few weeks I have begun to realize she had been showing me and preparing me my whole life for this by teaching me to see sigils and patterns in all things. She never told me directly... but she made sure that I was ready."

Needle drew in a sharp breath and looked contemplative for a moment. "So did my father!" he blurted. "I never realized it until just now. I...I never really thought about it before, but looking back, he was preparing me. I used to go out on digs with him in the desert. He taught me things. How to use a knife... how to pick a lock... how to free myself from rope bonds... things that no other Agrabi kid ever had to learn."

Needle noticed that Cael had a contemplative look on his face. Needle figured it was because his parents had been killed when he was a baby, and it was obvious that his grandfather had been preparing him in much the same manner. Mallet on the other hand, had a peculiar wounded look on his face, but said nothing.

The idea that his father had been preparing him his whole life... a fact that Needle now realized was unmistakable, instilled in him an even stronger sense of duty. The thought of traveling with these Buerdeleise had been distasteful, but it was different now. His father, Cael's father, and Brynn and Mallet's mother had been bound together as *Watchers*. And so he was now bound to these Buerdeleise kids. Needle sat back down on the crate, the yellowed parchment still in his hand. He suddenly perceived these three Buerdeleise kids differently. He wasn't just an Agrabi among Buerdeleise anymore. He... they together... were *Watchers*.

"So... there's one thing I still don't understand," Mallet said tentatively. "Who in the hells is Raju?"

"What? You're the only one that can have a nickname, dumbass?" Needle retorted. Leave it to the big oaf to make him feel small again.

Mallet's eyes narrowed menacingly for a moment.

"So. What do you say, Needle?" Cael asked, sitting back down himself.

What in the holy hells was Cael talking about? 'Say to what?' was all he could think to respond.

"You were about to leave us. I mean... you were about to swim off and go home. Will you come with us?"

Needle was astonished. He had completely forgotten his intention to leave. So powerful had been the appearance of his own name in the ancient prophecy that it had obliterated any thought of his leaving. His demeanor softened immediately. He even smiled. "We're a team, aren't we? We're *Watchers*." He couldn't remember the last time he had smiled.

"Thank you, Needle. We would be lost without you," Cael said. Needle studied his face for any hint of disingenuousness or sarcasm, but he found only sincerity. He wasn't accustomed to a Buerdeleise speaking to him so respectfully.

"Yes, thank you. Needle," said Mallet. "I, for one, am completely lost without you." There it was.

"Well then," said Cael quickly. "You should see these also."

Needle watched as Cael shuffled through three other parchments he was holding. "I found them along with the prophecy I already showed you."

Needle reached out and took the pages. He handed one page to Mallet and one to Brynn. He kept the third. They each read silently and exchanged pages until they had each read all three.

The circle of time will begin anew
The prophecies of Yex will come to pass
The stars will proclaim his coming
The Codicon will be opened once more and then again
The heir will beguile himself
The blind think they can see, but they cannot
The circle of time is beginning anew
The demon sees his prison at last
The path to evil is made clear
The Cult of Yex is rising again
They who are hidden shall hide no longer
The circle of time has begun anew

Accursed be the Blood of the Defiler!
Throughout the generations, even unto the end of days.
The Blood of the Defiler shall be the wellspring of resurrection.
Into the bowels of the earth will the Blood go.
First the Blood must fall so that the Blood can learn to fly.
In the earth the Blood will learn.
In the earth the Blood will choose.
In the earth the Blood will fulfill its great destiny.
Accursed is the Blood of the Defiler!

In the day of the great cataclysm the sundering of the earth shall be a signal to the stars in the heavens. At the moment of convergence the circle of time shall sunder much as the earth before it, and the season of dissembling will be at hand. The season of dissembling will bring the second cataclysm which shall be a signal to the stars in the heavens. At the moment of convergence, the great demon shall be set free. The epoch of glorious death and horror begins with the first great cataclysm. Blessed be the days of the sundering!

"That adds some clarity to what happened last night," Needle said as they finished.

"Clarity? How in the nine hot hells does that add clarity?" Mallet demanded. "It's all just a bunch of gibberish. The heir? The great cataclysm? The circle of time? The stars in the heavens? The blood of the defiler? What does it all mean?"

"I admit I don't understand a lot of it, Mallet," said Cael. "But some of it makes sense given what we saw last night."

"The great cataclysm was the earthquake," said Brynn. "And the sundering of the earth. That's the sinkhole. That couldn't be clearer."

"But it talks about two cataclysms," said Mallet. "Which one happened last night?"

"The circle of time," Needle said, rubbing his chin thoughtfully. "That's the belief that time flows in a circle and not in a line. Things that have happened before will happen again... it's an Agrabi idea. Maybe it refers to the fact that the cult was once powerful and will become powerful again."

"Like maybe their power ebbs and flows in long cycles?" Brynn asked. "So maybe there was a cataclysm that ushered them in five thousand years ago, and the second cataclysm happened last night?"

Needle just shrugged.

"Who is the heir then?" Mallet said.

"Boxxaway doesn't know the answers to most of those questions either," Danilus replied from the tiller. "But remind me to show you the stars tonight when it gets dark. The stars in the southwest have drifted from their proper place in the sky. They are on the move. I noticed it several nights ago. Boxxaway mentioned it to me yesterday. He said it was to do with the return of the Cult of Yex."

"So then he knew about the prophecies... these prophecies?" Needle exclaimed waving the parchments he held.

Danilus looked at Needle and shrugged. "Pass me some of that ham would you?"

"Yes," Cael said. "He knew."

"Then why didn't he just tell us?" Needle demanded.

"Would you have listened?" Cael asked.

Needle felt sheepish.

Danilus broke off a hunk of ham and tossed it to Dheke. The old mastiff woofed appreciatively.

"We would have been swallowed up by that sinkhole if he hadn't saved us," Mallet reminded them.

A pair of ibises, flying side by side just barely above the water, passed by the port side of the *Riparian Scout.*

"There is something that has been bothering me, Cael," Brynn said as she turned her head back from the birds with an anxious look on her face. "Can I see that prophecy, Needle? The one with our names in it?" Needle handed her the yellowed page.

"This prophecy talked about other things, Cael. I mean, we've been focused on the fact that our names are in it, but what about the rest of it?" She was studying the text intently. "It basically says here, Cael, that you will turn evil. And together with us, you will usher in the Demon's reign. It says the cult is going to turn us to their side."

Needle stood up and snatched back the parchment, poring over it. He had been so stunned by the appearance of his own name in the prophecy that he had glossed over the rest without considering its meaning.

"What in the holy hells?" Needle muttered. "Cael, it says you will stand at the precipice and answer the call of evil. What's going on?"

"We should talk about that," Cael said.

Needle listened in amazement as Cael recounted the story about how he had gotten separated from Mallet and Brynn the night before as he stood on the edge of the sinkhole. How a voice from deep in the earth had called to him, how he felt compelled to leap into the great chasm, and how Boxxaway had pulled him back from the edge.

As Cael related all of this to them, Needle watched as Brynn grew more and more anxious.

"No wonder they haven't tried very hard to kill us!" Brynn blurted when Cael concluded. "They're using us!"

"Not if we don't let them," Cael said calmly.

"Let them? *Let them?*" Brynn said. "We're just kids Cael. How can we possibly hope to fight against something so evil and so powerful? That prophecy says we will turn to evil. Led by you! This is out of order. It's all completely out of order."

"Now, wait just a minute," Needle said to Brynn. "You have been trying to convince me that this was all real, and we are the world's only defenders against the cult! And now suddenly you aren't sure anymore? Well, here is a fresh idea for you sister! We *are Watchers*. I wanted to deny it but I can't. My father was a *Watcher*, and your mother was a *Watcher*. You know what? Don't do your duty if you're scared... but I damn sure am going to do mine! I'll make my father proud."

"I was doing my duty when you had one leg over the railing and were this close to swimming home," said Brynn. "That's not what I'm talking about. Don't you get it, Needle? It's not a question of doing our duty. I'm willing to do my duty, but that prophecy changes everything! It names each one of us as turning to evil. Are we just going to disregard that?"

"It named us because we are the *Society of Eyes* now," said Needle. "Yes. They got that part right, and the Cult knew we were *Watchers* even before we did. Okay. I'll give them that. But you are implying they have the power to make me choose evil. Well, I won't. So I'm not worried about that. Besides, you heard

Cael. Boxxaway pulled him back. He resisted the call, so the prophecy got it wrong."

"It's not as simple as that, Needle," said Cael. "Boxxaway did pull me back, but he said it didn't simply end there. The Cult won't give up that easily. He said that I... we... will have to continue to resist them. They will work hard to turn us."

"Just what makes you think you can resist it, Cael? Brynn asked. "When an ancient prophecy... one that predicted an earthquake, and our very existence... says differently?"

"I admit that is troubling," said Cael. "But Boxxaway said the same thing that Needle just said. He promised me that the cult can't make me do anything I don't want to do. No matter how hard they try, they just can't make me turn evil if I resist them enough."

"But the prophecy says you do," Brynn said. "Are you saying its wrong?"

Needle watched Cael closely as he hesitated. Cael didn't really want to answer that question.

"Well," Cael finally sighed. "That's a hard question to answer, Brynn. But you already know the answer."

"He means they will constantly try to kill or turn us," said Mallet. He had been sitting quietly on his stool on the deck. He was slumped over, rubbing the black bristles on his scalp. He still hadn't looked up, but he had been listening. "We either kill them," he continued, "Or they kill us. It's the only way it can end, Brynn."

"Do you think we really have a chance?" Brynn asked.

"Yes I do," Cael said forcefully. "The cult fears us. If they are so damn powerful, then why do they need us to usher in their return? If they really need to convert us to their side in order to succeed, well then, they can't be all that powerful, can they? If that prophecy is true, then it is *we* who have the power. The cult knows it too. It's why they tried to kill us. Me, at least. Twice that I know of. That proves they would rather have us dead. But having failed to kill us, their only option is to turn us to their side. Read between the lines of that prophecy, Brynn. They fear us. As long as we stand in their way, they cannot succeed."

"That... that sounds right," said Mallet looking up. His normally deeply tanned face looked frighteningly pale.

"Cael's right, Brynn," Needle said, feeling a growing confidence even as he spoke. "We're more than just kids to them. They're afraid. It's the only sensible explanation for why they would even mention us in that prophecy. I mean really... why would they even bother?"

"Maybe they are afraid," said Brynn. "But we'd have to be insane ourselves not to fear them. Forgive me for stating the obvious here Cael, but how do we know your story is even true? Maybe you already joined them and you are just leading us along. Maybe this whole thing is a setup."

"Come on Brynn," said Cael. "If I was really trying to deceive you, why would I have shown you that prophecy?"

"Why did you show it to us?" Brynn asked. Mallet nodded, looking worried.

Cael thought about it for a moment. "Because for one thing, Needle needed to see it. And for another, you all need to see it. Brynn, you are right in one respect: we should fear the Cult of Yex. They are powerful, but we *can* beat them. If we are going to beat them, there shouldn't be any secrets between us. If we don't work together, we will fail."

Needle watched Brynn and Mallet's reactions carefully. Mallet was nodding and the muscles in his chin were tensed, jutting his lower lip upward. Cael had swayed him back. Brynn, however, still looked concerned.

"But Cael," Brynn said. "There is more to that prophecy than just wishful thinking on the part of the cult. From far in the past they saw our time. They saw us, and surely they saw things that haven't even happened yet. How could they do that if it wasn't all supposed to happen? What if it's your destiny to join them? Our destiny?"

Needle felt a sudden rush of anger at Brynn's words. She sounded like his mother. Like all the rest of the hopeless Agrabi that accepted their plight as if there was nothing they could do about it.

"So what are you saying, Brynn?" Needle demanded. "That we don't control our own choices? That just because some damn piece of paper says we are evil, we have to be? Hells no! Not me."

"Some damn piece of paper just named you *Watcher*," said Mallet, "And you went from running away to joining the cause!" He pumped his fist in mock enthusiasm.

"Needle, you just don't understand," Brynn responded. "If it is your destiny you *will* choose it. You'll think that you've exercised your agency, and you'll justify your choice in those terms. But if it is predestined then it is predestined, and there is nothing we can do about it."

"By that logic, Brynn," Cael said. "You can't quit this even if you wanted to. I mean, if evil is truly our destiny... if we are destined to unleash a demon on the world... then do you think you could stop it by simply getting off this boat and going home? Hells. For that matter, we should just turn around right now and go sign up with them."

Brynn had no answer to that.

"At the edge of that sinkhole last night," Cael continued, "After he saved me, Boxxaway promised me that I have the power to choose a different path than the one laid out in that prophecy. He said that destiny was indeed a powerful force, but it was opposed by a force just as strong: freewill."

This brought Mallet to his feet, nodding enthusiastically.

"Cael, you don't understand," Brynn continued. "I'm not trying to be difficult."

"But you are being difficult," Needle observed.

She ignored him and continued: "There are patterns that appear in life... powerful, inalterable patterns. Most people can't see them. But they *are* there. Our entire life is governed by them. You can't just break out and live as if the patterns didn't exist."

"What in the holy hells kind of gibberish is that?" Needle demanded. "What are you trying to say?"

"I'm trying to say that you can always believe that you can choose, but that your choices exist inside a larger pattern of pre-destiny that governs your choices. Go ahead and choose what you want, but it won't change the eventual outcome."

"Oh, I ain't believin' this!" Needle laughed. "You sound just like a crazy old Agrabi shaman."

Brynn blinked several times. Needle knew she was trying to comprehend what he meant.

"Did you ever stop to wonder why the Agrabi don't just rise up against the Buerdeleise?" he asked her.

"What's that got to do with anything?" Mallet demanded. "Rise up for what reason?"

Needle ignored the implicit insult and pressed on. "The Agrabi outnumber the Buerdeleise in Demon's Bluff. If you count all the Agrabi who live on the outskirts and out in the nearby desert, we outnumber you almost three to one. Didn't you ever wonder why the Agrabi don't just rise up and take back what is rightfully theirs?"

"Ho!" Mallet yelled, as he started toward Needle. Cael jumped between them and held Mallet back.

Needle pressed on, undaunted. "It's because they believe the same load of tripe Brynn does. That magical circles and invisible patterns in time govern them, and there is nothing they can do about anything. All Agrabi believe that all they have to do is just sit back and wait until some circle in time comes back around and then they will once again rule the desert as they once did. So they pointlessly suffer in poverty and indignity, when any damn fool could see that they don't have to. If the Agrabi would just choose to act, then they would control their own destiny. But instead, they abdicate to some imaginary time circle."

"So..." Brynn said expectantly.

"So choices *can change* eventual outcomes," Needle said, flabbergasted. "My choices... our choices... can change them." Needle hesitated in what he was about to say next, because he didn't want to say it. But Brynn needed to hear it. "Our parents... my father... died to protect us. We are *Watchers* and *our choices* shape the destiny of the Cult of Yex. Not the other way round. We each have a duty and I *choose* to do mine!"

Brynn let out a long sigh. "None of you understand. Being aware of the patterns gives you freedom within them. We can't just pretend it's not happening.."

"I understand, Brynn," Cael said. "I really do, and I am worried about it, too. Don't think I haven't thought about it constantly since I saw that prophecy last night, because I have. Yes, my grandfather assured me that I can choose a course different than that prophecy says, and I believe him. But I had to come to that conclusion myself, and here is what you are missing, Brynn. You are assuming that the prophecy *is* our destiny, that it is the true pattern... that somehow, just because it was in the prophecy, it must happen. You don't know what our true destiny is, and neither does the cult."

Cael took a deep breath, and continued.

"What if the cult did see some unalterable future, but it was a future they didn't like? Do you think they would have written it down in their prophecies? Do you really think you'd see a prophecy that said, 'yeah, we will make another run at it, but it won't work because some pesky meddlers named Cael, Brynn, Needle and Mallet will stop us'?"

"Yeah!" said Mallet, giving a real fist pump this time.

"No," Cael continued. "They wouldn't. They would alter their own prophecy to say what they wanted it to say."

"So you are saying the prophecy is a lie?" asked Brynn.

"Finally!" said Needle. "You are seeing some reason."

"If we know anything about the cult Brynn, we know they are liars and deceivers," Cael continued. "Of course they would lie in their own prophecies."

"So where do we go from here?" Brynn asked after a long pause.

"There are only two possibilities, Brynn," Cael said with deliberation. "If that prophecy is a lie, then we proceed together to fight them, because our destiny is unknown. If the prophecy is true and we are destined for evil, we can't know it's true. So therefore, we proceed to fight them, and hope that my grandfather is right, and our freewill can beat their destiny."

Needle could see that her concerns were fading. Not gone, but fading.

"You're right," she said. "We have to fight them. We just have to stay vigilant."

"And I'm counting on you to keep watch on the larger patterns," Cael said.

Needle marveled. Maybe there was more to this Cael kid than he thought. In that whole argument, they had all lost their temper, except for Cael. He stayed calm and talked sense into Brynn in a way that he, Needle, never could have.

Their boat made slow steady progress upriver in the afternoon sun. The rare south wind was dying down and much more familiar gusts from the west were picking up. Danilus angled the large square sail to catch the emerging west wind. The sail popped as it caught a gust and the boat rocked to starboard.

Needle sat in the front of the boat, dangling his feet in the water and catching the occasional spray the prow created as it hit a wave.

He considered all he had gone through in the last day and a half. Poverty and near starvation had driven him to try to join the thieves' guild, which had ultimately landed him in Boxxaway's dinghy. Brynn's concerns about destiny echoed in his mind. What if he hadn't gone to the guild yesterday? What if he hadn't been captured and then escaped? Would Boxxaway have divined that and found him a different way? What if he hadn't escaped from that crate, and had been enslaved in Balankov? But he knew that wasn't really even a possibility. He would never have assented to being enslaved. He always would have chosen escape. Needle didn't like where his thinking was leading him. He tried to imagine numerous different paths he could have chosen yesterday, and ultimately they all probably would have led him to this boat today. Maybe that is what Brynn meant. Perhaps destiny meant that he could choose any path he liked, but all paths led to the same place. The idea that he wasn't ultimately in control of his choices was intensely unpleasant. His thoughts drifted to his mother, and how Wheizer had murdered her before his eyes.

Wheizer. Needle recalled the deep satisfaction of plunging that silver dagger into Wheizer's chest, and watching that rat bastard clutching his chest and gurgling blood. But a feeling of uncertainty nagged at the back of his mind. He had been propelled onto the boat before he could watch the wererat take his last breath. He had left him there dying on the dock, but he had not seen him actually dead. But surely the silver dagger his mother gave him had done its job? Were-creatures were vulnerable to silver; his mother said so. It had been one of the last things she ever said in life. But what had Wheizer said last night about the silver weapon? Needle thought back. He couldn't remember exactly. Only that Wheizer had claimed not to fear the weapon. Needle recalled how Wheizer had approached him closely as he held the dagger just inches from his filthy rat face. He showed no fear of the dagger, and upon reflection, that was troubling. But Needle had jammed the silver blade into the wererat's chest hilt-deep. No man could survive that wound. But still there was a nagging doubt.

Under a normal circumstance, the newfound sense of purpose he had just discovered would have him floating upon a cloud. But the only clouds he could imagine were dark and ominous. After his father had gone missing, he had spent his days brooding about what might have been, pouting over his lowly state, and pondering that there was nothing in his future. No greatness. No heroic adventures in the desert with his father. He could never be the artifact hunter that his father was. He knew he could never be as great as his father had been. But the revelations of the past days had changed all that. His father had been preparing him for greatness. He was a *Watcher*. He was descended from a long line of *Watchers*, and he had a secret duty to safeguard the world. This was exactly the type of thing he had hoped and dreamed for himself... and here it was, and there was no joy in it; only a sense of foreboding and a hard duty that must be done. He knew one thing. He would make his father proud.

Needle's thoughts lingered on his father. He had convinced himself over the past year that Kemano had simply gone missing, and would return; his faith had been unshakable. The discovery that the Cult of Yex was back, and that they had assassinated Cael's parents was deeply worrying. The implications were frightening. Needle had just lost his mother to a foul creature that was surely an agent for the Cult of Yex if not an outright member. He didn't want to think about what that might mean as regarded his father, and he put it out of his mind.

"So, there's still one thing I don't understand," said Mallet later, as they gathered for an afternoon meal. Blood was seeping through his new bandages, and he looked extremely pale. Needle didn't understand how the big lug could even be out on the deck with them, given his wounds. For that matter, how he even survived them in the first place?

"What was in the sinkhole that was calling to you, Cael?"

Needle was taken aback by that question: he hadn't considered it. By the look on Cael's and Brynn's face, he could tell they hadn't either.

Cael was about to speak, when Mallet's eyes suddenly rolled up into his head and he slumped sideways onto the deck.

CHAPTER SEVEN
The Whisperer

"It was not known at the time, but the true origins of the Bystle Moss were terrible indeed. The enormity of its power was enough to warp dimensional space and create a shadowy realm in its vicinity that co-existed with our own world. The horrors of that shadowy dimension were held at bay by only the thinnest of veils."

- Caed the Chronicler

2nd Day of Summer - 2:15 AM – The Moss Garden - 13 Days to the Full Moon

Tharchelon turned his back on Nelcherath as he felt the eldritch power of the moss infuse his mind with lucidity. The augmentative power of the moss heightened his intellect, his judgment and his senses. Moments ago, in his agitated state, he would doubtless have confirmed his own guilt by flying into a rage at Nelcherath's audacity. He would have been justified, as none but the Kings of the Vale were allowed into the sacred Moss Garden.

No, shrewdness was needed here and shrewdness and control were now in him. Under normal circumstances, Nelcherath would have merited execution for such sacrilege. But the circumstance was far from normal. The seed of an idea began to sprout... perhaps Nelcherath could prove useful...

Tharchelon turned and fixed Nelcherath with a self-assured kingly gaze, and waited for his adversary to speak first.

"M...m...my Lord?" Nelcherath clearly expected Tharchelon

to show some sign of guilt but Tharchelon knew he would find none.

Tharchelon waited in silence as Nelcherath broke from his gaze and his eyes flitted to the moss and back to Tharchelon several times. Tharchelon could see the doubt growing in his once-trusted advisor.

"I... thought..."

"Clearly your thoughts have led you astray. You have committed a grievous offense."

"The moss... M'Lord," stammered Nelcherath.

"What of it?"

"It... it doesn't look good."

"How did you get past my guard?"

"We... he and I... we were worried..." As Nelcherath began to speak, Tharchelon, his hearing magically enhanced, picked up the faintest of gasps around the corner.

"Corporal, return to your post," commanded Tharchelon quietly, never taking his eyes from Nelcherath.

Even Nelcherath could hear Thock exhale as one who knew he had been discovered. His footsteps faded down the stairs.

"And how do you know that the moss doesn't look good?" asked Tharchelon.

"Well... I supposed--"

"That is your problem, Nelcherath." Tharchelon felt his confidence growing by the second as the magic of the moss continued to flow into him. "Your arrogance. You suppose to know things that you could not know. You presume to question me about things that are none of your affair. Your arrogance has led you to commit a most unholy and treasonous sacrilege!"

"But M'Lord! I saw you! You have been eating the--"

"You forget yourself!" snapped Tharchelon. "I am your King, and once again you suppose that my actions are not in keeping with the prerogative and tradition of the Guardian Kings of the Vale!"

Nelcherath hesitated. Tharchelon could see that Nelcherath's mind was racing, trying to determine if he was bluffing. Tharchelon knew as well as anyone that his behavior must have seemed erratic over the past several months and that surely Nelcherath was considering that. He must have been suspicious for a long while now... the whispering bastard.

But now his foul deeds were uncovered and he must convince his advisor that nothing was amiss. He had to know what the apparition had told Nelcherath.

"Tell me of your dream." It was not a request.

"My memory has failed me for much of it, M'Lord... but I... I... remember that the ghost in my dream said... seemed... worried that you were not yourself."

Tharchelon kept an expectant glare upon Nelcherath.

"And... well... it...he... commanded that I should investigate." Tharchelon could see he was frightened and mustering the courage to continue. "He.. he... said that your purpose... the purpose of all the kings throughout the generations was to preserve the sacred moss..."

"Go on."

Nelcherath cast a furtive glance at the sickly moss, but continued. "He said that the time approaches when you will have an important task to perform as regards the moss. But the apparition seemed worried that you... would not have the will to do it when the moment was at hand. I... I'm to help you."

"And what was the task he said I should perform?"

"He... he didn't say," Nelcherath stammered. "Or my memory fails me".

Tharchelon studied him carefully. He was badly frightened and it showed. Tharchelon judged that he was not lying. That was good. He quickly began to formulate a plan.

"The apparition has visited the Guardian Kings from time to time," Tharchelon said. "Bearing counsel that has protected the vale." His faculties were sharp and his mind crafted the plan only one step ahead of his words. His confidence was absolute. "I expect that the apparition came to your dreams as well as mine, because this time, the threat to our vale is grave. Perhaps more grave than any in our history."

Nelcherath seemed to doubt. His eyes again flitted for an instant to the scraggly moss.

"I sense your concern, and assure you that it is misplaced," said Tharchelon, changing course to deal with his worry over the moss. "The Kings of the Vale have always partaken of the moss. It is strong, and grows quickly."

Nelcherath's expression was strange... unreadable. *Was he being swayed?*

"Kings throughout the generations have partaken of it. It imparts wisdom."

"What then, is the threat to the vale my, King?"

Damn hells, Nelcherath, Tharchelon thought. He simply didn't know if this whispering worm was being convinced. He couldn't risk trusting him. His mind raced through options to deal with him. He could kill him right here? No. He'd have to kill Thock too and how could he know that idiot hadn't said something to some passerby already? Or for that matter, that Nelcherath hadn't already whispered here and there to others about his dream? He needed to stall him. Co-opt him. Find a way to use him.

"The threat, Nelcherath, is the end of our way of life. Even now, outlanders are journeying to the vale, intent on taking our moss for themselves."

A flicker of recognition crossed Nelcherath's face. "Yes! I remember something about that from my dream. That's right! They are coming for the moss."

Elation! Finally there was the chink in his armor. He would twist the fool's muddled memories to his own purposes.

"I remember that they would bring something with them," said Nelcherath.

"That's right. They bring ancient tokens of great power that they will try to use to steal that which is most sacred to us. It's no wonder the visitor to your dreams is worried. He visits me and I'm worried. We have to find a way to stop them."

Realization suddenly flashed on Nelcherath's face. "So that's why... the shepherd!"

Tharchelon had this whisperer right where he wanted him.

"So now you comprehend the burdens of a king, Nelcherath. The apparition in our dreams has chosen you, Nelcherath, for clearly you are important to our cause. Your entry into this garden room is no crime, as it is clear to me now that you have been chosen as a champion to help me defend the vale against the interlopers. Even now the outsiders approach and may be here in mere days to make their attempt. I sense now that your coming in this moment was foreordained by the powers that watch over and protect this vale."

Tharchelon detected a flicker of pride in Nelcherath's eyes as he listened. *There is your weakness, Nelcherath, you whispering fool! I should have guessed long ago... your arrogance betrays you!*

"Your entry into this garden is forgotten," Tharchelon continued. "As for my acting strangely... yes... I admit it. But why do you expect such has been the case?" Tharchelon watched Nelcherath's face intently for what his words could not convey.

"M'lord, many in the vale are unsettled, and some have begun to whisper."

You chief among them.

"But I see clearly now," said Nelcherath, "that indeed you carry burdens heavier than I understood. Forgive my ignorance of the weight of your duty, M'Lord."

Tharchelon did not respond for several seconds as he looked deeply into Nelcherath's face, desperate to get an absolute read on him. Was this whispering weasel to be believed? Tharchelon strained to detect the slightest untruth or doubt but he remained unsure. He would have to trust for the moment, that Nelcherath had been swayed. What option did he have?

"We must work together to defeat this most grave threat," urged Tharchelon.

"I am yours to command, My Lord," said Nelcherath after a silent moment of consideration.

His momentary hesitation annoyed Tharchelon.

"I have been considering various options," said Tharchelon. "And your heroic actions have now confirmed to me the right course of action. We must take the initiative and strike at the outsiders before they approach the vale. We will send out an expeditionary force to ambush and destroy them. You, Nelcherath, will lead it."

Nelcherath straightened and breathed in deeply, "M'Lord, I would be honored, though I am not a warrior."

"Nelcherath, we must be wary of traitors in our midst and use care in who we trust. We must not allow word of this to get out amongst our people. You understand that, don't you?"

Tharchelon pressed on before Nelcherath got out an answer. "Nelcherath. I have duties yet to perform here. Go and fetch Sergeant Deth. He can be trusted. Have him select a small but strong force of his best warriors. Include Corporal Thock among them. We will meet in my council chambers at mid-morning to finalize the plan. I'm counting on you, Nelcherath. What say you?"

Tharchelon knew that Nelcherath's arrogance could not resist such flattery. Yes. He had played this encounter properly. Nelcherath *was* with him!

"I am yours to command, My King," Nelcherath said, bowing. He turned and strode purposefully out of the garden room.

Tharchelon smiled. It seemed he had avoided disaster and gained room to maneuver. He had an armed force to deal with the interlopers, but he knew that wasn't enough. If he had learned anything as king, it was that there should always be a backup. All he had to do now was find one; a way to kill the four if Nelcherath failed. And what if Nelcherath succeeded? The whisperer could not be allowed to live.

Tharchelon reached down and took another pinch of the blood red moss. Never had he taken two pinches so close together, but damn hells, hadn't he earned it? He smiled a wicked smile as he enjoyed the extra indulgence.

CHAPTER EIGHT
Spy in the house of the Night

"The most powerful warrior in your army is the one who does not exist, but that the enemy believes is there."

- Yazak Thuune, General of the Armies of Yex

7th Day of Summer - 7:00 PM – Eastern Shore of the Demon River - 8 Days to the Full Moon

The disk of the sun kissed the western horizon, igniting a panoply of colors that danced through the remaining clouds. As they had traveled several days upriver, the fertile fields of the flood plains slowly gave way to undeveloped desert. The winds shifted and the breeze came from the north, further dissipating the clouds. Danilus said that with the square sail of the *Riparian Scout*, it wasn't possible to sail against the wind. He had seen sailors with triangular sails do it, but he didn't know the trick, even with the right kind of sails. So, until the familiar west wind returned, it was best that they not fight it. He had scanned the mottled, reed-choked bank of the Demon River as they slowly drifted backwards. He and Cael used push-poles to beach the boat at a suitable open spot on the eastern bank.

Mallet convalesced in the cabin. He had spent much time resting there after his collapse almost a week earlier. Danilus regularly tended his bandages and provided his herb-infused tonic to help Mallet sleep.

Brynn was napping in the cabin, and Needle dozed in his customary spot between the tarp-covered barrels in the bow. Cael tossed a mooring line to Danilus, who secured it to a stump at the riverbank. He motioned for Cael to look east; the setting sun behind him had lit a copse of mesquites in the distance about a mile from the river. "I reckon I could go for a nice camp on shore and a proper cook-fire," Danilus said in a low voice. "Come help me find some firewood?"

They left Dheke napping on the boat and walked in silence through the desert for a while, the only sound was an occasional desert cricket starting up its nightly serenade. "You 'member I promised you Boxxaway had something to help you protect yourself?" Danilus asked.

Cael had all but forgotten.

Danilus passed him a leathery bundle--a belt wrapped around a scabbard and dagger. Cael began to unwrap the bundle when his blood ran cold. He'd caught a glimpse of the dagger and it was emblazoned with the Cult of Yex symbol. It was a dagger he'd seen before...

"Now, your ol' grandfather told me to give this to you in private where we could talk," Danilus said.

Cael stopped walking and pulled the dagger from its sheath, half expecting it to be encrusted with his mother's blood, but it was shiny and clean. "This is the..." Cael trailed off as he tried to fight back tears.

"Your grandfather told me what it is," Danilus said quietly, walking back the short distance to Cael. "He said the assassin who killed your parents dropped it as he was trying to flee. Your grandfather fretted about whether or not to give it to you."

"Why did he then?" asked Cael, tears now streaming down his cheeks.

"In the end, I reckon he figured you'd want to have it. He said it would help you always to remember what your true purpose is."

They resumed walking as Cael considered the dagger. He put on the belt and took the blade out again, examining the hilt.

"I'll never forget, dagger or not," Cael said. "I'll keep it, but I don't want to have to look at that evil symbol."

"I reckon I can take a strip of leather and wrap the hilt for you tomorrow," Danilus said.

It was near dusk as the two of them finally approached the trees.

"You been awful quiet, Cael," Danilus observed as they weaved their way through the sage scrub and prickly pears. Cael knew Danilus well enough to understand what he meant. Cael indeed had something on his mind, and the old ranger sensed it. The problem was that Cael didn't have the courage to say it. The implications of the fourth prophecy weighed heavily on his mind.

Well? Danilus asked after a long moment, a gust from the north wind ruffling his red hair back away from his sun-browned, freckled forehead. Still, Cael hesitated.

"You sounded pretty convincing to me." Danilus reached down and plucked a pale leaf from some sagebrush as he ambled by.

Cael furrowed his brow. "About what?"

"That prophecy, I reckon. You convinced the others... but I wonder if maybe you was trying to convince yourself?" He rolled the leaf into a gummy ball between his fingers and flicked it away.

Cael was amazed. Despite his unlearned manner, the desert ranger often displayed a keen wisdom.

"I figgered you'd want to talk about it is all," said Danilus, and then sniffed his fingers.

Cael failed to respond to Danilus' question as he deliberated how to express his worry. A single concern gnawed at him, but he was far too ashamed to admit it to himself, much less to his uncle.

They reached the copse of mesquites about an acre or so in size. The trees had grown around a slow, muddy spring that left much of the area with soft, grassy ground. In short order, Danilus zeroed in on a fallen mesquite. He pulled the axe that hung at his belt and began to hew the branches from the trunk. The thin dry leaves that still clung to the twigs rattled noisily each time he struck a blow. Cael broke a long seed pod off a nearby branch and began to chew it. He broke through the thin shell and tasted the sweet, thick sap inside.

It was starting to get dark when they headed back, each carrying a bundle of kindling and firewood wrapped in leather straps. A cacophony of desert crickets welcomed the oncoming night, their high-pitched chirps punctuating the dry desert air every few seconds.

"We should step lively, Cael. It ain't hard to lose your way in the dark, but we got just enough time."

Cael nodded, a seed pod still between his teeth. After a while he tossed away the pod and took in a deep breath. "You're right, I suppose. I don't think I'm as convinced as I sounded."

Danilus said nothing, but sort of shrugged as he adjusted the bundle to his other shoulder.

Danilus' silence felt uncomfortable to Cael. "I... I was going to do it."

Danilus gave him a look to acknowledge that he was listening, but he made no response.

Cael hesitated. It was hard to confess. "I was letting myself fall into that chasm." Danilus looked like he was going to respond, but Cael pushed on in a rush of words. It was out now, and it felt good to have Danilus share his burden. "The voice called my name, and I felt helpless. I couldn't resist it. It was so compelling. Nothing else seemed to matter."

"But you didn't fall in," Danilus finally said.

Cael desperately wanted to admit the truth; the *whole* truth; that some small part of him *wanted* to go. He wanted to fall in the chasm and answer the voice calling his name. "Only because my grandfather pulled me back. If he hadn't shown up to save me..." Cael almost choked up, but stopped himself from admitting the whole truth that he desperately wanted to confess. "The truth is... I was already going in when he pulled me back."

"Wow," said Danilus. Several seconds passed before he continued. "You sure sounded confident this afternoon."

"No words of wisdom?" Cael demanded indignantly.

"Mmmh. I s'pose not. Sounds like you done made your decision at that sinkhole, and that's that. May as well have signed your membership papers in that cult."

"It's not like that!" Cael protested. "I... I... I just don't know. It's all so confusing."

"Ahh. I see," said Danilus. "So you *are* redeemable, then."

Cael marveled. Without saying much, Danilus had clarified the issue substantially, and it made him feel better. Cael *did* have a choice, even now. But he knew that there would still be a lingering worry... no matter how he tried to put it out of his mind. The question Boxxaway had not truly answered would continue to haunt him: *Am I evil?*

What would happen if he heard the voice from the pit again? Would he have the power to resist? Would he want to go to it again? The thought of it petrified him.

"Cael, I reckon that all leaders have doubts," Danilus mused, almost reading his mind as they made their way back through the scrub and cactus. "Great leaders never show doubt to those they lead."

There was not much else that Danilus could have said that might have eased Cael's fear more than those words. "What you done today... convincing them kids..." Danilus continued. "That showed that you got the instinct of a great leader."

Or a great liar... Cael thought.

They walked along silently in the descending darkness until Cael could once again detect the subtle, musty smell of the river, now probably a hundred yards ahead. Danilus turned and walked backwards, looking toward the darkening eastern sky. Cael followed suit and looked back, too. The waxing moon was visible just over the horizon.

"Eight days. Seven, maybe," said Danilus, turning again and continuing toward the river. Cael knew what he was thinking. As if he needed more to worry about.

Suddenly Danilus froze and Cael almost bumped into him. "What? What is it?" Cael asked.

Danilus held a finger to his lips. He looked around, an intense look on his face.

"What's wrong?" whispered Cael.

Danilus moved his finger from his lips to his ear, indicating to Cael that he should listen. Cael was listening, but he couldn't hear anything. He gave Danilus a quizzical look.

"Crickets," Danilus virtually mouthed the word.

Cael suddenly understood: the desert crickets had gone silent. Cael knew from experience that the little blighters wouldn't quit their chirping at night even if you were jumping on the prickly pear they lived in. It certainly was peculiar for them to go silent. Only the faintest chirps could be heard in the far distance.

"What does it mean?" Cael mouthed back.

Danilus shrugged slightly, motioning that they should continue.

"Yeah. I reckon about another week 'til the full moon," said Danilus out loud. The look on his face told Cael that something was not right, and that they should continue on as if they suspected nothing.

"What do you reckon on for dinner, Cael?" Danilus dumped his bundle of firewood unceremoniously as they arrived at the bank. "Why don't you find us a camp site aways from the riverbank, and make us a cook fire? There'll be less skeeters apart from the river."

Cael looked around conspicuously, straining to see in the faint light, painfully aware of the silence of the crickets. "Umm. Yeah. Okay."

"I'll check on Mallet and fetch some cooking gear from the boat," said Danilus.

"Would you put this in that trunk for me?" Cael unbuckled the belt and wrapped it about the scabbard and tossed it to Danilus. The ranger bounded down the slope of the riverbank.

Cael worked for several minutes, gathering smaller sandstone rocks strewn about to make a fire ring, while the silence of the crickets thundered in his ears. Soon the fire was crackling, its yellow light casting undulating shadows on the nearby brush. The crickets had slowly resumed their chirping somewhat, but their odd and sudden silence, and Danilus' reaction to it was all he could think about. He scrambled down the muddy bank and over the side of the boat. Danilus was across the deck, lantern held high in one hand while rummaging through a trunk with the other. Dheke had leapt off the boat and was snuffling around the shore.

None of the others were around, but Cael could hear some clumping noises coming from the cabin, which he assumed was Brynn.

"Mallet's doing better," Danilus said, continuing to rummage. "He'll pull through, I reckon. I told him to stay and rest and we'd bring him some dinner."

Cael hunkered down next to Danilus as he slapped a mosquito at his neck, longing for the smoke of the fire to keep them at bay. "What do you suppose was going on with those crickets?" he asked in a low voice.

"I been ruminatin' on that, in fact," Danilus said, pausing in his dig through the trunk. "It weren't natural."

"What does it mean?"

"Well, I reckon you'd be the one to know. I figger it had to be magic what spooked 'em, cause nothing I know of will shut them bugs up."

Cael hadn't even considered this possibility. "A spell? But who? Nobody's around."

Danilus shook his head slightly. "You reckon somebody could be spying on us?"

"The cult?" Cael speculated. "Maybe Boxxaway watching after us?"

"I'm pretty sure it ain't your grandfather. Could the cult spy on us with magic? From such a distance?"

"Maybe," Cael said. "Yeah. I think so. But they'd need to have some knowledge of us, or where we are."

"I'm pretty sure they have some knowledge of us, don't you?" It was Needle. He was behind them, a chunk of half-eaten cheese in his hand. He had approached without a sound.

Cael, Needle and Danilus set up a camp kitchen while Brynn wandered the area. She had broken off the desiccated shaft from a serrated spoon plant and used it to poke around at the sagebrush and sand. Needle complained vociferously about her dawdling, but she made up for it when she commandeered the cooking and artfully used Danilus' spice collection to make a meat and root stew far better tasting to Cael than any of Boxxaway's bland fare. They delivered three large bowlfuls to Mallet, along with a loaf of bread, a hunk of cheese, and plenty of dark beer from Danilus' stores. He had virtually inhaled the food and quickly fallen back into a deep sleep.

Now they each sat, minus Mallet, on large sandstone rocks in a circle around the glowing embers of the fire. The chill of the desert night had set in. Dheke lay in the sand at the edge of the firelight with his muzzle on his paws.

"You really think the cult is somehow scrying us?" Brynn asked, holding her hands out to catch the warmth of the dying fire. "Isn't that powerful magic, Cael?" The desert crickets were back to their usual racket.

"Yes, I think so. Very powerful, but I think Danilus must be right. What, besides magic, would quiet the crickets?" Cael poked the fire with a stick, moving the unburned part of a log onto the bed of coals. "Seems like maybe they can somehow sense it and it makes 'em go quiet."

"Scrying?" asked Needle, looking up from his bowl.

"It means using magic to spy on someone. Watching from a distance," said Brynn, who then looked back to Cael.

Cael struggled not to laugh as Needle scrunched up his face and mouthed a phantom lecture in a sarcastic, head-bobbing mimic of Brynn.

Brynn either read Cael's reaction or noticed Needle out of the corner of her eye, because she turned back to Needle, nearly catching him.

"Is it safe to talk about... you know... where we are going?" asked Needle, having instantly dropped his mockery--the picture of innocence.

"Yeah, I think so," said Cael. "I mean, if we are right, the crickets are back to normal because the scrying is over for now, and it means we aren't being watched anymore. The crickets will fall silent if they try again."

"But then they have seen where we are. Right?" asked Brynn.

"Probably," said Cael. "But the important thing is they don't know we are going to the Bystle Vale, or why."

"As far as we know," said Needle mopping up the last of his stew with a hunk of bread.

Danilus rocked back and stretched behind him to grab the last mesquite log. He tossed it onto the fire, sending a burst of orange sparks rising skyward on the column of heat. Danilus watched as they mingled with the stars.

"Look," he said, and pointed to the southwestern sky with his chin. "You remember what the ballista constellation looks like?"

"Of course," said Brynn. "Everyone does. It's a giant cross-bow that launches javelins. You can't miss it."

"See if you can find it for me then," Danilus said with a hint of a smirk.

The three of them studied the sky where Danilus had indi-cated. The ballista was a constellation that even the youngest child in Demons Bluff could spot. It consisted of nine bright stars, arranged in almost a perfect arc, intersected by a long straight line.

"It's crooked!" Brynn murmured. "It's not supposed to look like that, is it?"

"I reckon not," Danilus said, bemused. "I don't know much, but I know them stars ain't supposed to move. But they been slowly wanderin' out of their proper place for a short while now."

"How can that happen?" Needle asked. "Stars don't move."

"Most stars don't," said Danilus. "There's about half a dozen that move all over the sky. But they always done that. The rest of the stars ain't supposed to move at all, Ballista included."

"But they *have* moved," said Cael, head tilted as he stared at the stars. "What does it mean?"

"Boxxaway pointed it out to me a few days ago. Said they was startin' to rearrange themselves. Said it was a sign that things was about to get busy for us. He weren't kiddin', nei-ther."

"He told you that?" demanded Needle, a flash of his earlier distrust of the old ember wizard crossing his face momentarily.

"Rearrange themselves?" asked Cael. "Into what?"

"Hey, Cael, do you still have those prophecies in your pock-et?" asked Brynn.

"Can't you guess?" responded Danilus. Cael rummaged around for the parchments in his pocket. He handed them over to Brynn, who angled them to pick up firelight as she studied them.

"The Symbol of Yex!" whispered Needle.

Danilus just nodded. "That's what the old man told me."

"I knew it!" Brynn exclaimed. "Listen to what this prophecy says: *'the stars will proclaim his coming'*," she quoted and then shuffled more of the parchments.

"Holy hells, that's right!" Needle exclaimed as he stood up and started pacing. He held his empty wooden bowl absently. "It's in that prophecy!"

"And here in another one," said Brynn, still poring over the parchments. "It talks about how the *'sundering of the earth will be a signal to the stars in heaven'*." She angled the paper again, trying to gather light. "And later it talks about how the *'demon will be set free at the moment of convergence'*." She looked up at them, and from where Cael sat, the fire lit her concerned face in an eerie glow.

"So that means that the earthquake and sinkhole and the stars means that it's starting," said Needle, more a statement than a question.

He was about to continue when Brynn cut him off. "Yes, but we already knew that from the prophecy that has our names. I mean, the part about the earthquake being a sign, at least."

Needle barreled on, his mind barely ahead of his words. "And the demon will be set free the moment the stars converge into the Symbol of Yex?"

"I don't reckon you could read it any other way," said Danilus, leaning forward and wrapping his arms around his gangly knees.

"Holy son of abyss," Needle breathed, sitting back down. "How much time?"

Danilus studied the malformed constellation. "Until the stars line up? I ain't got no idea. Months? A year?"

"So the Symbol of Yex," Brynn asked. "What's it look like, then?"

They all stared at her, dumbfounded. Cael had assumed they all knew what the symbol looked like.

"How can you not know?" Needle asked, incredulous.

"I never really thought about it, I guess," Brynn said. "What's it look like?"

Cael smoothed out the sand in front of the rock on which he sat. He quickly drew the symbol in the sand as Brynn stood for a better view in the dim light of the fire.

"That's the Symbol of Yex?" Brynn asked. "Where have I seen that before?" Cael could tell by the look on her face that her mind was racing.

"It was on some of the artifacts in my house in the Kuma," Needle offered.

"No, it was when I was young."

"Probably in Father's study," offered Mallet absently, suddenly appearing from the darkness. "That's where I saw it last."

"Yes! That's it!" said Brynn excitedly. "I was playing in Father's study when I was a little girl and there was a shield on his desk with that symbol on it!"

Needle made a funny noise as he expelled a breath of air between his lips. "Probably bought it from my father."

"It's a sigil, you know," Brynn said suddenly.

"What's a sigil?" Mallet asked, confused.

"The Cult of Yex mark. It's not just a symbol. It's a witch sigil."

"So?" Needle said. Mallet looked distinctly unhappy.

"What's the difference between a symbol and a sigil?" Cael asked.

"A symbol conveys meaning. It is meant to cause the mind to reflect on an idea or a concept, but that's all it does," Brynn said. "A sigil has a function... it does something."

"Like when you trace it?" Cael said.

"Kind of like that. Some sigils need be traced in order to be activated. Other sigils are always active to provide their function. They need only exist. I think the Cult of Yex sigil is one of the latter."

"So?" Needle asked again, but much less dismissively this time. "You're the witch... what's it do?"

"I... I don't know," Brynn said. "It seems incredibly basic."

"But you don't know what it does?" Needle asked again.

"No," Brynn responded. "I'm certain it's not in the book of sigils my mother left for me. I would definitely have remembered it."

Mallet glowered.

"But if it is so basic, why wouldn't it be in there?" Cael asked.

"I'm not sure. Maybe it has a function that my mother didn't want me to know?"

"It's evil, you mean," Needle said.

"No... I don't know. Maybe." Cael couldn't help but notice the disconcerted look on her face.

"So, can you figure it out?" He asked.

"I'll certainly try."

"So what's an example of what sigils can do? The kind that you don't have to activate, I mean," Needle asked.

"I'm still learning about them from the book that my mother left me, but from what I can tell they are usually protective. A sigil of hiding, when etched on an object, can make it hard to find, for example. I think there are blessing sigils that ward off evil spirits. Stuff like that."

They sat without talking for a long moment, the din of the desert crickets and occasional popping ember from the fire was the only accompaniment.

"So nobody ever answered Mallet's question," Needle finally said.

He was met by confused looks.

"What was in that sinkhole calling to Cael?" he clarified.

"Are you saying," asked Brynn after a moment's pause. "That you think Yex himself is down there?" She reached up and began to nervously twirl a lock of her auburn hair. Cael leaned forward on the sandstone boulder he sat on. This was a question he didn't want to think about, but he most certainly wanted to know what the others thought.

"I'm not saying I think anything," said Needle. "I just think it's a good question. It sounds like you think it might be Yex yourself."

"I'm not saying that either," said Brynn quickly. "But let's assume for a second that it is Yex down there. Does it change anything? It sounds like from the cult's own prophecy and Danilus' assessment, we have at least a few months left before he gets out."

Cael had intended to stay quiet and listen to the debate, but he couldn't help himself. "*If* he gets out. We are trying to stop him, remember."

"My point," Brynn responded, fidgeting with her hair. "Is that we have time. Now, suppose it wasn't Yex down there. What do you suppose it was, Cael?"

"How should I know?"

"Because it called out to you," Needle said. "Did it sound like a demon?

"And how should I know what a demon sounds like, much less a particular demon?" Cael shot back, feeling irritated with himself for letting these questions get under his skin so quickly. "Besides... I'm not even sure that I heard it."

"What the hells?" blurted Needle, standing up again and sending his empty bowl bouncing off his leg and landing near Danilus. "You either heard it or you didn't!"

"Easy, Needle," said Danilus, picking up his bowl and scooping up some nearby loose sand with it in a sweeping motion.

"What I mean to say," said Cael. "Is that something did speak to me, but I can't say whether I heard the voice with my ears or my mind. That's all."

"Oh," said Needle sheepishly, plopping back down. "It's scary to think about. I didn't mean to get so upset, Cael."

Cael was surprised. Thinking back on their long history, it was the first time he could remember Needle apologizing for anything, especially to him. "It's not a big deal."

"I'm not trying to pry here, Cael," said Needle. "But if you aren't even sure you heard it, how do you know it was real? I mean, how do you know you didn't imagine it?"

It was a hard question for Cael, and he didn't want to confront the answer. It forced him to think about that which was most worrisome. It was basically the same question Danilus had forced him to confront as they gathered wood earlier. "All I can tell you, Needle, is that it was real. I don't know if I heard it in my mind or not, but it consumed my consciousness. I don't know much, but I know I didn't imagine it."

"It don't matter what's down in that hole," Danilus said, as he started to scrub Needle's bowl with sand. "Boxxaway has a plan to deal with it. So you just let me worry about that sinkhole, and you kids focus on getting that moss from the Bystle Vale."

"What are you doing?" Brynn asked Danilus, a horrified look creeping onto her face.

Danilus looked at her, baffled, as he continued to rub sand into the interior surface of Needle's bowl.

"Are you trying to clean that bowl with... with... *dirt*?" she continued, the look of horror growing on her face as she realized that she had eaten out of a wooden dish that had doubtlessly been 'cleaned' in the same manner in the past.

"How else do you reckon I should clean it?" said Danilus, bemused.

"Ewwww! With water and lye soap of course!"

Danilus snorted as he emptied Needle's bowl and knocked it on a big rock to get the clinging sand out. "I ain't got money to waste on no fancy soap, princess," he said as he started on his own bowl. "'Sides, sometimes nothing gets stuff cleaner than dirt itself."

Brynn stared at him, mouth agape. "Do you even hear yourself?" she demanded after a few moments.

Danilus just smirked as he continued rubbing sand in his own bowl.

Needle snatched Brynn's bowl from where it lay next to her rock, and instantly scooped up sand and got to work on it. A big grin was spreading on his face, his white teeth a stark contrast in the firelight to his olive skin. "How much longer 'til we get there, anyway?" he asked.

Cael couldn't help himself and laughed out loud.

"You're all disgusting!" she hissed.

"Well, it depends on the winds, I reckon," said Danilus. "But I figger five days more. Maybe six to get to where I drop you off. But, we have a stop to make first. Maybe more."

"Stops?" asked Cael. "Where?"

"And don't forget," Danilus continued. "I reckon you got to add another half day or so get to the top of the plateau and walk to the Bystle Vale."

"Washing dishes with dirt," Brynn was muttering to herself. "I've heard a lot of stupid ideas..." she trailed off.

Danilus winked at Needle. "Boxxaway left more instructions for you," he said. "And I reckon now is as good a time as any. I'll go and fetch them."

Dheke looked up and woofed as Danilus returned with his glowing bullseye lantern after a few minutes.

"How you feeling?" Needle suddenly asked Mallet. Cael couldn't help but notice he glanced at the waxing moon as he did so.

Mallet just shrugged. "I've been better."

"Boxxaway said to give you this before we got to our first stop," said Danilus. "I figure since we will likely get to the marshes on the edge of the swamp tomorrow, it's time." Danilus handed Cael a scroll case. It was a tube carved from ivory, about as big around as Cael's bicep, and about seven inches long. It was sealed on each end with a green, tarnished, copper end cap designed to fit snugly over the tube to keep the contents inside. Cael had seen scroll tubes like this before; the wizards of the academy used them to store their magical writings and carry messages to one another. Usually, there was intricate designs etched into the ivory, but this scroll tube had a smooth exterior that looked quite yellow in the light from the fire and Danilus' lantern.

"Take a look," said the ranger. "I expect you'll want to read it to the others."

Cael opened the tube, and slid the contents out. There was rolled-up parchment wrapped around a peculiar device that looked at first glance like a tangle of wire and colored glass. Cael tucked the parchment roll under his arm to free up both hands to handle the device, which he recognized instantly as the spectacles he had used a week earlier. It seemed an eternity.

"What in the holy hells?" asked Needle, maneuvering in for a better look. "Why does that look familiar?"

"They are called *Lorgnettes*," said Cael, unfolding the device delicately. "It allows a wizard to divine the past. They are my grandfather's."

"Is that how he knew?" Needle blurted.

"About the earthquake?" Brynn asked.

"Hold on," said Cael.

"But I thought he was too old to do magic anymore," said Mallet, scratching at his bandages.

Cael held the unfolded *Lorgnettes* up and its multi-colored lenses glinted in the firelight. "You have it all wrong. They only allow a wizard to see the past, not the future. And it's a magical device like the flying carpet. With an artifact like this he doesn't have to spend his life to use it. It does the magic for him."

"Flying carpet... diviner's spectacles... what else does that old bastard have that we don't know about?" asked Needle.

"Hey!" Cael exclaimed.

"How does it work?" asked Brynn.

"He didn't mean nothin' by it, Cael," Danilus said.

"I could put them on," Cael explained. "And see what has happened in the past where we are now, for example. I could see the history of this place."

"I'm sure that'd be exciting," said Needle. "You certain Boxxaway can't use them to look into the future?"

"Certain," said Cael. "I remember from lessons my grandfather taught me that it is much harder to divine the future than it is to see the past." Cael slid the *Lorgnettes* back into the scroll tube and set it down on the sand. He unrolled the parchment.

Danilus angled the light of his lantern, and the others gathered in closer. His grandfather's scrawl was recognizable on the page in black ink. He read aloud:

Cael,
As you know from my prior missive, you will need to find three tokens left as beacons for the Rothkin who fled to hide the moss in

the Bystle Vale. They are small, black, magical orbs. King Tharchelon's duty is to protect the moss and he will give it only to those who have these tokens. You will need to find them on your journey. The first is somewhere in the Foetid Swamp.

Danilus knows where to disembark. Use the Lorgnettes and focus your concentration on the name 'Elija Abel'. He carried the moss to the vale to hide it from Adirak's agents. The Lorgnettes will allow you to follow his ancient path, and recover all three of the tokens.

If for some reason you are unable to collect all three tokens, you will need to find a way to convince Tharchelon to give the moss to you, or otherwise obtain it.

May the heavens speed you along,
Boxxaway

P.S. Remember Cael that you cannot use blood to augment a magical device. The Lorgnettes work by tapping the psychic afterimages in a place by focusing your concentration on the right names or events.

Everyone was silent for a moment, returning to their seats around the fire.

Cael looked to Danilus. "We ain't too far," the ranger responded to the unspoken question. He reached down and grabbed a handful of sand, and streamed it from his closed fist in the light of his lantern. "We'll get there tomorrow." The drift of the fine grains indicated that the northern wind had finally abated, and there was a mild breeze from the west. "I reckon the wind looks promising."

Brynn suddenly stood up with a panicked look on her face. "Someone is coming!" she hissed.

"How could you possibly..." Needle trailed off as a fountain of sparks erupted from the ground in a momentary burst about forty yards away from them toward the south. There was a guttural yelp and crash of sagebrush.

Danilus leapt up and instinctively pulled his axe, dropping

his lantern as he did so. It hit the sand and was extinguished. Despite the light from the fire, it suddenly seemed disproportionately dark to Cael. Danilus was already moving slowly southward in a crouch. "Get something to defend yourselves!" he said in a commanding voice as he turned his head back to them. "She's right. Someone is out there. Maybe more than one." Dheke followed the ranger, sniffing furiously as he went, alert and quiet.

Cael felt a sense of panic as he realized he didn't have a weapon. He cursed himself for sending the dagger back to the boat with Danilus. Needle was on his hands and knees searching for a sandstone rock. Mallet was also looking around vainly in the dark for something to use. None of them had brought their weapons! How could they have been so stupid?

"What in the holy hells was that flash?" asked Needle loudly as he continued his blind grope for something to use as a weapon.

"They are running away," Danilus shouted. "Heading south and angling a little west toward the river. I need some light over here!"

Cael tried to listen, but between the crickets and his companions, whatever sound there was of fleeing intruders didn't carry over the din. "At least they aren't scrying us," he said to no one in particular.

Brynn almost tripped over Needle and would have gone headlong into the fire, but she regained her balance. She felt around the cool sand for Danilus' lantern and cried out as her hand met the hot metal with a hiss. She found the handle and fiddled the latch open in a desperate attempt to relight it. "I drew a sentry circle around the camp," she said. "I was worried by all the talk of scrying."

Cael felt a sudden sense of calm as he decided on his own course of action. He abandoned his futile search for a makeshift weapon and instead centered himself and reached out to get a sense of the *Arcanus Navitas*. Here was another case where he had been stupid. A good wizard always had a sense of the *Arcanus Navitas*, and he had been oblivious to it most of the evening. He wanted to close his eyes to help him concentrate, but somehow that seemed like a bad idea. He reached out with his mind as he kept his eyes open and aware. The *Arcanus Navitas* was thinner than in Demon's Bluff, but there was enough background magic that he could begin to gather it in.

"Sentry circle?" asked Mallet, hefting a sizable sandstone rock he had found. "That's not a witch thing, is it?"

"Light! Lantern!" Danilus called. "We are losing them!"

"I'm trying!" Brynn shouted, just as she managed to relight the lantern with a flaming twig from the fire.

Needle, with a sandstone rock of his own in one hand, took the lantern from Brynn with the other and headed out into the darkness toward where they could hear Dheke barking. Mallet followed.

Brynn looked imploringly at Cael. "Hells no," said Cael. "We aren't staying here alone." They followed the dancing light of the lantern ahead as Needle bounced and bobbed over and around sagebrush and cacti.

"I reckon they done run off," Danilus said as they caught up with him about fifty yards or so from camp. "I could hear 'em tearing through here," he said, taking the lantern from Needle and angling its light onto the sand. Dheke had stopped barking but still sniffed around excitedly. "Stay right where you are and hold that dog. I don't want anyone messin' up what's left of the tracks."

They all stayed put as Danilus walked back and forth along the path of the intruders, trying to decipher their tracks.

"What's a sentry circle?" Needle asked Brynn. Mallet's eyes narrowed in suspicion.

"It's a very large sigil that I traced in the sand around the camp. It warns when someone enters the perimeter."

"What were the sparks?" Cael asked.

"Looks like there was only one of 'em," Danilus called from about twenty yards away as he continued examining the ground by lantern light.

"It was just a flash to indicate where the breach was," Brynn said. "It didn't hurt him, but it probably scared him pretty bad."

"Yep. For sure, just one," Danilus called again. "Wore boots. He lit out at a full run. He'll be picking out some prickly pear spines."

"What will we do now?" Brynn asked as Danilus came back

toward them.

"Well, the wind from the west has picked up a bit more, and I ain't in no mood to sleep out here tonight, are you?"

"Who do you think it was?" Mallet asked.

"It's obvious, isn't it?" Needle said. "The cult is onto us."

The sobering thought stayed with them as they broke camp in the dark and resumed their journey up river, the west wind propelling them.

Cael couldn't be sure, but as they had worked to break camp a sudden movement in the sky caught his eye, and he turned in reaction to it.

He could have sworn that a shadow passed in front of the moon.

CHAPTER NINE
Realization

"Oh betrayal! I have been betrayed and now revenge is what I seek. My pain is so great I would die to end it, yet only my thirst for revenge keeps me alive."

- Agrabi Psalm

3rd Day of Summer - 7:00 AM – The Moss Garden - 12 Days to the Full Moon

He could hear his own ribs crack when the second blow landed, but it was nothing compared to the shock of the first kick to his chest. Tharchelon had the wind knocked out of him many times before, but it had always been from a blow to the stomach. As unpleasant as that always was, it was nothing compared to the desperate feeling of having the wind forced out of his lungs from a blow directly to his chest. It was as if his breath had been squeezed out, and a cork forced down his throat. His diaphragm flexed mightily in a futile attempt to draw in air, but none came.

He heard voices directed at him but he couldn't focus on the words. His mind had only capacity for his increasingly desperate need for air. He cracked his eyelids open. It felt as if he was dragging them over sand and gravel. The brightness of the yellow light felt like daggers being driven through the back of his eye sockets into his brain. He heaved again trying to pull in a breath... nothing.

The last thing he remembered was savoring a second, well-deserved taste of moss after his talk with Nelcherath. As his eyes adapted to the searing light, he realized he was still in the Moss Garden, lying on the polished wooden floor. Many feet and legs milled about him. Doubtless they were both the source of the voices he was hearing and the boots that had been kicking him. The susurration continued, but the words were as indistinguishable as his blurred memory.

Something monumental had occurred between the second taste of moss and the blow that kicked him awake just now. He was certain that something of great importance had taken place, but the memory was ethereal... shadowy. The memory was as vital and elusive as the air that still refused entry to his lungs.

His diaphragm heaved involuntarily and he used all his will to amplify the effort. Air surged suddenly into his lungs in a massive rush, as if a dam had burst. Great tidal waves of blood pumped up his neck and pounded into his head. His ears rang loudly and he suffered the worst headache of his life.

When he was younger he had a propensity to overindulge in Bystle Mead and the headache the morning after was indeed miserable, but it was nothing compared to the hammering in his head now. He gasped several times but the pain in his head only increased with each breath.

"Pick him up," a disembodied voice commanded flatly. It was Nelcherath. He was grabbed roughly by each arm and jerked to his feet. He became aware that his face was bruised, swollen and scratched. His tunic was ripped in many places, hanging off of him in tatters. His arms were scratched with claw marks encrusted with dried blood.

"Let's go." Nelcharath commanded. Two brutes dragged him down the stairs and out of the Moss Garden. Aside from the two kicks to his chest, the rest of his wounds had occurred earlier as blood had clotted and scabbed over, but he still couldn't recall the events after he took the second dose of moss. He couldn't avoid the sense that it had been of vital importance. *Something* had happened to him... something that superseded the troubling events of the current moment. He focused on remembering as he submitted completely to the will of Nelcherath and his thugs as they dragged his limp form through the halls of the Bystle Tree.

Tharchelon felt the sting of humiliation as he was dragged out through the front ceremonial entrance at the base of the great trunk into the bright light of the morning. Crowds of his people were already there, and more streamed in as he was dragged unceremoniously past the murmuring throngs. It hurt to breathe deeply, and the pain in his head was constant and virtually overwhelming. His head hung between his shoulders, but he chanced a few surreptitious glances through his locks of disheveled, blood-matted hair. Most of his people watched his humiliation with a clear sense of relief on their faces.

Was he such a tyrant?

He thought he detected sad glances from a few. Or was he simply hoping that some were still loyal to him in this treasonous coup?

He must have been passed out for quite some time after taking that second dose of moss, because clearly the traitor Nelcherath had plenty of time to plan for his maximum humiliation. Ahead, at the end of the row a wagon awaited, drawn by two ponies and piled high with fresh manure. He knew what was coming but was too weak to resist. He was hurled face first onto the stinking dung cart. A cheer went up from the throng. The driver clucked twice and snapped the reins, urging his team into action. The wagon, flanked by heavily-armed members of his own personal guard, moved slowly along the main road through the western end of the vale. To see Thock there didn't surprise him, but Deth's resolute face filled him with despair. He had thought him completely loyal. Nelcherath followed behind with a bevy of his other advisors. Tharchelon scanned their familiar, treacherous faces. The betrayal ran deep; it was utter and complete. The only face missing among the traitors was Rathenel, his adjutant. Perhaps he was still loyal? There was no telling where he was now, nor would he ask. Despite the throbbing in his brain, he was capable of deciding that he would not give the usurpers the satisfaction of hearing him speak.

He rode in silence along the road past fenced fields and open meadows toward the wooded groves of younger trees at the western edge of the vale. He would have liked to smell the blossoms so evocative of his childhood, but the searing smell of dung and ammonia filled his nostrils like the pain that filled his head.

They continued westward for what seemed more than an hour when the driver pulled back suddenly and the cart jerked to a stop at the edge of the western boundary of the vale.

"Your chariot has arrived, my prince," said a sarcastic and disturbingly-familiar voice. The driver turned and to Tharchelon's horror, it was Ockler, the shepherd bully from his youth. Nelcherath had indeed orchestrated humiliation upon humiliation. Tharchelon kept his resolve and did not respond. He worried that a moment of horrified surprise had shown on his face. He did not want to show weakness but his head hurt so badly it was difficult to feign either strength or dignity. He was jerked off the dung pile by his boots. His head hit a plank on the way out, sending a searing jolt of pain through his brain. The impact with the unforgiving ground sent another burst of sharp pain through his broken ribs and bruised lungs. On any normal day, he could whip them all, such was his training, strength and speed... but not today. He was as helpless as a newly hatched sparrow.

He was dragged again to his feet and frog marched a few dozen yards past the end of the old dirt road and propelled forward as they loosed him. He tried to keep his feet under him as he stumbled, but he knew he was going down. He put his hands forward to help break his fall. Before he went down completely, he felt an odd sensation, as if he were falling through a curtain. Pain rocketed up his left forearm as he struck the ground. If his wrist wasn't broken, it was badly sprained at least. The pain however, was still nothing compared to the pounding throb in his skull.

He heard the gravel at the end of the road crunch behind him. He stood and turned to face the approaching traitor. He was not surprised to see it was the unsmiling Nelcherath.

"You almost convinced me last night, you know," the whisperer said. Tharchelon seethed with hatred. "You would have too, had you not made one fatal mistake."

Tharchelon glared at him, saying nothing, picking out the gravel embedded in the heels of his hands.

"I obeyed your orders. I spoke with Deth, who began gathering a force as you commanded. I retired to my quarters to get a quick nap since you kept us up all night with your asinine judgments. That was your mistake. The visitor came immediately to my dreams. In my dream, I told him all that had transpired. He seemed extremely distraught when I told him you had eaten nearly all the sacred moss."

Tharchelon was furious with himself for his lack of foresight. Of course the unctuous visitor would come to the whisperer's dreams! But Tharchelon remained resolute and said nothing.

"My discussion with the dream apparition was very enlightening, and I will spare you most of the details, as I'm sure you already know them."

Tharchelon did indeed.

"The visitor commanded me to execute you and tend to the moss and help it recover. I was to give it to four who will come to retrieve it: the fulfillment of generations of preparation."

Panic surged in Tharchelon. *My moss will end up in the hands of the interlopers.*

Nelcherath misinterpreted. "I see your fear, but I won't kill you. Neither will I give away that which is most sacred to us. I awoke after the dream and contemplated the options available to me. I first concluded that no dream could make me betray our people as you have done. I owe no allegiance to a nightly revenant, but to our people and our way of life."

Tharchelon felt a moment of relief, though it was overshadowed by the ache in his brain.

"What to do with you, on the other hand, took quite a bit more deliberation. As much joy as it would give me to slit your treasonous throat, it would be a punishment too good for you. If Deth and most of your councilors hadn't agreed with my plan so quickly this morning, I might have been resigned to carrying out the wishes of the dream visitor by my own hand. But fortunately for me, your tyranny has left you with few friends in the vale."

Tharchelon glared, unblinking.

"The druids proposed your fate. This morning, they harnessed the remaining magic of the waning Bystle Fruits and erected a magical barrier that now encircles the entire vale. You passed through it moments ago. You stand now outside that barrier. It will *never* let you come back."

The words came too quickly for Tharchelon to process, and he knew the confusion showed on his face.

Nelcherath allowed himself a humorless smile.

"No, my King. Death is too merciful a punishment for you. Exile is the punishment worthy of your crimes."

Ockler grinned as he clucked his team into motion and the procession turned and headed back along the road without another word. Tharchelon sat in the dirt next to a boulder and watched them go. The boulder was a well-known landmark marking the western boundary of the vale. His people called it 'goat head rock', as it looked uncannily like a giant goat head when seen head on. Bruised, beaten, humiliated and suffering an unbearable headache, he watched them disappear.

He sat for a while, squinting in the morning sun, contemplating the baffling turn of events. He finally walked forward, his right hand outstretched and trembling. His heart sank as it came in contact with an invisible wall, just as Nelcherath had said. He pressed forward against it, but it was immovable. He picked up a rock to strike the invisible wall, but the rock sailed right through the barrier, though his fingers which held the rock impacted it with full force, sending shooting pain up his arm. As a capstone to a perfect morning, he was certain he had broken a finger, maybe two.

Tharchelon, head pounding, touched the unseen barrier with his left hand, being careful to keep pressure off his sprained wrist and began walking south, feeling the barrier as he went.

There was something vaguely familiar about feeling along the barrier as he walked. It was a peculiar feeling; a hint of déjà vu. But he had more important things at hand, so dismissed the feeling.

He walked for what he guessed was several hundred yards and satisfied himself that all Nelcherath said was indeed true: there was a barrier around the vale to keep him out. From his vantage here, he could see all the way to the center of the vale where the giant Bystle Tree towered above all else. It was then that the most horrifying thought of his life struck him. It suddenly dawned on him what Nelcherath had meant about death being too merciful.

He was about to suffer a fate indeed worse than death. He was cut off from his precious moss...

CHAPTER TEN
The Temple of the Damned

"The cause of our worst fear from the Cult was not their great sorcerers. We too, had great wielders of magic. No, our greatest fears were the Ruukus ob Thaaxo, the Damned, fearless agents whose single minded fanaticism and devotion to Yex made their every move unpredictable and utterly terrible. One of my own sons, Eldirak, sought out their infamous secret Temple of the Damned. His last report was that he believed he was close to finding it, but we never heard from him again."

> \- Excerpt from the lost Journal of King Adirak of Taglyon

8th Day of Summer - 7:45 PM – The Temple of the Damned - 7 Days until the Full Moon

Cael looked up into the eyes of Elija Abel and screamed.

One hour earlier

"This is the place," Cael said excitedly. He stood in knee deep, putrid swamp water. He held his cedar staff, and his leggings and tunic were stained brown up to his waist from walking through the muck.

"I just see more trees and stinking, foggy swamp," Needle complained. "Oh, and don't forget more bastardly mosquitoes sucking me dry. What makes you think this is it?"

"I saw it," Cael said. "I saw *him*. Elija Abel. He came here... right here."

"It occurs to me," Brynn said, standing next to Needle. "That our Agrabi friend might just be correct in his assertion that this mosquito and leech infested stretch of mist enshrouded swamp is by all appearances that the eye can perceive, exactly the same as the previous four miles of swamp through which we have slogged since this morning."

Cael rolled his eyes. Brynn had surprised him, complaining as much as Needle about the oppressive heat, stink and muck of the swamp. She really was a duke's daughter at heart. Even Danilus had made more than one snide comment. Only Mallet had remained silent.

Cael was skeptical of letting Mallet come along due to his injuries and said as much privately to Danilus.

Danilus had shaken his head: "Cael... that boy, I ain't never seen anyone heal so fast... wounds on his shoulder and chest are free of scabs, just turned into angry red scars."

"You sure he's okay to come along, though?"

"Do him good," said Danilus. Then he shrugged.

"What?"

"You realize why he's healing so fast, dontcha?"

"The wererat bite?"

"It's healing him... keeping him safe and fighting off other infections..."

Cael sucked in his breath.

"It wants him alive..." Danilus whispered, leaving Cael with a sinking feeling.

Now, walking through the swamp with Mallet, Cael couldn't help but constantly scan the evening sky, though there was no moon out. Only fleeting glimpses of the clear sky were possible with all the low fog about. How many days 'til the full moon?

They came upon a rise in the ground. "Well, your suffering is over," Cael said to Brynn. "This is definitely it. Look ahead on that big hillock. Do you see it? *The Temple of the Damned*."

Ahead of them, through the nebula, they could indeed make out the form of a massive hillock rising out of the muck. Upon it was the shadowy outline of a long-dead giant tree, its leafless branches reaching skyward through the mists.

8ᵗʰ Day of Summer - 7:00 AM –Western Shore of the Demon River – About 12 hours earlier

"This is where Boxxaway told me to take you," Danilus said. The sun was above the eastern horizon and they had the whole day ahead of them. He guided the *Riparian Scout* over to the western shore where the hull crunched up onto the sandy bank. After five days of travel up the Demon River, they had arrived at the place where Cael was to use the spectacles as instructed by Boxxaway. The wind blew from the southwest in sandy gusts, sending up sprays of water in rainbow mists. To the north and west of them lay the first evidence of the flooded, fog enshrouded valley where the Demon River long ago created a dangerous swamp, the deepest reaches of which were even now uncharted. Nebulous mists whirled masking the hints of dead trees reaching up through the water, stretching into the swamp as far as the eye could see.

"There is the petrified Eklon tree," Danilus said. "The northern reaches of Demon's Bluff's territory." Indeed, a singular dark and petrified tree jutted from the ground thirty or so feet from the bank of the river. It was an unmistakable landmark.

"Get them spectacles ready, Cael," said Danilus, "We should get after it."

Cael shielded his face from the blowing sand by pulling his new white linen tunic up over his mouth and nose.

Cael heaved the anchor onto the sand and then leapt into the warm water, splashing through the mud which sucked at his feet. Wading ashore, he bent down and grabbed the iron anchor with both hands and lugged it up past the sand to a lichen-encrusted pile of rocks. He dropped the anchor with a grunt and adjusted it to make sure it was secure and the rope was taut.

Needle leapt off the boat and waded ashore. He climbed past Cael, going on all fours, grabbing the rocks to pull himself up the bank.

At the top of the bank, he headed toward the petrified tree. The ancient gnarled, grey thing looked like it had been carved from stone. "My father told me about this tree," said Needle, passing his hand over the stony wood.

Mallet leapt to the sandy bank over Brynn's protestations to be careful. He had recovered remarkably since his near fatal encounter with Wheizer, and it showed. Danilus and Brynn followed and the three of them climbed the slope and headed over to the petrified tree, its branches forming a spidery umbrella over them.

"How long has this tree been here?" Cael asked as he approached, looking up at the ominous grey branches arching over him in the twilight, like they might suddenly come alive to snatch him and hurl him into the desert.

"Look at that desert to the south and east," Needle said, sitting down next to him. Cael stared out at the line of the horizon.

Cael looked and shuddered. The eastern horizon stretched out straight and broad like a hand drawn line, even with the distant dunes fading into uniformity. It was a haunting emptiness made all the worse because something had once been there: A vibrant, green valley of trees, crops, towns and roads.

And now? No trace, no sign, not a single identifying mark showed proof of an ancient civilization, but he had been out there before with his grandfather and had seen them firsthand. The cult was all too real, as were the battles that ultimately defeated them. All that remained was the distant, perhaps imagined, trace of mnemonic emotion. Cael's recurring worry returned suddenly... the cult was still around. Out there now, perhaps?

"This is the place, kid," Danilus said, relieving Cael of his troubling thoughts.

Cael nodded as he stuck his hand into his pocket and pulled out the *Lorgnettes.* The very ones he had worn a week ago to see his mother murdered on the night she had given birth to him. It seemed at the same time an eternity ago, yet as fresh as if it had only just happened.

Cael was to concentrate on the true name of the Rothkin,

Elija Abel, as Boxxaway's letter had instructed. The note from his grandfather had helped him to better understand the nature of the *Lorgnettes.* They functioned through intense concentration on the target subject, not by blood augmentation or anything else so exotic. He realized he had finally been able to see his mother when his focus was entirely upon her. He tried with all his might to block out everything but the name *Elija Abel* as he donned the jumble of wires and lenses. To Cael's amazement, within several seconds of concentration, he could see a vision of the ancient past unfolding before him...

Five Thousand Years Ago – Six weeks before the fall of the Cult of Yex

Elija Abel was tiny compared to the tall, blue-robed wizard who stood over him. The two met in a lush green forest, next to a large tree, its leaf-laden branches heavily-bowed over them to form an umbrella-like canopy. The trills of birds echoed down around.

Elija fell to one knee, and bowed his head: "My Lord Xylex, you have summoned me." His voice was lower than might be expected, considering his childlike size.

Xylex was a gaunt man, with black wavy hair streaked with gray and the shadow of a mustache on his upper lip. His skin bore the scars of a demonic case of childhood acne, but his brown eyes were gleaming as if he were on the verge of an emotional epiphany. He had the heavy air of authority, and a sad sort of wisdom about him. He seemed to radiate sorcerousness and a gargantuan will.

"Have you heard the news from the Valley of Oar?" His voice was soft, yet commanding.

"Thune lost Malevolent, Black Widow, and Blot. Rumors swirl that Nepharus and Smolder survived, but barely."

"They did not," Xylex said.

"It would seem that our enemy Adirak is gaining the advantage."

"More than you know," Xylex coughed. "Our time is short."

"What would you have me do?" Elija entreated.

Xylex looked up into the branches of the tree beneath which he stood. Sunlight, golden and warm, filtered through the canopy. The air was hazy and dust motes swirled in the light.

"I'll not dissemble. Things have gone poorly. I fear we are defeated."

"Is there no hope for us?" asked the little one after a long pause.

"I hope that we may yet finish the gate and bring Yex into the world to reign, but as you say, Adirak is gathering strength. His armies are ringed about and the noose is closing. I fear his forces may overrun the Citadel before the gate is completed."

"What then?"

"While we may yet finish the gate in time and triumph, I believe we must take precautions if the worst should happen. I have spent my energies in these last weeks finding a way that, if we should fail now, we will ultimately triumph. Should we fail *now*, we must secret ourselves away... lay up resources. As long as my will burns, our purpose will be fulfilled, but this is not a time to be foolish. Our hope may lie far in the future."

"And my task?" Elija asked with an air of resignation.

"Hold out your hand."

Elija didn't hesitate; he stuck out his hand, palm up.

Xylex pulled a small, cherry-sized black ball from a belt pouch. He set the ball on Elija's hand. The ball immediately sprouted needle-like legs that bent and jointed back down. Cael could see it clearly through his vision. It looked like a black spider with six legs forming the disturbing pattern of the Symbol of Yex.

"This is a *Balizar*: a spider golem of dark magic. Each emits a light that only those who bear the proper mark can see, even through obstacles. It is a beacon that guides people through the darkness, to secret places."

"This creature," said Elija Abel. "Will guide our refugees to a secret place where we can hide if we lose this war?"

Xylex smiled. "I chose you wisely," he said. "Not just hide, but hide and wait. If we lose now, then a time will come when we will rise again to finish our great work."

Elija whistled. "I see," he said.

"And many of your people, the Rothkin... have we not branded those who are the strongest and best among them?"

Elija pulled his black hair back, revealing a cryptic symbol seared into the flesh of his forehead.

"If the worst occurs, I will send the surviving Rothkin who are thus branded to follow the light."

"I am to prepare the way, then. And prepare a sanctuary?

The gaunt wizard nodded. "I have prepared four *Balizars* for you."

"Where shall I place them?"

"Go first to the Temple of the Damned. Deposit an orb there and transmit my order to shut down the temple. All there are to converge on the plateau with due haste. We need every available resource for the defense of the Citadel. We may be able to buy enough time."

Elija nodded.

"When you leave, take moss spores with you. You will need them to establish a new crop in the place of refuge.

"And where is that?"

"Next, go to the Shrine of Ophidia and leave a *Balizar* there. Tell those who are there to come and help defend the Citadel. Do the same at the Fortress of Rovule on the eastern rim of the canyon by the dam."

"So far to the north?" asked Elija.

"Make haste and tell them to do the same. Reinforcements serve no purpose if they don't arrive in time."

"And the place of refuge?"

"Journey east from Rovule. You will find a secluded vale. You will know if for the mighty oak that grows in the center, brother to the one that grows at the Temple of the Damned. You will find a hollow high in the trunk. It is small, but adequate to make your home. Place the final *Balizar* there as a beacon and sow and cultivate a new crop of moss."

"How long before the refugees begin to arrive?"

"I expect the final battle for the Citadel will occur in mere weeks. Longer, if we are lucky."

A slight breeze rustled through the canopy of leaves above

them.

"How long before the new crop of moss is ready?" Elija asked, looking up at the swaying branches.

Xylex smiled sadly, "It grows slowly, and will be of no help to us now. The purpose of the crop you cultivate is preservation, not production. If indeed we must hide ourselves away, we must have the moss when we rise again."

"And how long will that be?"

"Not in our lifetimes. Generations, perhaps."

"Have we enough left to help defend the Citadel?" asked Elija.

"Precious little remains. We spent far too much at the Valley of Oar. We hoped it would be a decisive blow that would turn the tide, but it was all for naught. The supply at the Temple of the Damned had dwindled and what little we already harvested, we must have to complete the gate."

"And if we should succeed and finish the gate in time?"

Xylex smiled broadly at that thought. "There is indeed hope, but the odds are long. Should we triumph I expect you will know soon enough as Yex's reign spreads out over the world. But if refugees begin to arrive, then you will know we have been defeated... for a time. Know this; your Rothkin will not be our only hidden enclave."

Elija nodded.

"Do you accept this task?"

"Yes, my Lord."

The *Balizar* skittered up his wrist and began to dig violently into his forearm. It burrowed down into his skin and muscle, kicking flecks of skin, blood and fatty tissue behind it as it dug. Elija cried out, but held his hand still. When the little thing had burrowed into his arm, the wounds healed over in seconds leaving a faint scar as the only evidence.

"You impress me," Xylex said. He produced another *Balizar* and set it on Elija's palm. This one burrowed down like the first one. Then a third, and finally the fourth. When all four were embedded into his arm, Elija lowered his hand. Sweat beaded on his brow.

"One more thing," Xylex said.

Elija waited.

"My plans are thorough. When the time is right, the Cult of Yex will arise again, and our great work shall resume. The moss is one of our most critical resources and we will once again require the power it imparts. As you and your descendants cultivate and preserve it for the time of resurgence, never surrender the moss to anyone unless they bear three *Balizars*. No matter how distant in the future, no one will know of the *Balizars,* nor how to find them, except for the appointed agent. The agent will present them as the sign of their allegiance."

"Is it not possible that someone might randomly find them? Worse, what if Adirak finds them?"

Xylex nodded and smiled, "A *Balizar* beacon can only be seen by one who bears the mark, as you do."

"I understand, my lord," Elija said. Without another word the Rothkin strode purposefully off to the west.

The vision faded, and Cael came aware in a cold sweat.

"So?" demanded Needle. "Did you see him?"

"Yes," said Cael, standing up and folding the *Lorgnettes* away. He pointed west and a little north, toward the misty heart of the swamp. "This place used to be a forest." Cael made a sweeping motion of his arm. "All this was forest. No desert to the east, and no swamp here and out west. I didn't see the Demon River, either. It must have changed course over the last five thousand years."

"I reckon we should commence to walking," Danilus said.

"How do we know where he goes?" Mallet asked.

"I can use these again every so often and follow his path," Cael said.

Five Thousand Years Ago – Six weeks before the fall of the Cult of Yex

Elija passed effortlessly through the dense foliage of the forest. His movements reminded Cael of the lizards he used to chase behind his house. Elija darted quickly and easily through any obstacle, sometimes emerging from under a green wide leafed bush, eyes flashing, head still as if listening carefully before he slithered off again.

Cael picked his way along with his staff. He and his companions stopped periodically in the foggy swamp so Cael could use the *Lorgnettes* again to follow the little Rothkin. Needle made snide remarks about Cael making it all up as they journeyed deeper into the mist of the swamp.

Finally Cael watched Elija as the small man made his way through the forest until he came to a landmark impossible to forget: a large and peculiar oak tree. It dripped with long mossy vines, its gnarled bark grey, thick and wrinkled like the skin of an old man. The oak leaves were larger than any Cael had ever seen, and cancerous burls grew all over the trunk and branches.

Elija circled the tree, his eyes flashing as he paused twice to sniff and listen. Apparently satisfied, he deftly scaled the trunk until he came to a crook formed by three massive branches.

Perching there, like a kid playing fort in a tree, Elija grabbed a massive knot on one of the trunks and twisted it to the left. A section of trunk before him slid open silently, revealing a secret passage.

Pausing again, Elija cocked his head, sniffed and listened. He pushed his head forward into the opening to look down. From his vantage, Cael could only assume that the passage went straight down through the thick trunk.

Elija pulled his head back with a jerk and sat still in the arms of the tree for a long time, his face crinkled in thought. After what seemed like an eternity, he pulled a steel dagger from his belt scabbard, spun it artfully by the hilt for a moment, and then holding it in front of him, entered the secret opening and disappeared. The passage closed behind him.

8ᵗʰ Day of Summer - 6:15 PM – The Temple of the Damned – 7 Days until the Full Moon

The tree was long dead and in a state of progressive petrification. The nodules were still as pronounced as Cael saw in the vision, but the branches were completely devoid of leaves. Danilus made some torches from swamp reeds and then they all climbed up into the tree, which was a comedy in itself. Dheke remained below, forlornly looking up at them, emitting an occasional whine. The mists still enshrouded them at this height, though they were thinner. Mallet was peering down into the dark opening that Cael had triggered, having seen how to do it.

"I'm not going down there," Mallet observed.

"For sure," Danilus added.

Cael looked at Needle.

"Oh holy hells, you little girls," said Needle. "You want me to go first?"

"I don't reckon I should let any of you down there," Danilus said.

"Boxxaway wants us to get that orb," said Cael. "Look, there are rungs going down."

"Yeah, like I trust those," said Needle sarcastically.

"Use this; I brought it from the boat," Mallet said, holding up a coil of hemp rope.

"What if there is something alive down there?" Brynn asked nervously, leaning into the opening and staring down.

"The rungs seem sturdy," Cael said, "I'll go first. I need to use the *Lorgnettes* again when I get down there."

"Not without this," Mallet said, shaking the rope in his hand. "Just in case."

"Here," Brynn said, and dropped a stone down the hole. Needle leaned over to listen.

Danilus gave a low whistle.

"Shhh!" Needle hissed.

"Did you hear it hit the bottom?" Cael asked, taking the

rope from Mallet.

"I didn't hear anything, thanks to all the yapping," Needle said, snatching the rope from Cael. "Here. I'm going first." He tied the line around his waist.

"How you gonna see down there?" Mallet asked.

Danilus quickly lit one of his torches with some tinder, flint and steel. He handed it to Needle, who tested the top rung with his foot.

"You and Mallet going to stay up here to hold the rope?" Needle asked Danilus as he began to lower himself into the opening, torch held gingerly in one hand.

"I got you," Mallet grinned.

Needle paused, looking at Mallet. "Danilus, can you just make sure he doesn't drop me?"

Five Thousand Years Ago – Six weeks before the fall of the Cult of Yex

Elija climbed down the hollow in the trunk, which descended into the hillock.

He was in a chamber hewn from rock, a single wooden door to his right. His steel dagger gave off a faint yellow light. He listened at the door and then opened it by pulling on the iron ring in the center. It screeched open, its bronze hinges badly in need of oil. A dank narrow passage opened before him, hewn straight as an arrow into the rock. The passage was invaded by occasional tangles of deep roots from the trees above. He moved silently down the passage at a steady pace for what seemed to Cael like fifty yards or more until he reached another door, this one made of stone. He paused here for a long time, listening and sniffing.

Finally, he cautiously pushed against the stone door. It opened silently, but only about one quarter of the way before being blocked by something. He peered out into a large square chamber hewn from rock. The light from his dagger created menacing shadows. The room was in disarray, scorch marks marred the walls and floor. Corpses were strewn all about.

He waited, but heard nothing. He put his shoulder to the door and pushed. It skidded open slowly, as whatever was blocking it slid back with a wet squish.

The *Lorgnettes* allowed Cael to hear and even smell, and he almost wretched at the odor of death and decay that came to him.

Elija Abel stepped cautiously into a room full of rotting corpses. They hadn't been dead long, maybe two days, three at most. Four saplings in clay pots stood against a wall, charred black and burned.

The corpses were human mostly, but a few were Rothkin and Dwarves. Some looked to have been killed in whatever conflagration erupted in here, but terrible wounds and blackened arrows sticking from some of the bodies testified to a battle that killed most of them. The chamber looked to have been a last bastion for the denizens of this dungeon, for they had erected barriers of tables and benches in a defensible position around the four charred saplings.

Elija surveyed the destruction. His eyes finally fixed on the far dark corner of the room.

"What ho?" Elija said into the darkness, his voice quavering.

"So a last warrior has returned to this infernal place," a deep voice spoke from the darkness. From the shadow emerged a man who looked to be in his mid-thirties; handsome and fierce, with sharp cheeks, he carried a simple, yet elegant long sword. A blue cloak draped around him, and his eyes were dark in the low light.

"Warrior? N-no. I am but a simple messenger. You slew all these people?" Elija breathed.

"I and my companions, but only I survived the blast."

"I k-knew them. Most of them," Elija said, backing up slowly toward the door behind him.

"Why do you return here, little one?"

"I'm just returning from an errand." He reached the door.

The man nodded slightly toward the door and by the power of sorcery it slammed shut behind Elija. There was no going back.

The man smiled.

"You don't seem a mere errand boy." He took a step toward Elija, his long blade glinting in the light from Elija's dagger. "That knife you hold seems too valuable a trinket for an errand boy. Slide it to me along the floor... move slowly."

"You have been here for days. You don't know everything," Elija said, doing as the wizard commanded.

"Very good little one," the wizard laughed, bending down to retrieve the glowing dagger without taking his eyes off Elija. "I hoped someone like you would return here, as I have so many questions. And lo... here you are."

"I know things about this place. I can tell you things you will want to understand. I know all about this place..." Elija offered obsequiously.

"And in return I'm to spare your life, then?" said the wizard approaching even closer. He tucked the dagger into his belt, its light still providing illumination.

"I have no illusions," Elija said. His back was to the now closed door. The man had come forward and stood a single yard away.

"Then speak, little one. My little errand runner," said the man with a sneering laugh. "Start by telling me about the moss you cultivate here."

"What happened to it?" asked Elija, casting a furtive glance to the charred saplings.

The man took a step back and turned his head slightly to look at the burned trees. "Your people made their last stand here. They fought valiantly to defend those trees. The red stuff grew on them, though there was very little of it."

"You burned it, then. After you killed everyone?"

"Your own people did that," the man said somberly. "When it was clear they could not defeat us, one of them set flame to the red moss. The explosion killed everyone but me."

"Is there none left, then?" asked Elija.

"Only this," the man pulled a stoppered vial from his cloak. The clear glass container held a small quantity of red powder. He watched the powder settle after swirling the vial. "Spores, I expect... locked in a metal chest on the other side of this complex. Our alchemists will find this fascinating, I'm certain."

Elija said nothing in response.

"It must be of great import for your people to have died so willingly to protect it. What does it do?" the wizard asked.

Elija was silent.

"Come, now. How do you expect me to hold up my end of our bargain if you won't hold up yours?" the man smirked.

"Our wizards use it, but I don't know the details," Elija sighed resignedly. "It makes their magic stronger, somehow."

"The Valley of Oar!" the wizard exclaimed.

"You were there?" Elija asked.

The man nodded. "I have never seen such a release of magical energy in my life. I would not have thought it even possible. How is it used? Eaten? Rubbed on the skin? Brewed into a tea?"

"I don't know."

The wizard held the sword blade menacingly closer.

"I swear, I don't know!" Elija stammered.

"No matter. Our alchemists will solve it." He tucked the vial back into a pocket of his cloak. "Tell me of the *Ruukus ob Thaaxo.*"

"How do you know that name?" Elija said, his eyes widening. "No one knows we even call them that."

"The Fingers of Yex? *Ruukus ob Thaaxo* in the accursed language of the Abyss? We too have spies, little man. This is where you trained them, no?"

Elija trembled and nodded. He sucked in breath between his teeth, making a whistling sound. "What do you want to know?"

"What do you think I want to know?"

"They'll kill me..."

"They're already dead," the warrior said sweeping his hand around the room. "Besides, your cause is lost. You must know that. The Battle at Oar went very badly for you, despite your secret magics."

Elija paused, scanning around at the piles of corpses. He trembled again, looking like he wished he could step back even further. He looked like he wanted to bolt and run. "They are assassins, fanatical agents that do the bidding of the cult leadership."

"We know that part!" the wizard warrior said impatiently, gesturing for Elija to hurry. "How do you make them so rabid?"

"We start with children... always *your* children, captured during raids or stolen from your homes in the night."

"Keep going," the wizard warrior said.

"The core of the *Ruukus ob Thaaxo* is their willingness to do *anything*."

"That, I have noticed."

"You have met one?"

"He isn't alive to tell about it," the wizard said.

"But you bear the scars?"

"How do you train them to fight so fiercely?"

"You don't understand. Their training is no more than any other warrior or assassin receives."

The man stared at Elija, his eyes gleaming. The sound of air could be heard as he breathed in and out through his nostrils. "They fight as if they are possessed," he said. "They take risks in combat that no sane man would take. They fight as if they have no fear."

"Exactly," said Elija. "We take away their fear. That's what you are seeing when you fight them: the complete absence of fear."

"Evil assassins that willingly undertake suicidal missions," the wizard said flatly, incredulity evident in his tone. "And pray tell how does one remove fear from a person?"

Elija pointed to the charred saplings. "The moss has many uses. We feed the moss to your captive children. They receive it regularly for a week or so. From the moment they first taste it, they will always crave it desperately."

"And that takes away their fear?"

"No. We feed it to them... then we take it away."

"And?" asked the wizard expectantly.

"And they will do anything to get it back. *Anything*. Their indoctrination and training begins: weapons, poisons, stealth... all for the promise of another taste of that moss. We keep their hope alive by giving them an occasional taste."

"How long?"

"Back in the day, they were conditioned in that manner for

a couple of years. Nowadays, the need is more pressing. We are lucky to train them for a few months before testing them."

"Testing them?"

"Once their training is complete, we keep them dosed for a full day and then the moss is once again taken from them. We send them out on their first mission to prove their willingness to do whatever is asked."

"That would be what, then?"

"They are told that they will never receive another taste unless they bring back the severed heads of their own parents."

A look of horror breached the wizards face. "And they do it?"

"Always. From that time forward they are damned and fearless. They belong to us... utterly."

8ᵗʰ Day of Summer - 6:30 PM – The Temple of the Damned – 7 Days until the Full Moon

Cael led Needle and Brynn through the dank corridors of the Temple of the Damned. Mallet and Danilus stayed back in the tree to hold the rope. Cael had paused a few times to don the *Lorgnettes* in order to follow Elija Abel and the tall wizard. He had watched their discussion in the chamber with the charred trees and then followed them as they navigated labyrinthine corridors into other, deeper parts of the complex.

Over thousands of years, things had changed. Anciently the temple had been under a forest, now it was in a swamp and it smelled of mildew and mold. The air was thick with humidity, clogging the lungs and nostrils. It was so thick, they could taste the foulness as much as smell it. Decay had long since erased most bodily remains, though a few lumps of rust or bronze had persisted. Only a few bones remained. To their surprise, the corridors were not flooded with swamp water, but puddles at this depth were in no short supply. They wound around the dank puddles where they could, and tiptoed through ones too large to avoid. Cael surmised that the complex had been carved into the dense rock of the hillock and still remained well above the water line.

"Brings back great memories, huh?" Cael said to Needle. They had spent a lot of time as youngsters following Boxxaway and Kemano down many an ancient tunnel in search of artifacts.

"You sure you know where you are going?" Needle asked.

A giant centipede, as long as Cael's forearm, slithered out from a crack in the wall. He stepped aside to avoid it, and it crawled right over Brynn's foot. She stood petrified, but did not cry out.

"What do you think Boxxaway wants this moss for?" she asked.

"I'm not sure," said Cael, "But I gathered from his letter, that he will tell us when we give it to him." Cael had considered the question constantly since watching Elija explain to the blue-cloaked wizard. He had learned of at least two distinct uses for the red herb. First, it was used to condition the cult's fanatical assassins. Cael thought back to seeing his own parents murdered and wondered if that assassin was one of the *Ruukus* things that they talked about. He couldn't imagine anyone being capable of such horrors were they not twisted by the cult and the moss. Second, it was some kind of magical augmentative, and apparently from Boxxaway's letter, the Cult's wizards also ingested it. Was there another use Boxxaway had in mind? Eating it was certainly not an option. Indeed, there were lots of questions he had for Boxxaway.

"It makes me nervous," Brynn said.

"Well, for one thing, we need to make sure the cult can't get it," Cael offered. "And now that I think about it, the cult wizard I told you about, the one that sent Elija... he mentioned that the moss was needed to construct a gate. I'm not sure what that meant, but I got the sense that it was of paramount importance to them."

"Seems like an important detail you forgot to tell us about there, wizard boy," said Needle.

"So maybe they will try to rebuild the gate thing again?" Brynn wondered aloud.

They had come through a series of winding damp corridors

and rotted out doors to a descending stairway. The torch light shone in a small radius around them, showing slime and mold clinging everywhere.

Cael's feet slid on the slimy stair, and he waved his arms to keep his balance. "Watch out," he warned.

The three linked hands as they descended the stairs. Near the bottom, they reached a hallway flooded with swamp water. Cael prodded for the bottom with the end of his staff. "It's only about a foot deep," he said, taking a tentative step forward into the water. They continued through the fetid water until the flooded passage turned and ended in a wide spiral staircase leading up.

They reached the top in short order and emerged in a short, straight passage. Continuing, they soon found themselves in a small square chamber that ended in a tall stone door with a tarnished metal ring inset in the middle of it. The room was muggier than the rest of the complex. Everything was wet. Cael guessed that they must be in a section in the complex at the base of the hillock. In the middle of the room was a pile of debris.

"Once more," Cael said, donning the *Lorgnettes*.

Five Thousand Years Ago – Six weeks before the fall of the Cult of Yex

"Well, this is it," Elija Abel said to the man as they reached the base of the spiral stairs. Faint light from Elija's dagger, still tucked in the wizard's belt, provided illumination. "There is the main entrance, though how you managed to find it, much less open it, amazes me."

"Like I told you," the wizard said looking at the door. "We too have spies."

Moving with catlike speed, Elija produced another dagger seemingly out of thin air, and stabbed at the man. Cael was stunned by the sudden assault he was witnessing. The man moved quickly, barley blocking the first blow.

But Elija struck again. And then again, the blade flashing like a scorpion's tail. The man had his footing now and deftly blocked each blow.

"I knew you were no mere messenger," he said as he stepped back, drawing his sword with his right hand. He held forth his left hand, palm out, and fired off a bolt of fiery blue energy into Elija's chest. The little man absorbed the blow, his leather vest burning away down to his charred skin.

Still Elija relentlessly attacked, the dagger flashing in the light as he struck. The wizard was unused to coping with an opponent of such small stature. He stepped forward with a mighty thrust of his sword, but Elija dodged it with incredible dexterity. He counterattacked the stunned wizard, plunging the dagger deep into his stomach, doubling him over.

Elija didn't pause. He pulled out the dagger and rammed it home under the wizard's chin, sending the blade into his brain.

"You judged correctly. I am no messenger. But it seems you still underestimated me." They were the last words the wizard ever heard. He fell twitching to the floor. Elija stood over him, breathing easily. He held out his arm. His skin rippled and jerked, like a flower blooming in the spring, the skin split apart and a *Balizar* emerged, covered in blood and pus. It skittered to Elija's upturned palm and leapt on the corpse of the wizard. It burrowed through cloth and flesh with the enthusiasm of a dog searching for a buried bone, disappearing down into the chest cavity of the dead man.

Elija sheathed his dagger and leaned over the wizard to reach into his cloak. He emerged with his glowing dagger and the stoppered vial of red spores. He paused to examine the spores in the light before he stepped around the corpse and ran his finger along the door, which popped open at his touch. He walked out into the late afternoon light. The door slammed behind him with a boom.

8th Day of Summer - 7:45PM – The Temple of the Damned – 7 Days until the Full Moon

"What did you see?" asked Brynn.

"He hid the first orb in that pile of debris in the middle of the room." Cael walked over to it and nudged it with his toe.

"Bring the torch closer please," he called.

He bent down and dug through what had to be the man's five-thousand-year-old remains with his hands. There were only bits of bone and corroded metal, but he soon found the small black ball.

He picked it up gingerly with his thumb and forefinger and examined it in the light. There was no doubt they had found the first token. He had a sudden worry that it would try to burrow into his arm. Boxxaway hadn't mentioned that possibility, though, of course, how could he?

He risked it, cupping his hand and letting the ball roll around in his palm.

A flash of black passed before his eyes and a stabbing, agonizing pain shot through his palm and up his arm. At first he thought the orb had indeed turned into a spider, but then he realized that a long, sharp object had come down from above and pierced the orb, destroying it and then pierced clear through his hand.

The pain made his heart skip a beat and he bit down hard on his own tongue. Blood gushed into his mouth. He staggered back into Needle, who shoved him forward. He slipped on the damp floor and fell to his knees.

A shadowy figure appeared before him. Cael looked up into the eyes of Elija Abel and screamed.

CHAPTER ELEVEN
Delirium Trigger

"You know what's delicious? Bystle Moss. That's what."

\- King Tharchelon

5th Day of Summer - 7:00 AM – Just Outside Bystle Vale - 10 Days to the Full Moon

The bugs feasted upon Tharchelon. The constant itching of their ferocious little bites was the most maddening thing he had ever been forced to endure. The pain of his headache had not abated, but had grown steadily more prevalent. The pain in his skull was a welcome distraction to the constant desire to scratch. He focused on the pain in his head and allowed it to engulf him, pushing the desire to scratch to the back of his mind, if only for a while. He sat shivering in the morning light and allowed himself a furious round of scratching at the little blighters. He looked at his blood-encrusted fingernails. He had once again scratched off the scabs of previous scratching. He looked at his arms, blood flowing freely. His rent tunic was covered in blood spots. He tried to focus his bleary eyes in the cold, grey light of the dawn. The bugs must be very small, because, though he was infested with thousands of them, he could not see them; they must have burrowed into his flesh. He examined the coagulated blood under his finger nails, and carefully picked through it, looking for the remnants of one of the vicious insects that he might have scratched out... nothing. He could feel them burrowing deeper into his skin. He resisted the urge to scratch again by focusing his mind on the pain in his head. To distract himself from the pain and the growing sense of hopelessness, he tried to focus his thoughts on the events of his last night in the vale. He had taken a double dose of moss, and something important had happened. He had tried again and again over the past two days to remember, but the memories would not come. All he could remember was a vague sense of shadows and low, whispering voices.

He had spent the last two nights shivering, sitting upright against trees, trying desperately to sleep. But even the fleeting moment of respite that sleep offered, refused him. The protrusion at the base of his spine ached, but he didn't care. It was just one more agony in a long list of agonies. He trembled and shivered constantly, even during the day when it was warm. He could not lie flat, for the pain in his chest overwhelmed him. If he could see his own lungs, he knew they would be bruised black and blue. Sitting upright at least allowed him shallow breaths with bearable pain. The first night, he had apparently chosen poorly and sat against a tree infested with the tormenting bugs. They must have found him one by one, as the itching began slowly at first and then became a constant torment as the entire colony assaulted him. He hadn't slept in the two days and nights since his exile, nor had he eaten. He yearned only to taste the moss; its soothing and calming flavor would bring him instant relief and clear his mind so he could think. The hankering was constant, utterly overshadowing the want for food and everything else. He checked the pockets of his tunic and robe again, just in case there might be a pinch of dried moss in there. He had checked a thousand times already, though he had never put any moss in his pockets before. He always ate directly as he picked it in the Moss Garden. If only he had planned ahead and stashed some extra in his pockets! A torturous headache and an unyielding itch were his constant companions. He had started to tremble persistently now. His tongue tasted like tin, and he couldn't get the ever-present smell of burning hair out of his nostrils.

Tharchelon forced himself to stand, using the tree to steady himself. He walked on wobbly feet, holding his hand out until he found the barrier again. In the last two days he had almost circumnavigated the entire vale, hoping to find a weak spot. He had tried digging under the barrier, but it continued several feet deep below ground. He had even climbed a tall tree whose branches extended across the barrier high above the ground. Climbing in his condition was extremely foolish but such was the hankering that compelled him. To his dismay, the barrier was higher than the highest branch and he was once again thwarted. He longed for the moss... ached for it. He *needed* it.

Tharchelon limped along, dragging his left palm against the invisible barrier. He tried to keep his mind focused on the events after he had taken the second dose of moss. The act of feeling along the barrier for a way through was growing increasingly familiar to him... somehow connected to his lost memories of the night before his exile. As he focused on this sense of déjà vu, he suddenly experienced a sense that he had been transported to some shadowy place, after taking the second pinch of moss.

He clung desperately to that idea, trying to plumb its depths as he limped along. Every step was agony. He scratched at his bloody sores continually as he went, hoping against hope to find a weakness in the invisible wall. He had only a few miles more to go before he would arrive back to the point where Nelcherath had dumped him and his exile began. So far, he had not discovered the slightest flaw or hint of weakness in the barrier.

Once again, the act of feeling the barrier triggered another vague memory. It wafted through his mind and he clutched at it. In that shadowy place, he had spoken to someone... some *thing.* Many somethings? He had been in that shadowy place for what seemed like a long time, and then suddenly he awoke to a kick in the chest the next morning. Was it a dream, like the dreams that fled his mind within moments of waking? It seemed more real. It seemed to have great meaning. The details were maddeningly elusive. The memories sometimes drifted to just within his grasp... taunting him.

He stumbled along, sprained left hand on the barrier, right hand scratching at the bugs under his skin, favoring his broken fingers. What happened that night in the shadowy realm? It was important. Something *had* happened. He was sure of it, and he had a sense that he had been pleased with whatever had occurred. If only he could remember, the memory might clue him a way back to the vale... back to his birthright... back to the moss.

Just ahead, he noticed the goathead rock. He had circled the entire vale and returned to the place of his exile. Hope abandoned him as he covered the last few feet to complete the vast distance, verifying that he was indeed cut off, utterly. Despair overwhelmed him. He slumped against the invisible barrier and slid slowly to the ground. No creature had ever been made to suffer so.

Then, in his abject hopelessness... he remembered.

CHAPTER TWELVE

Castaways

"The Rothkin are the least trustable race in existence."

-Written by an unknown author in the margins
of Adirak's original History of the Wars with the
Cult of Yex

*8ᵗʰ Day of Summer – 7:45 PM – Swamp – 7 Days until the Full
Moon*

Brynn had been staring at the orb on Cael's palm in trepidation as Cael rolled it around, when she suddenly noticed something that took her breath away. *The little ball had a sigil on it!* Or at least it was a partial sigil. It had definite aspects of a sigil, but it didn't seem fully formed. Of all places to see a sigil! Her mind did a back flip. How did it get there? What was its function?

As she pondered, something suddenly struck through it, destroying it and piercing Cael's palm. Shards of the broken orb lay scattered about the floor.

Cael screamed. Needle almost dropped the torch as he staggered backwards.

A small, feral man stood before them. Something was desperately wrong with his right hand. It was badly deformed, having six bony fingers, each abnormally long and jointed in odd places. Each finger sprouted out from the wrong place in his hand, if you could even call it a hand. Blood dripped from one of the bony fingers that had pierced Cael's palm. It reminded her of a spider.

If the shock of the sigil and the deformed spider hand weren't enough, what really got Brynn was this: the little man had *a sigil tattooed on his forehead!* The symbol was visible through his long, black, greasy hair, centered a little above his eyes. This sigil was different than the sigil on the orb, but like the one on the orb, it also seemed only partially formed. His skin was pallid and gray, as bloodless as his eyes were soulless. Could this creature be the ancient Rothkin Cael had told them about? Was this Elija Abel? Impossible!

"What the...?" she said aloud.

The next thing that happened was as crazy as Elija being there in the first place. Needle lunged forward and jabbed his silver dagger straight into the fleshy part of the little man's forearm.

Cael's howl of pain was only exceeded by Elija's; it was a guttural, inhuman sound. His blood was thick and black as pitch as it surged from the wound like clotted cream. The little man lurched backwards in the air like he'd been struck by lightning. He flopped onto the floor, his spidery hand twitching.

Needle stood there with a comical expression of utter shock on his face, his eyes glancing down to his silver dagger, amazed at his own action. The torch blazed in his other hand.

"We have to get out of here!" Cael shouted as he ran toward the large door. Blood flowed freely from the gash in his right hand. Brynn stood frozen, looking down at the little man, trying to catch another glimpse of the sigil on his forehead. There was a smell about him that reminded her of sour milk. And those eyes! Just flat... no spark in them. She had never seen anything like it. He was out of order.

Needle sheathed his dagger and pushed her toward the large sealed door. Wet algae grew green around its fringes.

"Great, what do we do now?" Needle squeaked as he began jerking on the huge tarnished brass ring on the door. He had discovered the stark truth: it was shut tight and seemingly locked. Elija was between them and the hallway to the rest of the complex. They had nowhere to go. Cael looked frantic as he squeezed his right wrist with his other hand in an effort to stem the bleeding from his pierced palm.

Brynn looked back over her shoulder and sure enough, Elija was slowly and deliberately rising to his feet, staring at them dully. She feared his stare would haunt her dreams for years if she managed to live past the next few moments. She turned her head and looked away.

That's when Brynn noticed it. "What in the...?" she muttered again. There, by the brass ring, was a sigil carved in shallow bas relief on the stone door. It was a sealing sigil, and a simple one at that. She had seen it in her mother's book from the rolltop desk.

"Get the hells out of my way," she said, elbowing Needle aside.

"What makes you think you can open it?" Needle cried as he stumbled into Cael at the side of the door.

She raised her hand and triumphantly traced the sigil, unlocking the door. "It's sealed with a witch sigil!"

Her triumph was short-lived. With the sound of an ear-splitting crack, the door flew open and a wall of black mud and brackish swamp water surged in.

She would have been carried away in the deluge if Needle hadn't been so fast. He reached out and took hold of her collar and yanked her to the side in the nick of time. Fortunately, she had elbowed him to the side, so when the door burst open, he and Cael stood in the lee of the flood.

Elija was not so lucky. The little man with the spidery hand had just gotten to his feet when he was hit by the full force of the tidal wave. He howled as the muddy, black froth swept him away down the hall. Brynn exulted at the sound of each pathetic note of his despair. His inhuman, spidery hand groped frantically as the flood carried him plummeting down the spiral stairs.

Brynn recalled seeing young Agrabi girls, their clothes scandalously pasted to their glowing olive skin, the sparkles of sunlight in water drops cast into the air from long black hair as heads were thrown back in laughter. It was a common scene she had only witnessed but obviously never participated in. The Agrabi grew up swimming in the muddy Demon River, but up until their journey with Danilus, Brynn had never so much as set foot in it. It simply wasn't the sort of thing Buerdeleise nobles did: at least not the women. No, Brynn couldn't swim, and the stark, sudden reality of it was as real as the swamp water rushing in.

The Elija creature hadn't seemed any better at swimming as he disappeared over the edge of the spiral stairway. But then again, who was to say whether the best of swimmers could have coped with that torrent? Perhaps he was drowning and would soon be dead?

Somehow she knew this was a vain hope, but she hoped it nonetheless. She never wanted to meet *him* again, though she wouldn't mind getting a closer look at the sigil on his forehead. *That* was fascinating.

Despite her fears, the gushing flow was slowing and Needle bravely waded through the open door, fighting against the current, his torch held high above the tide. The water would soon be waist-deep and was still rising, but it looked like they had an opportunity to escape. "Come on, we can make it," he said. "It's dark outside... and foggy."

Brynn put on her brave face and followed him, Cael right behind her, holding his bleeding, punctured hand high out of the rising water. The current was strong but they made slow progress against it.

"We need to get out of here in case it survived," Cael said, giving voice to the fear they all had. Fear of the little man propelled Brynn forward through the filthy water. Her hand shot out and took Needle's.

He gave her the most puzzling look, but he didn't let go, instead gently pulling her forward as they waded out of the Temple of the Damned. Beyond the door they were in a natural cavern that looked to be partially submerged.

Needle led them out where they found themselves at the base of the hillock where it met the swamp. He helped Brynn scramble up the slope and get clear of the water. Cael followed, holding his wounded hand to his chest, blood staining his tunic. Brynn took out a small knife and cut away a dry strip of her own tunic and wrapped it around Cael's pierced hand.

Due to the fog, visibility was limited, but she could still see water flowing into the cave opening, though the pace was slowing. There was nothing to indicate it would have been an entrance to an ancient underground complex. No wonder it had gone undiscovered for these thousands of years.

"Let's get the hells out of here," Needle said.

Brynn felt a hearty agreement. The little man might wade out after them at any moment. "But where are we?" she said. The stars were not visible through the fog.

"We have to get back to the big tree," said Cael. "But where is it from here?"

Needle pointed off toward the swamp. "That way is north," he said confidently. "That means the tree is... that way," he turned and pointed in a different direction up the slope.

"How could you possibly know that?" Cael asked, incredulous. "The stars aren't visible."

"My father taught me," Needle said. "Anytime you are in a strange building or cave or anything, you should always refigure north at every turn."

"And you did that? Down there?" Brynn said.

"Of course," Needle replied. "I thought everyone knew to do that."

"Well, we have no better option, and we had better hurry," Cael said.

The fog seemed to be thickening as they tried to keep a straight line in the direction Needle had indicated, but that was no easy task with only the light of Needle's torch to cut through the darkness and fog. The sounds of the swamp were disconcerting and it was impossible to discern from which direction each noise came; a splash of water here, the croak of a frog there, the snapping of a twig over yonder.

They didn't speak as they slunk along as quietly as possible for what seemed like an eternity but must have been about twenty minutes. There was every possibility that Elija had survived and was now out there in the fog... stalking them. They did have some trouble finally locating the giant tree in the fog, but Needle's sense of direction had been basically true.

"Mallet?" hissed Brynn, looking up the fog enshrouded trunk.

"Danilus? Dheke? Where are you, boy?" Cael hissed a little more loudly.

"Where in the hells could they be?" Needle whispered. "You don't think that creature beat us to them, do you?"

"What do we do now?" Brynn asked, feeling a deepening sense of helplessness.

"Maybe they are up there and can't hear in the fog," Needle said, suddenly scampering up the tree.

"But where is the dog?" asked Brynn looking around. Needle didn't respond as he climbed higher and disappeared into the mists.

"What are the chances that creature survived?" Brynn asked Cael.

"It was Elija Abel," Cael said flatly.

"I wondered about that," Brynn said. "But how is that possible? It would mean he has survived for thousands of years."

"It was him, all right, but I don't think he is alive anymore."

"How can you be so sure the flood killed him?"

"No, you don't understand, Brynn," said Cael. "He wasn't alive when he attacked us."

It took a few moments for the horror of what Cael was saying to sink in. "You mean..."

"He's undead."

"So he didn't drown in that flood then?" Suddenly it made sense to Brynn. He *was* dead! It explained the haunting, dead look in his eyes.

"I think we have to assume that he didn't drown."

Needle scampered down the trunk and jumped the last few feet of his descent. "They're gone, all right."

9th Day of Summer - 1:00 AM – The Swamp – 6 Days Until the Full Moon

"What in the holy hells possessed them to wander off?" Needle demanded in exasperation as they trudged through knee deep swamp water back toward the boat.

The swamp was almost completely dark but the fog was thinning progressively as they journeyed back toward the river. Needle was able to get an occasional glimpse of the stars, sufficient for orienteering. Brynn had no idea where they were, and was too tired to care. They had been trudging back through the swamp for hours, as fast as they could go. She estimated the time to be after midnight, and she was exhausted. The waxing moon provided barely-sufficient light. They had decided to extinguish the torch, as neither Cael nor Needle felt it wise, as it might provide a beacon to Elija. The moon provided another uncomfortable reminder of their predicament with Mallet. The moon would be full in seven days, maybe six. What then?

"I'm sure they had a good reason, Needle," Cael said. "We just have to hope they are ahead of us and waiting at the boat."

"And if they aren't?" Needle grumbled. "What if they're lost in the fog? What if the palm stabber got them?"

"They'll be there. We'll meet up with them and get back on track and I'll use the spectacles to find the second orb."

"Should we bother?" wondered Needle. "Can we succeed with one of them destroyed? Your grandfather's letter said we need all three."

"Yeah, I've been thinking a lot about that," Cael said, adjusting the bandage on his wounded hand. "The letter also said that we should find a way to succeed, even if we couldn't get all three."

"Yeah! That's right!" said Needle. "So do we even bother about the other two?"

"I think we should. I think it will be easier to convince this Tharchelon fellow if we show up with some of them, at least."

"How is your hand, Cael?" Brynn asked.

"I could probably use a clean bandage," he said. "I hope Danilus has some medicine that can fix it up. My whole arm aches."

"Here," Brynn said, cutting off another strip of her tunic. She stopped to rebind his wound. She could now see that the puncture went all the way through his hand; it was still seeping a little from both sides. The blood looked dark by the dim light of the moon.

She marveled at Cael's resolve. She couldn't imagine that she could have held up so well had the injury been to her. Maybe the Cult of Yex was right to fear him in their prophecies. No wonder they wanted to turn him to their side.

"I've been meaning to ask," Brynn said. "Did you notice the mark on that little black ball and a different one on the creature's forehead?"

"There was a mark on the orb?" Needle asked, surprised.

"Yeah, I didn't recognize them," Cael said.

Brynn had been pondering the odd sigils as they mucked their way through the swamp. What was their function? Neither the sigil on the orb, nor the sigil on the little man's forehead, seemed fully formed, and that made her have the persistent feeling that somehow the two sigils were connected in some way. As far as she could remember, neither sigil appeared in her mother's book and that seemed odd to her because each sigil was so simple, simpler even than she had come to expect from minor sigils. Odder still, the tune each elicited in her head was discordant and meager.

She recalled the Cult of Yex symbol. It too was a simple sigil, but it wasn't a partial sigil like the ones on the orb and the little man's forehead. She still didn't know the function of the Cult of Yex sigil. The appearance of these two new sigils forced her to confront a very unpleasant thought that she had been pushing from her mind since several nights ago, when they camped and discussed the shifting stars. She realized she had deliberately been avoiding the inescapable truth: the cult employed witches in ancient times. The idea was extremely disturbing to her. She assumed that witches were good, but simply misunderstood. Her mother was a saint, after all.

"I think we are getting close!" Cael exclaimed. "Can you smell the river?"

Brynn tried to see the sigils in her mind. She had gotten a good look at the sigil on the orb, and it was clear in her memory. But she had only gotten two fleeting glimpses of the sigil tattooed on the little man's forehead. She strained her memory for the details. She had a handle on the basic pattern, but it was fuzzy. Brynn desperately wanted to get to her mother's sigil book and pen the patterns into one of the blank pages at the back before she forgot more. But the swamp was no place for that, not to mention Elija could be closing in on them even now.

"There's the boat," Cael said as they emerged from the swamp.

"Son of abyss, it's about time." Needle cursed.

"Danilus!" Cael called out, in a voice louder than they had used for hours. "Dheke!"

"Mallet!" Brynn called.

There was no answer.

"They're not here, Cael!" Needle complained. "What in the holy hells do we do now?" They had searched the boat and scouted the riverbank for about a quarter mile in both directions, but there was no sign of them.

Brynn sympathized with Needle's despair; she felt it too. Cael was still nursing his wound, so she and Needle helped him into the boat.

"I bet Mallet ratted out early... or the creature found them," Needle speculated as he slumped down upon a crate on the deck.

"Shut up, Needle," Cael said flatly as he began working to light a bullseye lantern. "We must have beaten them here, that's all."

"Shouldn't we go back and look for them?" Brynn asked. She took out a quill and immediately started to sketch the sigils from her memory in her mother's book.

"They'll come here. They have to. We just need to wait."

No one said anything for a long while. The only sound was water lapping against the hull.

"They were sigils," Brynn said matter-of-factly, as she finished the second pattern in her book.

"What were sigils?" Needle asked.

"The mark on that orb. And the mark on Elija's forehead."

"Everything's a sigil to you, isn't it?" Needle asked sarcastically.

"That makes sense, I guess," Cael said. "What else would they be?"

"Are they in your book there?" Needle asked. "Are they the tracing kind, or the always-functioning kind?"

"I'm not sure yet," Brynn said. "They aren't in my mother's book, but I drew them in there. What I could remember of them, anyway." She held open the book for Needle and Cael to see.

"They look pretty simple," Needle said scrunching his nose as he studied the marks. "Are you sure they are sigils?"

"They're definitely sigils," Brynn said. "I'm just not sure how they work yet. They are different from sigils I'm familiar with."

"They're evil, you mean," Needle said.

Needle had said that before when they were discussing the Cult of Yex sigil. It was a very troubling thought to her at the time, that a sigil could be evil. It was one thing that there might be evil witches, but for a sigil itself to be inherently evil was something else entirely. She wasn't sure what the implications of that were. It would require a lot more uncomfortable thinking.

"I don't think so. I think most sigils aren't good or evil. It's how you use them."

"How long before you figure out what it does?" Cael asked.

Brynn just shrugged. They sat in silence for a moment, their exhaustion evident.

"I don't know about you two, but I need some sleep," Needle announced with a yawn. "How about you do another one of those big sigils around the boat, like you did a few nights ago? I mean, what if Mister Crazy Fingers shows up while we're waiting for Mallet and them?"

"I can't put that sigil over the water."

"What about just on the shore?" asked Cael. "That's where he would come from if he does."

"Hmm. I could maybe make an arc of several sigils in a

semi-circle," Brynn wondered aloud. "I have to get some sleep somehow."

"You got that right," Needle agreed. "I don't think any of us could stay awake for a shift of watching."

"How's your hand, Cael?" Brynn asked.

"I hope Danilus shows up soon. I definitely need his medicine."

9th Day of Summer - 8:00 AM – The Swamp – 6 Days until the Full Moon

"Hey, wait up," Needle yelled as he sloshed through the swamp to catch up to them.

The night had passed uneventfully and they had caught up on much needed sleep. To Brynn's dismay, however, Mallet and Danilus had not returned. The feral little man hadn't shown up either, but it was small consolation.

The sky was completely overcast with thick dark clouds when they woke, subduing the daylight. They decided that their only option was to head back to the swamp to search for their companions.

Cael's hand had begun to swell and Brynn wished desperately that she knew how to use Danilus' medicines. She felt helpless and resolved to learn. In the meantime, they needed to find Danilus and her brother as quickly as possible.

"Well, hurry up then," Brynn snapped. The sun had been up nearly an hour now and they had frittered away precious time debating their course of action. Needle's pace wasn't helping them make up for the lost time. Only she and Cael seemed to have any sense of urgency. The air was hot and humid, and the swamp mists were thin. She wiped away the sweat that dripped into her eyes.

"Shhh! Did you hear that?" Cael hissed.

"What?"

"Shut up!"

They were silent; the swamp was not. It was filled with all

sorts of sounds, a cacophony of insects and birds. It sounded like a twisted symphony with no conductor and nothing in tune, but it all made music, nonetheless.

Then she heard it.

Barking. Distant and faint.

"It's Dheke!" Cael exclaimed triumphantly, struggling forward through the muck.

When they finally found them, Brynn's heart leaped into her throat when she laid eyes on her brother.

He lay with his back against a tree on a little knoll that rose out of the swamp. His glaive lay across his lap. Danilus sat next to him. They both looked exhausted. Dheke looked overjoyed, racing back and forth at the water line, tail wagging furiously.

"What happened?" Cael asked as they approached. "Where in the hells have you guys been?

"Just takin' a rest afore we went on. We didn't get no sleep last night."

"Why weren't you at the tree last night?" Brynn asked, kneeling at Mallet's side. "Are you okay?"

"Fine," he said. "Just real tired."

"We heard a thunderous clang that come from out in the fog," Danilus said. "Big loud cracking sound. You'd been gone more than six hours and we figured you was in trouble. We climbed down to look for you, but we got lost in the fog for over an hour. No sooner did we find our way back to the big tree, when out of nowhere some little bastard attacked us. There was something wrong with him. Had dead eyes and some sort of monster hand."

"Elija," Needle breathed, looking around frantically.

"He's out of order, all right," Brynn said.

"We fought him, but he's fast. Strong too, despite being as tiny as he was. He came at us with that weird, deformed hand. I reckon he would have had us if Dheke hadn't a been there. Dheke could get behind him quicker, and kept nipping at him, and Mallet kept him at bay with that pole arm. It was a site to see. Good dog, Dheke!" Danilus reached down and patted him. Dheke responded by wagging his entire hind end uncontrollably.

"So you drove him away?" Needle said.

Danilus nodded. "I reckon he didn't know how to cope with ol' Dheke so he run off into the fog. We was too nervous to risk the swamp in the fog an dark so we stayed put and didn't sleep a wink in case that little bastard came back. We lit out at first light this morning, hoping you was ahead of us or already back to the *Scout*."

"We need to get you back to the boat," Brynn said. "Cael's hand is wounded and we need to tell you what happened to us." She felt sick. They had confirmation that Elija was alive, not that it was a surprise. She looked around the swamp. He was out there. Somewhere. Maybe watching them right now, waiting for the right time to strike. Brynn had a momentary image of spidery fingers wrapping around her throat to throttle, crushing her windpipe while her tongue wagged out from her frothing mouth. She wouldn't feel safe again until they were on the boat together sailing upriver.

Danilus and Mallet stumbled to their feet. "Tell me about your hand, Cael," Danilus said as they started, but Cael didn't have enough energy to relate the tale. Brynn explained their story as they trudged back toward the boat, Danilus leading the way.

"Wait a minute!" Cael rasped, his voice sounding dry and unused. "We have to go back to the Temple of the Damned!"

"The hells, you say!" Needle said. "Why?"

"We have to follow Elija to the next orb."

"I think *he's* following *us*," Brynn said.

"No, you don't understand. I have to use the *Lorgnettes* to follow his ancient trail. The only place I can pick it up again is from the door to the Temple."

"Aww, hells!" Needle almost shouted. "How damn many times do we have to traipse back and forth in this forsaken swamp?"

"So do we go back to the temple now?" Mallet asked.

"I think we..." Cael trailed off. "No. We have to go back to the boat first. I left the *Lorgnettes* onboard."

"Good," Brynn said. "We should do that, anyway. Danilus can fix your hand."

"Did you move the boat?" Danilus called back. They had journeyed all the way back to the river with Danilus on point.

"Holy hells," Needle breathed.

"This is out of order," Brynn whispered.

The *Riparian Scout* was gone.

CHAPTER THIRTEEN
Between Darkness & Light

"It is doubtful that even the wizards of the ancient cult understood what the Bystle Moss truly was. Its far-reaching effects were much more than just a simple magical augmentative."

- From History of the Cult of Yex, by Caed the Chronicler

2nd Day of Summer – 2:15 AM – The Moss Garden - 13 Days to the Full Moon

Tharchelon savored the flavor of the second pinch of Bystle Moss. The exquisite taste would momentarily become the surging feeling of power and calm that so enthralled him. The engulfing sensation was an odd mixture of pleasure with a hint of pain.

The rush of the second dose began to effervesce inside him. It was an ecstasy beyond what he had ever experienced. His encounter with Nelcherath faded from his mind, replaced by the pleasantness coursing through him. He stood with his eyes closed for several minutes, just focusing on the feeling. When he finally opened his eyes, something was strange. He looked down to the moss upon the altar but found that he had difficulty focusing upon it. This was peculiar, because in the past, whenever he had taken even the smallest amount of moss, his vision, and indeed all his senses, were sharpened.

He tried harder to focus his eyes on the moss, but he was still seeing double. It was like when he would cross his eyes slightly as a child, but this was not quite the same. There were two nearly identical bunches of straggly moss upon the altar next to each other. One was blood red as it should be. The other was also red, but appeared as if it were immersed in shadow. Everything was double. The altar was also double but the difference was starker than the moss. One version of the altar was golden hued, polished and well lit. The other version was identical, except it utterly lacked color. It appeared much darker, the grain in the wood appearing in varying shades of gray.

Tharchelon slowly became aware of a hissing noise around him. It sounded like whispering voices. The hissing felt foreign, alien. It seemed to be coming from all around him, and nowhere at once. He could swear there were jumbled, individual words whispered in the milieu, but he could not discern them.

He turned, looking for the source of the hissing, but he was alone. He noticed the bright yellow Bystle Fruits hanging from the inward-growing branches. Next to each in his double vision, was an identical companion, but the companion was like an evil twin. Instead of bright yellow light, it was a dark, black mass, emanating not light but shadow. He strained to focus his eyes to merge the two images but they remained separated in his vision. He tried to cross his eyes to bring them together, and for a moment, the images seemed to move toward each other, but remained apart.

The whispering grew louder and then more quiet as he crossed and un-crossed his eyes. He looked back toward the moss, and for a moment thought he saw shadows coalescing around the moss, but they faded in the yellowy light. An idea struck him. He tried to focus more on the dark and shadowy of the two images. Suddenly, the shadows he glimpsed earlier became visible around the altar. They seemed formless, indistinct. He concentrated on them, mentally ignoring the yellow lit half of his double vision. The shadows seemed to take form as he did so, appearing almost humanoid, but bent and twisted. The shadowy figures huddled around the moss, holding out their hands to it, as if warming themselves around a fire. The whispering reached its loudest.

He switched his focus to the light as an experiment. The whispering quieted and the shadows faded. What was happening? The double dose of moss had sharpened his mind and he somehow understood that he was glimpsing another dimension that coexisted in the same space as the Moss Garden.

In a flash of inspiration, he focused not on the double images he saw, but on the pleasant pain of the moss coursing through his being. He unfocused his eyes and willed his double vision, light and shadow, to merge. By the force of his will, they drifted toward one another until they were perfectly overlapped.

He heard a loud '*pop*', as if a cork had been pulled from a bottle. He felt a terribly disorienting sensation as if the floor on which he stood suddenly jolted out from underneath him. The feeling passed and he regained his sense of balance and direction. Something had changed. His double vision was gone. All around him was only shadow; black, white and shades of gray, and it was very cool here; almost cold. The Bystle Fruits were dark, emanating shadows. The only color was the red moss on the altar, but it seemed enshrouded in darkness as if it were drinking in the shadow given off by the black Bystle Fruits.

Hundreds of insubstantial, shadowy creatures huddled around the moss. They reached toward and through the moss, desperately clawing at it with incorporeal limbs. Then, at once, the shadows became aware of his presence. They turned and set upon him howling, penumbral fangs bared and shadowy claws raised to strike.

The mob engulfed him. He raised his arms in panic to protect himself and steeled himself for the pain, but the incorporeal claws reached right through him. He felt the rage and hatred, but not the claws. He stood amidst the fury of shadows, feeling more confident, about to lower his arms, when suddenly one of the incorporeal claws managed to connect and raked across his forearm. He stared at the claw marks on his arm. His flesh looked gray, and the blood seeping into the fresh scratch marks looked like black ochre. He stumbled and fell over backwards. The mass of shadows pounced upon him, furiously clawing, punching and biting. As before most of the blows passed through him harmlessly, but occasionally one found its mark. Before he regained his feet, he had been clawed, bitten and punched half a dozen times.

Unless he could escape, the hateful shadows would eventually destroy him, one scratch at a time. *He had to get out of this place.* He looked around for an exit. He was still in the Moss Garden, but a strange and alien version of it. It was devoid of color, except for the moss which grew upon the greyish altar, soaking up the shadows cast by the lightless Bystle Fruits.

Looking around he noticed for the first time, standing on the far side of the altar, a wiry creature with pale skin. The creature was clearly a Rothkin and a little taller than he. It stood stock still, watching Tharchelon's predicament, its dead eyes staring out between locks of long, black greasy hair. Some kind of tattoo was on its forehead, but it was impossible to make out through his hair. This being did not seem to be a creature of shadow and darkness like the mob that assailed him, but a creature of flesh and bone. In the rush of shadows that attacked him, Tharchelon had not noticed it.

The creature did not seem intent to act, so Tharchelon turned his attention back to escaping this place. He looked about for the hallway that should have been to his right but there was only a wall of colorless Bystle Wood. Surely he had become disoriented when he fell? The chaos of shadows raging about him certainly didn't make it easy to concentrate. He scanned the walls of the circular room, expecting to find the two exits, but there were none. He moved over to the wall, the mob of shadows following, their attacks unabated. He touched the wall; it felt distant and cold. He quickly circled the entire room, hand on the wall as he went, feeling for the exit that should be here, but wasn't. The creature that stood by the altar did not move as he circled the room. Even his head, perched on a scrawny neck, did not turn to follow his movement. As Tharchelon moved, he was able to get a better look at the gangly creature. His right hand was oversized and grotesque, with long, spindly fingers--six by his count, though they were hard to number as each moved out of sync with the others as if by its own independent will. The hand reminded Tharchelon of a spider in the throes of an agonizing death. *Who or what was this strange person?*

Tharchelon completed the full circle, dragging his hand on the wall as he went. There was no way out of this place; fear gripped him. Eventually the shadow attacks upon him, rare though it was that one struck him, would wear him down. Was he to die here in this dark, hellish place? Doubting himself, he circled the room once more, feeling again for the exit that surely must be there. *Where were the exits?*

An idea took shape in his mind. Perhaps he could escape the same way he had become trapped here? He stared at the Bystle Fruits, looking earnestly for the yellowy twins to the overpowering shadowy versions.

Yes! They were there! Almost imperceptible, but they were there. He focused on the yellow light from one twin and his double vision became more pronounced. Was it as simple as repeating the trick of willing his double vision to overlap and simply slide back, escaping back to his proper dimension?

He focused on feeling the power of the moss surging inside him. The double dose of moss was still strong. He stared at the Bystle Fruits, the dark and light versions now distinct. He willed them together, and as before they began to converge. Suddenly a claw reached out of the undulating blob of shadows and scratched across his face. His concentration was broken and not only did the dual images diverge, but the light version faded from his view. He tried again in vain, but his focus was interrupted by a raking claw or punch from the shadowy attackers.

For what seemed an eternity, Tharchelon tried repeatedly to focus his concentration enough to see and merge the double visions, but he could never maintain his concentration long enough to achieve success. Scratches and bruises covered his arms, neck and face. His clothes were rent in many places. He felt as if he could not survive much longer, and hope began to abandon him. The thought of dying here in this alien place filled him with dread. He wanted to live! Would he die in this place, slowly clawed to death by these vicious, hateful shadows?

He slumped against the wall and slid slowly to the floor, the shades enveloping him in a maelstrom of claws, fists and fangs. At the moment he was about to give himself up for lost, the shadow creatures suddenly retreated from him. It was as if they had obeyed an order only they could hear.

The hateful shades parted and the lanky, pale creature came forth. His steps were slow and deliberate, his greasy black hair swaying side to side with the rhythm of his gait. He came to a stop a few paces before Tharchelon and stared at him with soulless, uncaring eyes. Tharchelon somehow understood that this wretched thing was neither living nor dead. He was a Rothkin, same as him, but there were differences. He was taller than most, even taller than Tharchelon himself, who was quite tall for his race.

"Curious," his voice croaked with an eerie, otherworldly tone. Tharchelon had the impression that the word the creature just spoke was the first it had uttered in an impossibly long time.

"Who... what... are you?" Tharchelon replied, rising to his feet. Blood seeped from his lacerations.

The creature stood stock still and silent for quite some time, as the shadows milled about the altar in silence. "You should know the answer to that," he intoned with a rasp.

Bafflement. How could he possibly know who this creature was? "But..." was all he could muster. "Who *are* you?"

The creature just stared at him, saying nothing. Tharchelon's mind raced. Who and what was this creature? What were the shadows that inhabited this place? Deep in his mind a speculation began to form, but he instinctively shut it down. He knew he would not like the implication if it were true.

"I expect I am your grandfather of a hundred generations or more," the creature finally croaked.

Tharchelon stood, blinking... the worst fear of his shunted speculations coming true.

"And these," he said gesturing behind him. "Are the tormented souls of your forefathers back to my time. These are the spirits of my sons."

"My... my father?" said Tharchelon, looking frantically at the shadows that jockeyed for position around the moss and the altar. They were indistinguishable one from the next.

"I expect he doesn't remember you now... or more likely doesn't care. The shades care only to bask in the energy of that accursed moss."

The implications of what the creature was saying to his ultimate destiny were too awful to contemplate, so Tharchelon pushed them from his mind. "What is this place?"

"Have my progeny grown so dimwitted?" croaked the creature after several seconds of pause.

"What?"

"Can you not guess what this place is?"

Tharchelon, still simmering on the power of the double dose of moss coursing through him, understood what his ghoulish ancestor meant. He recalled his earlier speculation and instantly his mind began to fill in the details.

"It... it must be an alternate plane; a pocket or bubble that co-exists with the real world, occupying the same space, but in a different dimension."

"So. Cleverness is in you after all."

Tharchelon, his mind racing, continued with his suspicions. "This place must have come into being... *because* of the moss. Its power had carved out this place... shaped it. It exists in both dimensions at once, straddling the nexus between them."

The creature showed no expression of confirmation on his features or in his soulless eyes. "It indeed may stand in both dimensions at once, but for us... for *you* now... this place is not but a prison--your eternal prison."

A question suddenly occurred to Tharchelon. "So the spirits of my dead forefathers were drawn here at their death... but how did you come to be here? You are flesh and blood like me, are you not?"

"I am flesh. But true blood has not flowed in my veins for thousands of years. I persist in never-ending undeath. I came to be here the same way I expect you did. I died of thirst in this place, but my body and spirit did not separate."

Tharchelon's eyes grew wide. "You mean, you ate... tasted it?"

The creature did not say anything for what seemed to Tharchelon like an eternity. "I was instructed never to taste it before I brought the moss here to cultivate it. But in the end, I tasted it only once. After many years, I had grown despondent. I felt betrayed and disillusioned. All that I had worked for was destroyed and broken. The task that fell to me was a lonely burden and I began to feel it was without point or purpose. As time passed and I grew older, my despondency turned to bitterness."

"Instructed?"

"I established a good crop of moss and trained my oldest

son to tend the garden." Pausing, he turned slightly and cast a glance upon the writhing mass of shadows before he continued. "One day, I was alone in the garden. In a moment of supreme despair, I did as I knew the battlemages of old had done. I do understand why I suddenly felt compelled to eat. I did not fully comprehend the consequences. In some way, it was an act of defiance against those who had asked too much of me. The next thing I remember... I was here."

"How did you know I had been... tasting the moss?"

"I can see." He turned to look at the moss upon the altar. Tharchelon followed his gaze. It was indeed scraggly and unhealthy. The shadows around it reached for it, and through it, failing to touch it. "It has been diminishing of late."

"Can... could you see me? There... in the garden?"

"No, but the moss was slowly being eaten away. When you arrived here, it became clear to me."

Tharchelon's eyes narrowed. "You are not angry with me?"

"I myself partook."

"Why did you not continue?"

"The moss in this place exists only in its spiritual form. I can neither taste, nor even touch it... and neither can they, though they yearn for it desperately." The milling spirits continued to reach for the moss, in a sort of vain insanity.

"But they never tasted of the moss in life," said Tharchelon in bewilderment. "Why then do they seek it in death?"

"It compels them. Its power wrought upon them, though they tasted it not."

The creature had given Tharchelon much to ponder, but he still had questions unanswered. "You said you were instructed. If you were the first, and brought the moss here, who instructed you?"

"Did your father not tell you?"

"Tell me what?"

The creature seemed surprised, and contemplated for several seconds before he replied. "Don't you know the purpose for which the moss is kept?"

Tharchelon did not want to consider the question. What would his ancestor think? Would he find a reason for anger and set the shadows upon him again? The situation called for a bluff. "Purpose?"

"I was sent northward to this place with spores to establish and tend the moss in a hidden garden."

"Hidden? From who? Who sent you?"

"It was long ago, but my anger has seared it in my memory. I served an ancient religion in complete and total devotion. But the price I paid, imprisoned here, has been far too great. A wizard sent me with the spores near the end of a great war, to keep the moss hidden from the enemy, to preserve it for a time when it would be needed again. A time that I grew to believe would never come. My life's devotion was a purposeless lie."

Gaps in Tharchelon's understanding of the history of the Bystle Vale were suddenly becoming clear. There was so much his people had forgotten through the ages. "Until when?"

The creature cocked his head, indicating confusion.

Tharchelon pressed him. "You were to secret the moss away. Until when? For what purpose?"

"Did your father not tell you that also?"

Tharchelon just looked on expectantly.

"I was to tend the moss, and instruct my son, who was to instruct his son."

"Yes, yes!" said Tharchelon in exasperation. "To what purpose?"

"The wizard, Xylex was his name I think, said that one day, far in the future, our ancient religion would return and war might come again. He said agents would come to retrieve the moss."

Tharchelon fought to overcome his rising sense of panic. He suddenly recalled his discussion with Nelcherath and his plan to thwart the interlopers who indeed were coming. He needed a backup for Nelcherath, and if he was reading this undead creature correctly, he no longer harbored any loyalty to his original purpose in bringing the moss to the vale.

Tharchelon concocted a hasty scheme. It was a risk, to be sure, but he was confident he had read the creature correctly. His instinct called for lies, but something told him that the truth would be the best approach. "And what if I told you that those very same agents are even now coming to retrieve the moss?"

The ghastly being stared, revealing nothing on his stoic face. "I have been trapped in this prison for eons. A price too great to ask of anyone, don't you think? A price you are now fated to pay as well." The creature looked at the mass of writhing shadows forlornly.

Elation! Tharchelon knew he had guessed right. The rest of his plan began to crystalize in his mind. "What if I told you that I do not wish to give the moss to those agents who are coming to fetch it?"

The creature looked at him with a hint of interest. Tharchelon looked carefully for signs of anger or displeasure. There were none, just as he expected. Tharchelon continued. "I feel no connection to a purpose thousands of years old. The agents will destroy the way of life of my...our... people. But I may not be able to stop them... by myself."

The creature maintained his look of interest, but shook his head ever so slightly. "You can't stop anything from this prison you have stuck yourself in."

Tharchelon plowed ahead, growing more confident by the minute. "What if I told you that I *can* escape... and what if I could free you in the process?"

"There is no—"

Tharchelon cut him off. "But what if I could?"

"I don't understand."

Excitement was creeping into Tharchelon's voice. "If I could free you from this place? Right now. Would you help me?"

The creature laughed out loud. It was an ethereal, alien sounding laugh. "If! *If!*"

Tharchelon was losing patience. "What if I could?"

"I would help you then."

"Would you kill the agents for me? The ones who are coming for the moss?"

"If... you freed me from this place..."

"All I need you to do right now," said Tharchelon, walking toward the creature. "Is keep those shadow things away from me."

Tharchelon grasped the creature by its left hand; he wanted nothing to do with the terrifying right hand. Its flesh was cold and clammy. He kept an eye on the mass of shadows but they did not break their habit of milling about the altar.

Tharchelon took a deep breath, mostly confident about his strategy. He closed his eyes and allowed the odd mix of pleasure and pain from the moss to percolate, build and infuse his consciousness. He opened his eyes and focused on one of the black Bystle Fruits hanging from the gray branches around the ceiling. Sure enough, the yellow twin began to take shape. Tharchelon concentrated on it until his double vision was complete. He could see both dimensions simultaneously, and his confidence surged.

He squeezed the creature's hand and used the power flowing through him to will the two versions in his vision to converge. With the now-familiar feeling of the ground jolting out from underneath him, accompanied by a popping sound, he and the creature slid back into his warm, bright, home dimension.

A wave of exhaustion broke over him and he let go of the creature's chill hand, sliding to the ground of his familiar Moss Garden. The yellow light of the Bystle Fruits washed over them. The creature looked about, and the barest hint of a smile broke on his face.

"Those who come for the moss will die soon," the creature promised Tharchelon. It turned to the hallway, its greasy, black hair swaying as it began a loping stride for the exit.

"But how will you find them?" Tharchelon asked, on the verge of being overtaken by sleep.

"Those many generations ago, I left tokens to guide them here," the creature stopped and turned back to Tharchelon. "I will go to the tokens, and they will come to me."

Tharchelon, content, sighed and closed his eyes as the creature departed. One last question flashed into his mind before sleep overwhelmed him. "Grandfather... what is your name?

"My name is... Elija Abel," echoed the reply from the hallway.

CHAPTER FOURTEEN
The Shrine of Ophidia

"There just weren't that many people in the end that were willing to fight for the cult. They had a shortage of soldiers, and so they used their dark arts to simply make more in the form of Zombies. While they were ultimately defeated, the land and the people will forever bear the scars. Consider that the entire race of elves was exterminated by the Cult of Yex."

-Adirak's history of the Wars with the Cult of Yex

9ᵗʰ Day of Summer - 10:00 AM – The Eklon Tree, Western Shore of the Demon River – 6 Days Until the Full Moon

They made what amounted to a camp near the old petrified tree, sitting on rocks and logs in a huddled circle around a meager, smoky fire on the banks of the chugging Demon River. Thin rain fell from heavy black skies, promising a long wet day. They could just as easily have been a pack of vagrant beggars on the streets of Demon's Bluff, shunted off into the corner next to the mounds of fly-ridden camel manure. They had not much more than the clothes on their backs.

"Anyone remember the last time they felt this cold?" Brynn said. She ran her fingers through her hair, picking out knots from a spider-web-tangle of strands. No brush, no comb; just her fingers. She sighed and dropped her hands; it was useless. Better she found shears to solve the problem.

"Holy hells, we are completely defeated here," said Needle, waving the smoke out of his face. "Damn wet wood."

Brynn could only nod in agreement. Things had gone from

bad to worse very quickly. And to think they had just been on the boat! She felt like an idiot for going after Mallet and Danilus. They would have made it back eventually.

Then again, had they waited, Elija would have found them on the boat and likely killed them. *I would be dead instead of just miserable.*

This was so utterly out of order.

Danilus got up, went to Cael's side and examined his wounded hand. Dheke followed him, nudging Cael with his snout. The only herbs they had remaining were the ones Brynn had in her satchel, which Danilus supplemented with ones he had found growing nearby. Cael sat still. The light of the sun shadowed by the thick low hanging clouds cast his face in a zombie like glow. *Not unlike the pale skin of Elija Abel,* Brynn thought.

"He took my boat," said Danilus, swatting a lone mosquito as he let go of Cael's bandaged hand. "I'm going to find this little bastard and make him pay. How is the pain, Cael?"

"We've got to find the other two orbs," said Cael, shrugging.

"We're not gonna find him, or the other orbs," said Needle. "And, even if we did get the other two orbs, how are we going get the moss with only those two?"

"Anyone else curious," asked Cael. "How this Elija fellow is still around? He lived thousands of years ago... *five thousand years...*"

"You listening to me?" Needle asked, again waving the smoke out of his face.

"Five thousand years..." said Cael. "How can it be?"

Needle looked around at the rest of them with an incredulous look on his face. "We... lost... the... orb!" he said.

"Is he like one of those zombie rats we faced in Ganger's tomb?" Cael asked.

"He weren't right—them dead eyes," said Danilus, walking back to his seat and sitting down with a sigh. "But he didn't look like no zombie, neither. Not that I ever seen one, but I heard tell."

Needle shuddered, "I don't think he's a zombie, but I don't think he was alive either. But none of that matters. He destroyed the orb, yes?"

Cael held up his bandaged hand, "Yes, Needle. But Boxx-away said to keep going, so we keep going."

"Hey!" said Needle. "I'm not trying to be the gloom-sayer here, mister wizard, but... how? How exactly are we gonna find the next orb when you left your *Lorgnettes* on the boat? You can't follow the path anymore."

Cael's face tightened. "Son of ..."

Needle did the courtesy of not looking smug.

"We'll just have to find a way," Cael said after a moment.

"Hells," Brynn said under her breath, surprising herself by swearing. "How, Cael? Needle might be right."

"Might be..." Needle muttered as he tossed a pebble into the fire.

Brynn sighed. She was tired, she was afraid, and she was beginning to doubt they could complete their quest, even with Cael's optimism and drive. And now without the boat or the *Lorgnettes,* her heart sank down to her toes and the fight in her soul was on the verge of giving up.

I need to keep pace with Cael, she thought. *I need to believe we can accomplish this. But there is no way of finding the second orb. If it hasn't been discovered in 5,000 years, there is no realistic way we are going to find it.*

"You figure this Elija is the one pulling all the strings?" Mallet asked, running his hand over his freshly-shaved scalp. Trust Mallet to make sure his dome was smooth before anything else. Brynn ran a hand through her tangled weave of hair and momentarily envied him.

"I mean he's definitely part of the Cult, right?" Mallet continued. "Maybe he is the head of it? Maybe he went to sleep for five thousand years and just woke up to get things going."

"Can you be quiet?" Cael pleaded, kicking a log that sent up a plume of white smoke into Needle's face. "I need to think."

Brynn watched the smoke. It ebbed and flowed, unfolding like a fog, rising to surround Needle. The smoke made outlines, forms and then images; shifting shape effortlessly as it continued to evolve.

She heard a sound, the barest hints of a melody. The random patterns of the smoke reminded her of something... but what?

"Wait," she said loudly.

"For what?" Needle said, his image emerging from the cloud of smoke surrounding him as he waved his hand back and forth.

"I'm talking to myself," Brynn said. There was a thought flitting in her mind, like a moth, bouncing around. She tried to focus on it, capture it. What was it? *There is something I am missing.*

"What you told us, Cael," said Needle getting up and moving to a different spot around the fire. "Is that this Xylex fellow told Elija to give the moss to someone who comes along with all three orbs. That someone, turns out, is going to be us. So why is he not just waiting for us to arrive? Why is he attacking us and destroying the orbs? It doesn't make any sense. He's gone rogue, the dead-eyed Son of Abyss."

"How do you reckon he even knows we was coming?" Danilus asked. He reached down and rubbed Dheke on the muzzle.

"That's an interesting question," said Mallet, talking more than he had in a week. "This King Tharchelon fellow must surely be part of the cult, and we are supposed to show up with the orbs, which will convince him *we* are part of the cult, and he'll give us this moss. But if Elija is waiting for us, and he's the head of the cult, well hells, he already has the moss. He knows where it is because he put it there in the first place. I think when Boxxaway sent us on this errand; he figured Elija would be dead--long dead. But turns out Elija's still around. Maybe he's out to kill us because he realizes we aren't the real Cult of Yex. Could he know we is *Watchers*?"

"*Is*?" Brynn said to him. "You're starting to talk like Danilus."

"Will you both shut up?" begged Cael.

Brynn stared at the smoke and felt a momentary inspiration, but then it fizzled.

"Cael," said Needle. "We don't have a way to find the other orbs. And we have no boat. Everything has gone sideways! If Mallet is right, then Tharchelon is probably dead, or a servant of Elija. Either way, the cult beat us to the moss. Doesn't that make sense?"

Brynn had to agree with the Agrabi boy. Their situation was

indeed bleak. But she had that itch in her mind... and then, as everyone fell momentarily silent... that itch formed into a coherent thought.

The sigils!

She considered the sigil she had seen on the orb. She had gotten a less clear look at the sigil on the Elija creature's forehead, but something told her that those two sigils were important... and somehow connected. If her mother had taught her anything, there were patterns to *everything*, and so it stood to reason there was a pattern here that might help them, if only she could decrypt it. In any case, the itch in her mind about those two sigils was growing and begged to be scratched.

"It's all speculation. We'll press on to Tharchelon," said Cael. "We don't know if Elija has the moss."

"He's got my boat, that's what we know," said Danilus with a shrug. "I reckon we could make it to this Tharchelon in the Bystle Vale. But it'll be tough going without a boat."

"The Cult is winning," said Mallet.

"The battle hasn't even started yet," said Cael.

"What's immediately north of us?" Brynn asked.

"Looks like swamp," Needle said, waving his hand again. The smoke seemed to have followed him to his new seat.

"I mean after that," said Brynn.

"The ground begins to rise," Danilus explained. "It's hill country as it goes up to meet the mountains. Fairly tall cliff there, where the river comes out of the mountain gorge."

"Could we walk to it?"

"I reckon so. Hiking out of the swamp would be a slog for sure, but we are pretty close to the northern skim, anyways. I don't reckon we could follow the river up the gorge; too many impassible spots where the sheer cliff walls meet the river. We would have to find a way up the cliff, maybe take a few days to find it."

"Where do you think the second orb is?" she asked.

"I'll tell you what I think," said Cael after a long pause, "It has to be somewhere along the river route. We're going north along a similar path that Elija took thousands of years ago when he hid them. He must have put them along his route. We'll walk the river until we get to the gorge, then we'll figure something out. If we get to Tharchelon with no orbs, so be it. Boxxaway said we might have to improvise."

"Oh, we is improvising," said Needle, elbowing Mallet. The big boy looked at him with anger on his face.

Mallet's face shifted into a grin and lifted the haft of his glaive: "Oh I think we might be able to improvise..."

Brynn returned her focus to the sigils in her mind. She had sketched them from memory in her mother's book, but she had left the book on the boat. She turned around from their scrawny campfire and picked up a stick washed up on the shore. The sound of the susurrus water calmed her mind as she traced the sigils from memory into the sand.

Seeing them side by side, she could not escape the sense that these two sigils were indeed somehow related. Even the melodies that sprang to her mind, while different, seemed somehow connected... part of the same family, so to speak. On the one hand, each sigil was simple. Indeed almost *too* simple. All of the sigils in her mother's book were more complex than either of these. Even the learning pattern that her mother had secretly been teaching her all her life was more complex than either of these sigils, but only just so. Sigils as simple as these should be easy for her to decipher. Sigils held the message of their function in their very form. While she had much to learn, and the more complex sigils were currently beyond her understanding... these should not be. *They were so simple!*

Brynn was barely aware that Needle and Cael were arguing about their course of action, but she could not stop focusing on the sigils in the sand at her feet. Nothing in her mother's book prepared her to understand these new sigils. They were so foreign, so new... and that made the itch in her mind more pronounced. The feeling that these sigils were somehow related was overwhelming, but for the life of her, she couldn't see how.

Both sigils had the characteristic hallmarks of flowing curves and intricate patterns, yet each seemed somehow lacking... hollow. It was this hollowness, she decided, that made it impossible to decipher the function of either. It was as if each sigil, the one from the orb and the one on Elija's forehead were just partial sigils, each somehow... inexplicably... incomplete.

Then, as she stared at the sigils side by side, a waft of

smoke from the fire briefly obscured her vision. She rubbed the sting out of her eyes. In the blur, her vision momentarily doubled and one sigil image drifted over the other in her view. The answer came to her and she jumped to her feet and yelled: "I have it!"

Cael and Needle stopped their argument abruptly. Mallet glowered at her. She guessed he had been watching her work in the sand as the others debated their options.

"Did anyone notice Elija's face?" she asked. "I did. There was a sigil tattooed on his forehead."

"Yeah, I seen it," said Danilus. "Little pattern above his eyebrows. What do you reckon it meant?"

"I didn't see it yesterday," said Cael, looking down at his injured hand. "But I did see it in the vision with the *Lorgnettes*. I'm sure it must have been the mark that Xylex talked about."

"Yes!" Brynn exclaimed, waving them over to where she stood. "I'm certain now, that is exactly what that sigil is." She pointed down at the sigils she had traced in the sand as the four of them gathered around her. "I drew these from memory. What do you notice about them?"

"Um... they are chicken scratches in the dirt?" Needle offered, stifling a grin. "Men are talking here, Brynn."

Mallet laughed out loud. Brynn would have been annoyed, but she knew Needle was joking and it was good to see Mallet laugh. It was the first time she had seen him laugh since the night that Wheizer transformed.

"You finally warming up to her making the witch marks, are you rat-boy?" Needle said with a broad grin.

"What am I supposed to notice about them?" said Cael, holding Dheke back who was staring at the sigils in the sand and looked like he might walk over them. "I don't understand."

"Watch this," said Brynn hunkering. "Remember what this one looks like," she indicated the mark on the right, the one from Elija's forehead.

"Okay," said Cael. She noticed that even Mallet and Needle had stopped horsing around and were paying attention now.

She wiped the Elija sigil smooth with her hand. "Remember it?" She asked them again. They all nodded. "Then watch this."

She drew the Elija sigil in the sand *directly on top of the orb sigil.* Just as she knew it would, the one nested perfectly within the other. The two distinct melodies in her mind combined into a perfect harmony.

"Whoa!" Needle exclaimed. Even he could see that the two sigils fit together like interlocking pieces of a puzzle.

Each sigil alone was indeed, only partial. Seeing them together in the sand made it very clear. Neither sigil was complete without the other. They were a mated pair, working together to provide their function. These sigils were simple *and* advanced at the same time. When the two were combined, their function was evident in their form.

"What does it mean?" Mallet asked, scowling.

Brynn thought through the ramifications of what she was about to recommend. "It means... I think I figured out how to find the next beacon, even without Cael's *Lorgnettes.*"

No one responded.

"These sigils are a mated pair," she went on. "The beacon sigil makes it visible even from great distances. But only those marked with Elija's sigil can see it."

"That's what Xylex meant about the Rothkin being marked," said Cael. "They were marked with the same sigil as Elija so they could find the beacons."

"Exactly," said Brynn.

"Do the beacons still work?" Needle asked.

"If they bear the sigil, they should work. The one that Elija destroyed certainly had the sigil etched on it clearly."

"So what are you proposing, then?" Cael asked. "That one of us gets tattooed with the sigil to see the beacon?"

"No way, Cael," Mallet stood up. "Not letting you get a tattoo from the cult. Do you realize how close that comes to fulfilling that prophecy?"

"But without the sigil, we can't find the orb," Cael said.

"You're willing to tread that close to evil to find it?"

"Let me get this straight," said Needle. "The wererat is worried that *somebody else* might turn into something bad? Oh, that's rich! How else to do you propose we find the orb then, genius?"

Mallet clenched his fists into balls.

"Nobody said it had to be Cael," Brynn said.

Mallet looked at her and blinked. "What are you saying, Brynn? It should be you?"

"What's in a mark?" Needle asked. "After all, it's not like it's the Cult of Yex symbol or anything."

"Maybe Brynn should tell us," Mallet countered. "What *is* in a mark? You have no idea what the consequences of wearing those marks are. That mark may let you see the beacon, sure, but what else? I'll never let one of those things on me, that's for sure."

It irritated Brynn when her brother, not usually the most innovative thinker, brought up something she should have considered. She gave a renewed look at the combined sigil in the sand at her feet. The answer to the function was in the form, and she did not get the sense that there was any evil or negative consequence outside of its beacon and seeing functions. The combined sigil was fairly advanced, but not beyond her. But, maybe Mallet was right... could there be other effects?

"With the sigils combined, Mallet," Brynn said. "I can read their function. I'm pretty sure there is nothing inherently evil about them. They are what they are."

"Pretty sure?" he fumed.

"For once you're right, Mallet," said Needle. "That's why it shouldn't be Cael... just in case."

Mallet looked confused.

"But I thought the cheese-eater here threw all your ink overboard," Needle continued.

"He got my ghost flower tattoo ink, not the regular writing ink. But that's still on the boat."

"So how do we do the tattoo?" Needle asked.

"It doesn't have to be a tattoo," said Brynn. "I'm just going to draw it on with something else."

"So it won't be permanent?" Mallet said, looking relieved.

"What you reckon to use, then?" Danilus asked.

What else? There was only one universal substance readily available to anyone in need of a fast ink substitute. Blood would do fine, and she had a small mirror from her satchel. A reed from the swamp to use as a quill and she could make it work. The symbolism of tracing the same sigil from the Elija creature on herself in blood was not lost on her. While she was confident that the sigil was inert, there was still a worry that somehow it conveyed some evil meaning or effect. At least it would wash off.

"Needle," she asked. "Can I borrow your dagger?"

She took a deep breath, nicked the tip of her left thumb and squeezed out several large drops of blood onto a leaf. She only had to draw the 'seeing' half of the sigil. This turned out to be incredibly difficult to do backwards in the mirror. She had to replenish her 'ink supply' twice.

"Why does it have to be on your forehead?" Cael asked as he held the mirror for her.

"I think it acts sort of like an extra eye," she said. "It might work somewhere else, but I don't think so."

She finished. Looking in her mirror she had the same sigil as Elija, only hers was drawn in blood. What had she just done?

It worked. When she closed her eyes... she could see the beacon in the distance off to the north, and west of the river, the same side they were already on. The beacon was a sickly, almost flesh-colored glow. It beckoned to her, tugging at her mind. *I'm in it now*, she thought. *Have I become one of them? At least temporarily?*

11ᵗʰ Day of Summer - 11:00 AM – West of the Demon River – 4 Days Until the Full Moon

Brynn led them forthwith out of the swamp, into the hilly country, and toward the great escarpment which marked the beginning of the highlands where the gorge opened and the Demon River churned forth from between ancient granite walls. They had walked all through the rainy day, taking short, fitful naps with Dheke keeping watch. Then they continued through the dark night until they reached the end of the swamp. To a duke's daughter, one wouldn't think hard, rocky hills would have been such a welcome sight, but after slogging through mud and water it was nothing short of a miraculous blessing.

On the morning of their second day, they reached the escarpment, a wall of pale rock hundreds of feet high. Pine trees, healthy and abundant could be seen far above on the ridge.

The air was strangely silent, as light flooded in from the east through the breaking, low clouds.

"Seems desolate," said Needle. "In a weird kind of way."

"It's abundant with plant life," Cael said.

"But empty of... I reckon you would call it spirit?" Danilus said.

"Empty," said Needle. "It feels empty, in a way even the deepest desert doesn't."

"Reminds me of the black plain," Cael said. "The Battlefield of Oar."

"Yeah," said Needle. "That's it, only this *looks* normal, at least on the surface."

"The orb is inside the cliff face," Brynn said pointing, as her sight now gave her a closer view of the throbbing light from the beacon.

"That's an old landslide where you are pointing," Danilus said. Brynn hadn't noticed it at first, but now the telltale signs were there. The jumbled pile of rocks was now covered with centuries of shrubs and trees.

"Do you see the third beacon as well?" Needle asked.

Brynn closed her eyes, and nodded, "Yes, barely. It's pulling at me, too. Much fainter, but it's to the north and a little east, up the gorge on the other side of the river."

"Let's worry about this orb first," Cael said. "One thing at a time."

"The orb is straight *through* the landslide," Brynn said.

"Whoa," Needle said. "So it's buried?"

"Looks like it," Danilus said. "I reckon a long time ago by the look of it."

"Look!" Needle cried. From their vantage they could see the Demon River, not far off to their right, emerging from between the gash in the granite cliffs as the morning light sparkled on its surface. And there, moored to the western bank was the *Riparian Scout.*

Elija Abel was already here.

11th Day of Summer - 11:30 AM – The Riparian Scout – 4 Days Until the Full Moon

They crept up to the boat, weapons ready, but Elija wasn't aboard.

Danilus was overjoyed. You would have thought he had just found a long- lost family member.

His joy was soon turned to anger. Elija had sailed the boat ahead of them through drizzle of the previous day and presumably into the night. In what Brynn imagined was a gleeful fit of flinging stuff, Elija had strewn most of their food and supplies all over the deck, and a great deal of it overboard. The place looked a wreck.

Not so strangely, Brynn suddenly remembered her mother's displeasure at her for not cleaning and organizing her room.

"Look!" Cael exclaimed, holding up the *Lorgnettes.* In his destructive haste, Elija had overlooked the magical spectacles.

Brynn went into the cabin and found her mother's books, stored under her hammock. She breathed a sigh of relief, running her hands over the wooden covers. She emerged from the cabin. A dagger lay on the deck amongst the other scattered items in the wake of Elija's chaos. She'd not felt the need to carry a weapon up to now, nor did she feel confident in its use. But she dropped it in her satchel and felt just a little better for having it.

"If I lay hands on this creature..." Danilus said under his breath as he looked around his boat. His gaze lit on the tiller. He howled like he had been stung by a scorpion. Tajaa, his beloved idol, was missing. Elija must have hammered it off the railing and cast it into the effervescent flow of the Demon River.

Brynn disembarked and stood on the bank. She directed her gaze northward and saw the faint glow of the third orb far up the gorge. She turned west and saw the much brighter glow of the second orb, which seemed ensconced in the granite cliff wall.

"You can wipe that mark off now," Mallet said as he walked up to her.

Brynn considered that... with the *Lorgnettes,* they didn't need the sigil on her forehead anymore... and yet... some intuition told her to keep it on.

"Just a little longer," she said.

"You've grown fond of that mark, then?" Mallet said with divisive anger in his voice.

She shouldn't bother answering. He wouldn't understand.

"The mark got us back to the boat and the *Lorgnettes,*" Brynn said.

She pulled her new dagger from her satchel and held it in front of her. Would the slim blade do any good against a creature such as Elija? She considered the sigils she had been studying in her mother's book. Were there any that might provide protection or an advantage, from someone or something like Elija? She wasn't sure. Most of the sigils seemed specific in their protections, and not general enough to protect against a powerful foe they knew so little about.

"That dead bastard is just toying with us," said Needle, picking up some of the food strewn about. "Anyone doubt the little spider-handed freak isn't right now hiding somewhere, waiting to strike again? And with the landslide covering the second orb... looks we are down two orbs to give to this Tharchelon fellow." He dusted off a hunk of dried ham and took a bite.

"Are you saying," asked Brynn. "That we just sail up the canyon and forget about the second orb?"

Danilus shook his head, "I'm hunting that little bastard down and I'm taking care of him. Leaving him behind us would be a mistake."

Mallet nodded. "I agree. We should eliminate our enemy."

"Are we sure we can't get the second orb?" Cael asked.

"You just want to fight him," Needle said to Mallet.

Mallet nodded, gripping the haft of his glaive. "That would

be an accurate assessment."

Danilus leaped over the side of the boat and studied the bank. After a moment, he made a gleeful clicking sound and started walking. Dheke 'wuffed' and followed.

"Wait!" Cael ordered. "Let's see what the *Lorgnettes* show us first."

"Dheke and I don't need no spectacles. We can track the little bastard."

Cael concentrated on Elija Abel. There were no afterimages from distant past in the area involving Elija. The only afterimage was very recent.

1 Day Earlier

Cael watched, seemingly floating over Elija's head as the undead little man leaped off the *Riparian Scout* and onto the sandy bank. It was early morning, and the sun had not yet risen.

Elija left the ransacked boat behind and strode purposefully toward the landslide. But before he got to the rock fall, he turned toward the section of cliff face not covered by the landslide. He sniffed around, looking carefully until he found a protruding rock.

"Eh," he muttered and twisted the catch. A small stone door perfectly concealed on the face of the cliff slid open, revealing a hewn passage into the cliff face. Elija slipped past and the secret door slid shut behind him.

11ᵗʰ Day of Summer - Noon – The Western Shore of the Demon River – 4 Days until the Full Moon

Cael removed the *Lorgnettes* and pointed to the edge of the landslide off to the west. "There is a concealed door on that cliff face. He opened it and went in."

"All right then," said Danilus. "Let's get something to eat and then get after him."

A little later, they were following Dheke and Danilus as they tracked Elija's path, which was quite evident in the mud from the recent rain. He led them about a quarter of a mile straight to the base of the granite cliff, with Dheke sniffing and woofing all the way. The avalanche was still a few hundred feet further ahead and was covered with scrub oak and cedars.

"Yep," confirmed Cael. "This is exactly where he came yesterday morning."

"Another hidden entrance," said Needle, examining the footprints in the drying mud. "Secretive bastards, these cultists."

"The tracks stop right here," Danilus said. Dheke agreed with a wuff.

"Now what?" Needle asked. "How do we get in?"

"There is a secret catch here somewhere, but let me look again," said Cael, unfolding the wires of the *Lorgnettes*. In addition to the afterimage of Elija from a day ago or so, Cael could feel another afterimage, one much, much older. He focused it.

5,000 Years Ago

The little man appeared in his mind's eye, strutting along a road from the south. He was as Cael had seen him previously with the wizard Xylex; not undead and deformed, but alive and... normal. Cael hovered in vision, behind and slightly above the little man. The landscape in the area was much more vegetated, with trees and grass, in a time long before the landslide. As Elija walked, a large detachment of troops in formation appeared ahead, marching toward him. Elija took no notice of them as they drew closer. Cael realized they weren't soldiers. Hells, they weren't even alive. It was a regiment of zombies... perhaps a thousand of them, shambling along, following a single living commander wearing a black tunic with the Cult of Yex symbol emblazoned in red. He was wielding an ornate serpent staff. The zombies were in a frightful state: many were emaciated, and others had open sores in their pallid flesh. To Cael's horror, not all of them were men. There were women, children, old men and even toddlers--zombified and made mercenaries to serve in the legions of the cult. Elija passed them by without so much as a glance.

Ahead of him, built against the cliff face, lay a walled fortress, with earth ramparts around it and walls capped with dark granite parapets. A single road paved with dark stones led up to a portcullis. Ominous flanking towers with cruel pointed cupolas, buttressed the fortress, offering a formidable defense.

Cael shivered even though he wasn't really there: dread knotted in his stomach, just from watching the scene as Elija walked up the road toward the towering black walls. All vegetation had been cleared for hundreds of feet around the edifice.

Elija came to the portcullis gates. Two coiled bas-relief snakes had been carved into the pillars to either side of the gate. Their heads were etched with fierce, draconic features. Bony spikes protruded from their back, starting from the base of their head and gradually diminishing into nubs. Their mouths were open and their heads arched downward, staring at intruders. Was that venom dripping from glistening fangs, or just a trick of the light? Cael couldn't be sure.

Elija called out, "Ho!" and immediately the portcullis began to rise with an ominous clanking sound.

He passed through the barbican into the huge bailey, where what looked like a prison camp was located. Black smoke and moans of the dying filled the air. Guards with whips drove chained prisoners to and fro. Elija passed nonchalantly, and at one point, Cael even heard him whistling. He walked past rows of wire fence with gaunt faces of prisoners staring out pitiably.

Elija came to a place where dead bodies were piled high in a haphazard fashion. Flies and carnivorous wasps gorged on the bloated dead. The faces of many looked up as if crying out in desperation for some imagined mercy, a mercy that came only with death. Living prisoners pulled corpses from the pile and stacked them like cordwood onto a long flat wagon strapped behind a team of forlorn mules.

What in the heavens are they doing here? Where are they going to transport those bodies? Cael thought.

Elija picked up the pace past the pile and walked down a narrow road among some small wooden buildings, until he came to a finely-built house. Its previously white walls showed black soot smears all over it. He knocked on the door and was let into the home by an elderly woman.

"Sithik here?" Elija asked.

"The Lord High Curate Cypher Sithik," the elderly woman said in a haughty tone. "Is in his study."

Elija walked through the ornate wooden halls of the house past various objects of artistic excellence and obvious value, until he came to the study. Upon a couch of immense size and obvious worth, a small man with a pinched face, squinting eyes and white-tinged whiskers in his mustache sat watching a plain-looking young girl, perhaps ten years old, play the viol.

The music was beautiful, and when the man saw Elija, he held up his hand for him to wait. Together they listened until the song ended. Elija seemed as unmoved by the beautiful music as he was by the death and misery outside.

"My daughter, is she not gifted?" the man beamed. The young girl smiled, kissed her father on the cheek and then carried her viol over to a table where she set it down next to an ornate dulcimer, a pewter chess set and a bronzed serpent horn before she left the room.

"So what brings Elija Abel to my home?" the man asked, still sitting on the couch.

"Lord Sithik, I bear news from Archmage Xylex," Elija replied, still standing.

"Never good things these days, does Xylex say," Sithik said, standing up. "But his news can wait."

"This news is urgent," Elija said.

"I'm sure it is, but I guarantee I have something that is just as compelling for you."

Elija shrugged.

The Lord High Curate put on his cloak and led them outside. They wound their way a few hundred yards through the camp toward a huge pair of steel ornate double doors built directly into the face of the cliff.

As Cael watched Elija and his new companion pick their way through the misery of the bailey, he marveled at the fortress. The entire fortification was enclosed by a thick, formidable wall with periodic towers that looked like teeth, a defensive perimeter arrayed, without doubt, to protect these steel doors. Cael imagined it would take a powerful force of men and siege engines to break the fortress, but even then the assault would take months. What were they protecting inside? Cael was about to find out.

Together, Elija and Sithik approached the smoke-stained cliff face and pulled on huge iron rings. The foreboding steel doors creaked open, a wide, dark cavern before them. They entered and the doors boomed shut.

11ᵗʰ Day of Summer - 12:45 PM – 4 Days Until the Full Moon

Cael explained what he had seen in his vision with the *Lorgnettes*. Brynn stood with the others congregated in the lee of the landslide near the cliff face, holding her brother's arm. "That whole area," Cael indicated the landslide towering up to the west with a sweep of his arm. "It was all a mighty fortress that protected an entrance into the cliff face. Every bit of it is under the rubble of the landslide."

"Holy Hells," said Needle. "They are worse than we ever thought."

Brynn could only nod; so out of order. "And the cult is still out there... about to return..."

"Not if we can help it," Cael said grimly.

"Damn right," said Mallet.

"Well," Danilus said with a pensive look. "I reckon it's time to get after it. How do we get in there?"

"I know how he opened the concealed door," said Cael. "There should be a protrusion here, let's see... yeah, this it is." Brynn watched as Cael fiddled with the protuberance for several long minutes, but to no avail.

Needle stepped forward and elbowed Cael out of the way. Needle examined the protruding section of rock for a few seconds from every angle then reached out and fiddled with something on the underside and gave it a deft tug. With a grinding sound, a section of the cliff face opened, revealing a dark, narrow passage.

"The orb?" Cael asked Brynn.

"Yes," Brynn nodded. "Not far. In there." The fleshy glow pulsed deep inside the cliff wall, almost beckoning to her.

"Wait a minute," said Mallet, hesitating.

"That little boat pirate is in there," warned Danilus.

"It's too narrow and tight. How can I swing my glaive?"

"You all realize it's a trap, right?" said Needle. "Just like the trap he set for us in that temple complex in the swamp."

"Course it is," said Cael.

"For sure," said Danilus. "Little bastard is waiting in ambush, I reckon."

"Waiting to stab another hand and destroy another orb," said Needle.

"Maybe we'll get lucky and he'll stab you," said Mallet. "Bring us some rest from your smart mouth."

"I got an idea, Mallet," Needle said. "Why don't you go in there and rat out and kill him while we wait out here? You won't have to hear my smart mouth for a while at least."

A vein in Mallet's jaw bulged.

"We need to make a decision," Cael broke in. "Do we go in, or abandon this orb and take our chances with Tharchelon?"

"You know my choice," said Danilus. "Tajaa demands her revenge."

"I don't think we can intelligently take this risk," said Needle. "Come on, Cael, you and I grew up digging in crypts and caves in the desert. Neither my father nor your grandfather would want to enter a blind passage like this."

"I think we should get this orb," Cael said. "And that's not true. We entered Ganger's Tomb blind."

Needle shuddered. "And I almost got killed. In this case, we know for a fact that something bad is waiting for us in the dark in there."

"Well," said Danilus, "I aim to learn that bastard his final lesson."

"I reluctantly have to say I'm with Needle," Mallet said.

"What?" Needle exclaimed. "Big bad Bannon Bygrave is scared?"

"I'm not afraid," Mallet said. "But I'm not stupid, either. If I can't swing my glaive, we are all vulnerable."

Everyone looked to Brynn. "I'm with Cael and Danilus."

"Look," said Needle, "I get it, we got to have the Orb, and we should put this rabid little bastard down; he's certainly Cult of Yex. He dies. No argument from me. But Mallet is exactly right... going in there, *walking into his trap*... that ain't smart. I'm not going in there."

"Yeah," said Mallet.

Brynn gazed, seemingly through the cliff face, at the flesh-colored light beyond, entranced by the pulsating glow of the orb. An idea came to her in a rush of inspiration.

"What if we don't have to go in?" said Brynn. "What if we could make him come out to us?"

"Sounds good to me," Mallet said, pounding the butt end of his glaive on the earth and running his free hand over his shorn scalp.

"And just how are we going to do that?" asked Needle.

"Remember," said Brynn. "Having worn this sigil now for quite some time, I think that it does more than just allow me to see its mated pair... the orb I mean. I can feel the other sigil call to me. I can feel its pull."

"I knew it!" Mallet blurted. "Those witch marks *are* evil!"

Surprisingly, Danilus guessed it before anyone else could comment: "So you can make that other mark out here and it will summon Elija?"

"Simple," Brynn said. "Exactly. I'll draw the sigil out here;

he'll immediately feel it and see it."

"And you think it will summon him? What if he resists?" Cael asked.

"Well..." Brynn said. "I don't think it will *force* him to come. The pull I feel from the sigil on the orb inside the cliff is not overpowering. It's not *compelling* me, but it *is* pulling at me. But so what? When I draw one out here, Elija will feel it, and I'm betting he will come to investigate."

"Look," said Needle, "I don't mean to kill your idea here, but if you put a sigil out here, all you will be doing is alerting him to the fact that we're here."

Brynn frowned.

"Besides," Needle continued. "He has what *we* want, not the other way around. If he comes out, he gives up his advantage. He's been waiting for five thousand years. I'm betting he will wait in there for as long as it takes for us to come in after the orb or give up and go home."

"We can't just sit out here and do nothing," said Danilus.

"What you're all forgetting," said Cael. "Are these." He tapped his forehead where the spectacles were perched. "We go in, and I use the *Lorgnettes* to watch how he set his trap."

Brynn nodded, "That's it."

Needle looked up, then swallowed, "Yeah... I think. Son of Abyss, that's the way to do it."

Mallet looked worried, "But it's so narrow. If something goes wrong and there is no room to maneuver..."

"I'll protect you Mallet," said Needle with a grin.

Mallet's eyes widened and he took a step toward Needle.

"So we are decided," said Danilus. "Let's go find us a boat thief to kill."

Needle maneuvered behind Danilus, "Exactly. We find him, then... *BAM*," he made a chopping motion with his hand that he caught with his other. "We kill him."

"I reckon we're gonna need some light in there," Danilus said. "Give me a few minutes to make us a torch or two."

After Danilus had fetched some dry reeds from the river-bank to fashion torches, they slinked down the narrow winding passageway for several hundred feet, with Danilus and Dheke leading the way, burning torch held high. Cael, Needle and Brynn followed. Mallet brought up the rear, cursing in a whisper almost the entire time until the passage opened into a vast cavern. Mallet held his glaive with one hand and whirl-winded his other, the contrast between the tight passage and the huge cavern causing a moment of vertigo.

Brynn felt it too, and reached out to steady herself on Needle's bony shoulder. She sucked in a long slow breath, and looked up. They were inside a huge space... their torchlight was only strong enough to show the jagged silhouettes of a building ahead in the distance. The cold air made her shiver. Danilus' torchlight glinted off a large set of steel doors off to their left, against the wall.

"Those must be the doors I saw in the vision earlier that Sithik and Elija came through. We are on the other side of them," Cael said, looking in the same direction.

"So the landslide is on the other side of the doors?" Brynn asked.

Mallet flipped his glaive around him artfully, then held the shaft with both hands and lifted it high above his head and behind him to stretch.

"What is this place?" Needle asked, his voice shaky. There was a palpable heaviness in the air.

Brynn slumped her shoulders. What *was* going on? Suddenly the air felt thick and hard to breathe. There was an oppressive feel about the place. She could sense that something was out of order. For some inexplicable reason, her eyes were watering up. She brushed away a tear with the back of her hand.

Ahead lay the shape of a building with four towers at the corners, like a little keep. It seemed to Brynn that it was out of place here inside the cavern, and at the same time, it fit right in.

Danilus wandered over to the steel doors and examined them by the light of his torch. As he went, his light illuminated more of the place.

"What are those? Corpses?" Mallet asked, pointing to the left where a silhouetted pile about forty feet away revealed bent limbs, lifeless eyes and gaping jaws of countless dead bodies, stacked like cordwood. As they approached the horrid pile, they could see that it was actually a long, flat-bed wagon piled high with the corpses. A pair of emaciated dead mules lay on the ground before it, still harnessed to the contraption.

"All these corpses look recently dead." Needle said. "They should be long decomposed by now."

"Some foul necromancy," Cael guessed. "It doesn't stink in here. This place has been sealed, undisturbed for five thousand years."

"Didn't you say there had been more corpses outside when you looked through the *Lorgnettes*?" asked Brynn.

"Yeah," Cael said. "On a wagon just like this one. Out there, covered by the landslide now." He pointed at the double doors with his chin.

"What the hells?" Danilus said. "What on earth was they doing in here?

They walked closer to the pile of bodies.

"Holy hells," Needle breathed.

"There are children in there," Brynn said, her tremulous voice almost breaking.

They couldn't look away from the grotesque pile.

"You know what they were doing here, don't you?" Needle asked, his eyes fixed on the dead piled on the wagon. "They were making zombies out of these people."

"That's right," Cael breathed in a moment of realization. "That's exactly right."

"You said you saw a big group of zombies marching off toward the south away from here, right?" Needle asked.

"They brought their prisoners here to kill them," Cael said somberly. "They brought the bodies in here to raise them as zombies to fight for Yex."

No one spoke.

Brynn understood her earlier sense of oppression and sadness. The wickedness of this place had affected her even before she fully understood it. She did not want to tarry here.

"Let's head over to that building," said Danilus. "That's

where he's hiding, I reckon."

"You're up, Cael," Needle said. "The evil, spider-handed freak walked through here. Don those spectacles and gives us a look see."

"Wait," said Cael. "Brynn, can you see the orb?"

Brynn was thankful for an excuse to look away from the pile of dead bodies. "It's in there, in that building with the towers."

"Okay," said Cael. "Keep watch in case he attacks while I put on the *Lorgnettes.*"

Five Thousand Years Ago

Cael watched Elija and Cypher Sithik enter the large cavern through the steel double doors. The place was lit by flickering torchlight. Sconces spaced periodically revealed a high, stalactite-covered ceiling. The square, black stone building stood in the center of the cavern. At each corner stood an ominous tower capped with a cupola rising to a needle sharp point. Arrow slits in the towers were placed strategically to offer a complete field of fire to defend the smallish edifice.

Enslaved prisoners accompanied another flatbed wagon piled high with dead as it wound past the keep into some unknown destination deeper in the massive cavern.

Elija followed Sithik to the black stone building, entering it through a single steel door. Cael hovered behind them in his vision and followed the pair as they walked down a straight passage carved out of the black rock. It appeared the building was actually solid stone except for the hall carved out of the rock.

As he entered the building in his vision, Cael felt a sense of foreboding. Whatever this place was, it was unspeakably evil; the wickedness was palpable.

Large sigils spaced every dozen feet on the walls gave off a hellish red glow. After a short distance, maybe thirty feet, the passage forked in a 'y', ending in two different doors that were both visible from the intersection. Elija followed Sithik down the short passage on the right and entered a long narrow room. A large window, set directly into the black rock, covered most of the left wall. The glass was thick and crystalline, with just a hint of opaqueness. On the other side of the glass was a chamber, which could only be the room beyond the door on the left side of the fork in the passage. The chamber into which they looked had a single accoutrement: a heavy iron chair, bolted to the floor. It looked intensely uncomfortable to Cael, with its high back and wide armrests. No cushions of any kind, just cold, unforgiving iron.

"The Shrine of Ophidia," Sithik said in a reverent whisper.

"*This* is the vaunted Shrine of Ophidia that you've been working on for so many years?" Elija said with a hint of sarcasm in his voice.

"Do you know who Orwynne of Taglyon is?" the High Curate asked mildly.

Elija was silent for a pensive moment, until he said, "Adirak's wife?"

"We captured her."

Elija smiled. "Impressive."

"Everything changes for us now," Sithik said, his eyes widening slightly in excitement. "Two mages spent themselves and our witches went mad, more than one. The cost was high, but the Shrine of Ophidia is now complete."

"But I thought you've been raising zombies here to fight Adirak's armies for years?" said Elija.

"Indeed," Sithik frowned. "Deeper in this cavern, our necromancers use the red herb to sustain them as they raise the dead to swell the ranks of our armies. But Adirak's forces have learned to reap them like so many stalks of grain before the sickle. Now that the Shrine of Ophidia is completed... it will change everything."

"I highly doubt it," said Elija. "Especially considering the message for you I bear from Lord Xylex."

Sithik just smiled.

"And what does this great Shrine of Ophidia do?" asked Elija.

"It converts the living directly into an *augmented* undead warrior of Yex," said Sithik with an increasingly maniacal gleam in his eye. "These are not the *Ruukus ob Thaxxo*, nor are they the mere raised corpses of the dead."

Elija mimicked a shambling motion. "*More* zombies, Sithik? Adirak easily dispatched your last zombie army of near a hundred thousand."

"These new undead warriors will not be so easily felled by Adirak's scythe," Sithik said, shaking his head. "Your faith is failing you, Elija. Nothing can stop us, and nothing can stop the glorious coming of our Demon Master. Behold!"

They both watched through the window. The door to the chamber opened and two burly guards dragged a woman in her late-forties into the room. She kicked and fought but to no avail... they threw her down onto the cold stone floor before the iron chair and departed.

Sithik stepped over to the wall where two steel levers protruded. He pulled down on the left lever. The door in the woman's room clicked shut and three large steel bolts from the wall shot into receptacles in the door, locking her completely inside, alone in the room. She was dressed in rent, bloody and filthy clothing that was once some kind of finery worn by a noble woman. She had obviously once been very attractive, and age had only made her more so, despite the swelling and bruising on her face. Doubtless she had been beaten and tortured for some extended period of time.

The woman looked up at her tormentors through the glass, a proud defiance on her face. Cael was struck by the woman's eyes. They reminded him of his grandfather's eyes.

"This is a dark week for Adirak," said Elija. "I killed one of his sons a couple days ago and now he's going to lose his wife."

"A pity you didn't capture him," mused the High Curate. "This new Shrine of Ophidia will turn the tide." He pulled down the lever on the right, which made a dull scraping sound.

With a final grinding 'clunk', a small stone door on the right wall of the iron-chair room opened, and a host of long black snakes slithered into the room. The woman screamed and leaped onto the chair, standing on it in a crouched position.

Cael watched horrified as he realized the snakes were not alive. Elaborate sigils in glowing yellow adorned their backs, but gaps in their scaly hide revealed a bony skeleton underneath. Cael recalled Needle's description of the rats in Ganger's tomb.

The snakes slithered up the metal legs of the chair and swarmed over the screaming woman, wrapping in coils around her arms and legs and forcing her to sit in the chair, holding her fast. She struggled in vain, screaming continually.

"Watch," Sithik said in a hushed tone. Cael could see that the man was overcome by a twisted and inappropriate sort of anticipation. He licked his thin lips and his eyes grew wider as he watched the horrific spectacle. He was taking some sort of perverse and sadistic pleasure in the woman's terror.

Cael couldn't look away. This was Adirak's wife, and she was about to be killed... or worse. He knew the history. Adirak won, and the Cult was defeated, but did Adirak lose his wife? Cael didn't know. He didn't know anything about Adirak's wife. Adirak already lost his son, but Cael hoped with all his might that Orwynne of Taglyon would somehow manage to escape.

One snake, larger than the rest, emerged from the little opening and rose up in front of her to strike. Black droplets of venom beaded at the end of its yellowy fangs. Cael wished he could use the hold spell and save the woman like he had saved his grandfather. But he was a helpless, unparticipating spectator, watching the events of the past as though it were a play during the Festival of Drums in Demon's Bluff.

The large serpent struck, sinking its fangs into her cheek right below her eye. The yellow sigils on the snake's back flashed a pale green. The glands near the base of the serpent's head throbbed, pumping its dark poison into the woman's face. The snake withdrew. The woman evinced horror in her kind eyes as a strange pattern began to spiral outward from the puncture marks. Dark lines curved and intersected to form a grand, complex pattern that subsumed more than half of her face, tendrils of the black ink reached up onto her forehead and under her hair line.

Cael realized with awe that the serpent existed... was created... specifically to ensigil its victims. Brynn should see this, Cael thought. He'd never be able to describe the sigil to her. He felt a familiar nausea begin to cause a tightening feeling under his tongue as he looked at the monstrous pattern; he was entranced by the woman's tattooed face.

"That is an augmentation sigil," Sithik explained. The woman's body began to change. Muscles grew in bunches in her thighs, calves, arms and shoulders. Blades of bone broke through her skin along her arms and all the way up to her shoulders. Her fingernails extended into razor sharp claws. Fangs sprouted from the woman's mouth, and a cruel, feral red replaced the previous kind blue of her eyes.

"That certainly does look more promising than the usual zombies," Elija said. "Can the snakes hold her?"

"Yes," said Sithik, but Cael felt himself tense with anxiety as what was once Orwynne of Taglyon fought with augmented strength against the black coiled mass of snakes that restrained her.

"None have broken free yet," Sithik said, nonplussed. "And the glass is nigh unbreakable, if that's what you're worried about."

The snakes' bodies stretched, bulging as the coils tightened.

For one second, Cael thought she was going to burst free, but then she sunk back down into the chair as the snakes tightened their grip.

"Now we kill her," Sithik said.

"She's still alive?" Elija exclaimed. It was Cael's thought precisely.

Another enormous snake emerged from the opening, this one with glowing red sigils on its back. It slithered up and struck at the woman as she continued to scream. The snake's fangs sunk into the woman's open mouth, capturing the bottom lip and meat of her tongue in one hungry bite.

The snake's venom was powerful and killed Orwynne in mere seconds. She hung limp in the snake's hold, her tongue swelling quickly, wagging out of her open mouth. Her blackening lips peeled back in a horrific, deathly grin. Another dark sigil began to appear on her chin, spiraling tendrils down her neck, forming fractal curves and elliptical parallels cascading into a spinning infinity. The sigil was impossibly complex and Cael's nausea intensified as he studied the new pattern. *Complexly impossible* was a more accurate description, he thought. The pattern hypnotized him and he couldn't look away. The tight feeling under his tongue grew to a crescendo and then suddenly abated and he was able to return his full attention to the rest of the scene.

"Why must she be killed?" Elija said. "Your endless fascination with zombies and undeath eludes my understanding."

Cael felt an inexplicably intense sadness at her passing. It was if he had known her, though he had not. Up until mere minutes ago, he'd never even known she ever existed. And the manner of her death... Cael couldn't imagine how horrible and personal it must have felt to be bitten in the face and tongue by these snakes.

"It's not a fetish, if that's what you're thinking," sniffed Sithik. "A zombie can be controlled, while the living are... more difficult. Now we raise her."

A third snake, ensigiled in white, slithered up her bulging calf and coiled on her lap, poised to strike. It bit the dead woman on her chest, piercing straight through her sternum.

Cael trembled. Did Adirak ever have to face his zombified wife?

The woman's flesh turned a pallid shade of gray, as if all the red blood had been drained, and her veins refilled with the black serpent poison. She stirred and her eyes shot open. Instead of the kind eyes Cael had seen before, there was only a dead gaze glowing faintly red. Her face held no expression whatever. What had once been Orwynne of Taglyon was now a mindless zombie. Cael could see the twisting lines of a third sigil peeking up on her chest and shoulders from underneath her tunic. He was grateful to have the majority of that sigil covered by her clothing.

The newly-made zombie strained against the snakes that held her fast.

"One last sigil," said Sithik. Another snake with purple symbols upon its back sank it's fangs into Orwynne's other cheek.

"A sigil of control," Elija said as another sigil sprouted from the puncture marks, intertwining with the other sigils already present on her face and neck, covering her gray skin completely with a nest of ordered chaos. Her transformation was done. What remained was a willing servant of Yex waiting only to be commanded. The snakes released her and slithered out, but the newly-minted ophidian zombie did not make any effort to move from the iron chair.

"Now she's ours to command," Sithik said as he fiddled with something out of Cael's view. He turned with a demented smile, holding up a serpentine scepter topped with the bronzed head of a hooded cobra. He went to the right lever and raised it. The little stone door on the right wall ground shut. Sithik then raised the left lever and the bolts sealing the entry door clanked, allowing the door to swing open. The same two guards, one bearing an identical serpentine cobra scepter, entered and escorted her away. She obeyed perfectly.

"I must admit I am impressed," Elija said. "But I'm afraid it's too little too late. This all might have been helpful had you accomplished it two years ago,"

The Lord High Curate blanched.

"My news cannot wait any longer," Elija said abruptly. "Lord Xylex commands that this camp be abandoned. Kill all remaining prisoners and retreat with your men to defend the citadel at the plateau. Take everything of value with you. This is the command of Xylex. Therefore, it is the command of Yex."

Sithik stood stock still for a full breath.

"And take Orwynne. I'm sure Adirak will be glad to see her again. His forces even now are closing in on the Citadel. Our time is short."

Sithik stiffened and marched out of the room.

Elija opened his left hand and held it forth. A droplet of blood appeared on his forearm, and ran down toward his hand. More blood flowed, followed by the legs of the *Balizar* as it began to claw its way free from the little man's arm. Elija made no sound, but stood fast with an enduring grimace on his face. As before, the wound healed itself quickly.

The *Balizar* had fallen to the ground, its legs pulled inside of itself. It lay unmoving on the stone floor, the single sigil clearly visible upon it.

11ᵗʰ Day of Summer – 1:30 PM – The Shrine of Ophidia - 4 Days Until the Full Moon

Cael took off the *Lorgnettes*. All the blood had drained from his face.

"How do you feel, Cael?" Brynn felt her heart falter. "What did you see?"

He pursed his lips and blinked.

"You got puke on your face," Needle said, handing Cael a strip of cloth.

Cael took it with a confused look.

"Yeah, you were just standing there in that trance, then... blaaarrgh... vomit all over the place."

"What?" was all that Cael could say, wiping his chin with the rag and staring at the mess on the floor at his feet.

"Right in the middle of your trance," Needle went on. "Just puked all of a sudden, like it was no different than taking a breath. Never broke your trance."

"What did you see, Cael?" Brynn asked again.

"Can we take this a few steps to the left over there?" Needle asked, moving away from the puddle of vomit.

Everyone moved to accompany him as Cael took a deep breath and recounted his vision.

"That's out of order," Brynn said when he finished, staring at the smooth floor of the cavern.

"Way out of order," Needle whispered.

"Has anyone ever heard of this Orwynne? From history, I mean?" Cael asked.

Everyone shook their head.

Brynn let her gaze rise to the black stone building. "The orb is still in there."

Mallet swiveled his head back and forth. "It means he's probably in there, too."

"Maybe," Needle said.

"Then let's go," Danilus said, walking toward the black

building, torch held high. Everyone followed. They came to a stop at the iron door.

"No rust after all these years," Needle said.

"It wasn't locked in my vision," Cael said.

Danilus reached out to the iron rung and pulled. It opened silently as a reddish light poured out to greet them.

Brynn shivered. A wide passage opened before them, just as Cael had described. Brynn immediately noticed the source of the red light and went to examine one of the glowing sigils.

"It's just a simple light sigil," she said, "But a little different than I'm used to."

"What the hells?" said Mallet. "Why is it red?"

"No idea," Brynn said. "But it looks like light sigils can be modified slightly to control color. Hmm. I did not know that."

"Maybe red is their color," Needle said. "Not very efficient light, though."

Danilus put out his torch, then he, Dheke and Mallet led the way along the wide hall as Brynn confirmed they were moving toward the orb. The thick air smelled sulfuric.

After another fifteen feet or so, they arrived at the y-intersection Cael had described to them. They could see the two steel doors, each about ten feet farther down from the fork. The one on the right was shut, the one on the left was barely ajar.

"The door to the left is the one with the big metal chair," Cael whispered. "To the right is where Sithik and Elija watched."

"The orb is on the other side of the door to the left," Brynn said in a quiet tone.

"Hmm," Cael said, worry evident in his voice. "That's not where he left it five thousand years ago. It was in the room to the right."

"Put those *Lorgnettes* back on, see where he is hiding," Brynn said.

Cael put on the spectacles.

Brynn watched as he stiffened, eyes wide and unblinking. He didn't move for a few minutes.

Cael blinked and came to awareness. He took off the *Lorgnettes*. "Elija moved the orb to the chamber on the left. He put it on the seat of the metal chair," Cael whispered. "He's hiding in the room to the right, waiting by the levers."

"That little bastard," Needle whispered. "He wants us to go into the room with the chair, and then he's going to pull the lever and turn us into zombies that look like Mallet."

Mallet glared at Needle.

"I have an idea..." Brynn whispered.

She pulled everyone back the way from which they'd come. She stopped about fifteen feet away from the y-intersection in a dim area between red sigils and hunkered down. She motioned for the others to join her. "Cael, can you push the door to the left open wider?"

"Why him?" Needle said with an indignant grin. "I think we've already established that I'm better at opening doors than Cael."

Brynn sucked air in between her teeth and rolled her eyes. "No! I mean push it open with *wizard powers!*"

Cael considered. "Telekinesis!" he said suddenly.

"Tele-ka-whats-its?" Danilus said in bewilderment.

Cael closed his eyes, and then nodded. "The *Arcanus Navitas* is abundant enough here. I can use telekinesis to open the door. It means using magic to push and move things without touching them."

"So why not just--," Needle started to say.

"And then I can use it to grab the orb!" Cael hissed triumphantly, cutting Needle off.

"Well done, boys," Brynn whispered. "Glad you're all caught up to me."

"But what happens once that door swings open and the orb starts to magically float away? Old pasty-face in there is going to pull the lever, and that will close the door."

"Not if I move it out of there fast enough," Cael said. "His mistake was leaving the door slightly open. I can reach past it to the orb. I can pull the orb out quickly, *then* open the door enough to get it out. I bet he can't react fast enough."

"And then what?" Needle asked. "Run away with it?"

"We fight him here," Mallet said, grinning. Danilus nodded.

"I have a better idea," Brynn said. "What if we hide back here... in the passage. I can draw a darkening sigil on the floor here. It's the opposite of light sigil and will create a dark, shadowy area we can crouch in."

"That's not gonna fool him," Needle said. "He'll see this big weird dark area and come to investigate."

"*Then* we jump out and kill him," Mallet hissed eagerly.

"Not if Cael moves the orb slowly," Brynn said. "I'm betting that with a chance to keep control of the orb, he'll opt to do that first over investigating some dark patch."

"Hells, he might not even notice the darkness in that situation," Cael whispered. "He won't see us and he'll head through the door to secure the orb."

"So when do we get to fight him?" Mallet asked.

"Do we really want to risk fighting him?" Brynn asked. "If we can lure him into that room--," Cael cut her off. "Somebody can rush in to the other room and pull the left lever and we can trap him in there!"

"Hmmm," frowned Danilus, "I reckon that's a risky plan. We ought not leave someone like him alive, trapped or not. Besides, there is Tajaa and my boat. He needs to pay for that."

Needle chuckled. "But who would ever come in here to let him out? He'd be trapped in there forever. I can't think of a worse punishment, can you?"

Danilus showed a pensive look, but said nothing.

"So..," Mallet said slowly. "You're saying we don't fight him?"

"Work your sigil, Brynn," Cael said with a sudden resolve that told Brynn he'd settled on her course of action. "Needle, once he comes out, you sneak past into that room. Once he goes in for the orb, pull the left lever down to trap him in there."

"And what about us?" Mallet asked.

"You and Danilus be ready if something goes wrong. Be ready to push him into the room if needs be. If you can't, then do what you must."

Mallet grinned and nodded as he spun the shaft of his glaive in his hands. Dheke seemed to understand and began wagging his tail furiously but made no sound. Danilus held him by the collar, sword drawn.

"I'll move and bob that orb very slowly," Cael said. "Just like getting a fish to take the worm. Okay... Brynn, are you ready?"

Brynn realized she had a problem; once again, nothing to draw the sigil with. She dug furiously through her satchel but there was no ink or chalk or anything she could use. She considered blood again, but a sigil as large as she needed now would require far too much. Then it came to her.

"Hand me your torch please, Danilus," she said. The red-headed ranger dutifully pulled the doused torch from his belt and handed it over to her. She worked several of the charred reeds loose from the stub. She tested one on the stone floor, making a distinct line in charcoal. "Perfect," she breathed.

Now she prepared to try something she had never tried before. She understood a sigil for light and it had occurred to her that just like darkness was the opposite of light, a light sigil must also have its opposite. If there was a sigil for darkness in her mother's book, she hadn't gotten that far yet. She was alone in uncharted territory, but something instinctively told her that such a sigil must exist. She sketched the sigil on the floor from sheer intuition, and to her utter delight, it sputtered with shadow. She was close. After a few more minutes of refinement, she had the section of the hallway doused in a deep penumbra. It wasn't complete darkness, but it would suffice. She saw the others as vague shapes.

"I don't like this," said Mallet, a quaver in his voice.

Brynn touched Cael on the arm. He took a deep breath then reached out his hand in the direction of the orb in concentration. Brynn had no idea how he was doing it, but the hair on the back of her neck rose. From their vantage cloaked in shadow, Brynn could still see clearly down the hall beyond the shadowy area in which they crouched. She watched as the metal door down the left hall slowly creaked open.

From her angle, Brynn could see partially into the room. She could see a part of the big metal chair Cael had described, but she could not see the orb yet. She presumed Cael was manipulating it telekinetically. Would Elija bite? She hoped Mallet and Danilus were ready if things got out of order.

"I got it," Cael whispered, and she finally saw the orb moving ever so slowly, floating through the air toward the door.

A loud crash came from the right hall. The right hand door flew open and Elija burst from the room. He raced to the confluence of the y-intersection and looked directly toward them. He paused for a long second; the fingers on his deformed hand extending and flexing, as if of their own volition.

Brynn held her breath. Could he see them?

His head swiveled down the other intersection to the room with the metal chair, then back toward them. He paused again for several tense seconds, staring down the hall in their direction. He began to stride straight toward them. Brynn could sense her brother and the ranger tense up.

Mallet and Danilus sprang forward. Dheke followed, barking furiously. Whatever Elija thought might be down the hall, it clearly wasn't the onslaught that now barreled toward him. Elija stumbled backwards to the intersection. Mallet thrust his glaive forward at Elija, wielding it like a lance, but Elija had got his bearings just in time and stepped aside down the left fork, toward the chair room, as the sharp edge passed inches from his shoulder. Elija's monstrous hand grabbed the haft just below the blade and Elija tried to wrench it from Mallet's grasp. The big boy was too strong. Mallet made an adrenaline-fueled charge that dragged Elija, still holding the haft, further down the hall. Brynn watched as the door to the chair room swung fully open just behind Elija. She turned to Cael, who seemed to struggle to maintain his concentration with the melee before them. Needle slinked along the right wall and down the right fork in a lithe motion. Dheke, hackles raised, growled fiercely as he slowly advanced on the Elija creature.

Elija let go of the glaive and took a swipe at the mastiff with his deformed hand. He connected with Dheke's snout, sending the dog tumbling with a yelp.

Mallet lurched forward and connected with the undead creature's shoulder, shoving Elija deep into the room.

Danilus grabbed the door and swung it shut. He and Mallet put their shoulders to the door just as it began to buck from Elija slamming into it from the other side. The little creature might have been strong but he was no match for Mallet and Danilus.

"Needle!" Cael screamed. "The lever!" Cael sprang from the shadows, and ran full tilt, turning down the right hand passage and into the lever room. Brynn followed.

The clang of the bolts locking into place rang out above the chaos.

Brynn entered the room and in her quick assessment, found

it much as Cael had described it. It was lit by the red sigils but she found it surprisingly bright. There was the huge window of thick, rough glass, through which a scene unfolded she did not expect to see. Dozens of black snakes slithered from a small opening in the right wall, moving quickly toward Elija. Just as Cael had described, each was undead and covered with yellow sigils. Elija struggled as he was already being dragged toward the metal chair by several of the powerful serpents.

"Did you get the orb?" Brynn asked breathlessly.

Cael shook his head. "They slammed the door shut too fast. It's still in there."

Cael turned to Needle as Mallet rushed into the room.

Both levers on the wall next to the big window were in the down position. Needle was struggling vainly to push the right-hand lever up. "I panicked," Needle cried. "I got confused on which lever was the right one, so I just pulled them both. This one won't go up again!"

"Where's Danilus?" Cael asked.

"Tending to Dheke," Mallet said breathlessly. "I think he's okay. Be here soon."

The scene on the other side of the glass commanded their attention. Even Needle gave up trying to work the lever and watched. The snakes dragged Elija into a sitting position in the chair. Brynn watched with a mixture of awe and fear as the snakes, with their glowing, ensigiled hides, did their work. The first large snake emerged and bit Elija on the face. Brynn had thought Cael was exaggerating the complexity of the augmentation sigil, but he was not. It was much more advanced than anything she could even comprehend. And the fact that a snake could be made to pass on a sigil through a bite was incomprehensible. The evil of the Cult of Yex was exceeded only by their command of sigilic magic. There was no point in her even trying to comprehend or decipher these sigils: they were far too sophisticated. Brynn watched in rapt fascination as the sigil spread across Elija's face.

The little man began to grow muscles to a degree that Brynn would have thought impossible had she not seen it with her own eyes. The Rothkin's arms and chest bulged as stretch marks appeared across his gray skin. Blades and spikes of bone emerged from his back, shoulders and elbows. His teeth elongated into fangs and his fingers sprouted wicked looking claws. His mutant hand swelled with muscle into a powerful crushing claw-like fist.

"I can't believe this place still works the same way after so much time had passed," Cael said.

"Don't look directly at the sigils," Brynn advised. "They'll make you ill."

The next large snake emerged and delivered the killing bite. Brynn flinched, then froze in terror.

Elija didn't die.

"Uh... he's not dead," Needle said.

"I don't think he can be killed," said Cael, looking worried. "He's already dead."

Brynn fought back a moment of panic. *Don't look worried, Cael. Please... don't look worried.*

Elija bucked and strained against the zombie snakes that held him fast to the chair. The muscled Rothkin creature and the snakes fought an undead tug-o-war, Elija straining to free himself and the snakes straining to keep him in his place.

The third snake emerged and bit into Elija's chest, ostensibly to raise him into undeath. But he was already in that state, and the bite had no noticeable effect.

Elija began fighting against the snakes with a renewed ferocity that deeply worried Brynn. The bolts holding the chair seemed to loosen as he fought, causing the iron throne to buck and pitch.

Would the snakes hold?

"I don't think those snakes were supposed to hold someone for this long," Cael said, as if in answer to her unspoken worry.

The last large snake emerged from the hole and rose up prepared to strike at Elija. In a final surge of effort, Elija broke his deformed arm free from the snakes holding him, tearing several of them in two as he did so. Sections of snake spine and scaly hide fell twitching to the floor. Elija's muscled mutant hand shot forward with blinding speed and grabbed the final large serpent by the throat just as it was beginning to strike. His gnarled hand squeezed the serpent, easily crushing it just below the head. The snake's eyes bulged and popped out of its skull, each hanging by a bundle of nerve and sinew. Black venom sprayed in two long streams from the tips of its fangs.

Elija looked directly at the window, fixing them with his reddish, hateful gaze. Brynn felt as if she were staring right into the Abyss itself. He hurled the spasming serpent at the window with immense force. The snake's body bounced and fell to the floor, coiling and twitching.

"Time to get out of here," Needle said, but continued staring at the scene.

Elija used his meaty, deformed hand to tear himself free of the remaining snakes that held him fast. Chunks of rent zombie snake flew in every direction. In seconds, he had freed himself completely.

Elija howled deliriously.

He bent over behind the metal chair and picked something up. He stepped forward toward the window, holding the orb delicately in his overgrown hand as he flashed a wicked grin at them. In a single rapid motion, he crushed it in his monstrous, muscled fist. Shards of the black ball fell to the floor.

"This went well," Needle said.

Elija shifted into a rage and slammed at the window with his deformed spider-hand. Brynn felt the loud reverberation in her bones as it echoed through the room.

Elija moved back toward the iron chair and grabbed hold of it, wrenching it back and forth.

Needle scampered to the other side of the room and grabbed something that lay on the floor, thrusting it at Cael. It was a serpent scepter, identical to the cobra-headed one Cael had described. "Control him!" he begged.

Elija had almost worked the metal chair free from its moorings.

"It won't work!" Cael cried. "Elija didn't get the control sigil!"

"Oh hells," Brynn breathed.

A large metal chair was flying through the air toward the thick window separating them from the furious creature. It impacted the thick crystal with an incredible *clang*. A single crack appeared at the point of impact, and slowly grew to several feet long.

Elija stepped forward to retrieve the chair for another go.

Cael grabbed Brynn's arm and they fled. Mallet and Needle followed.

They rounded the y-intersection where Danilus and a whimpering Dheke joined their flight.

Another booming *clang* rang out behind them as they ran.

CHAPTER FIFTEEN
Soup

"My mother always said soup is the best medicine."

> - Favorite saying of Queen Doronela, Tharchelon's grandmother

12th Day of Summer - 9:00 AM – Camp of the Exiles – 3 Days Until the Full Moon

Something was being dribbled into Tharchelon's mouth. Tickling rivulets streamed down his chin and neck. The flavor was incredible. It reminded him immediately of his old grandmother's venison soup. He swallowed and more was dribbled into his mouth.

"There there, dear. We thought we might have lost you," said a motherly, disembodied voice. Where was he? Tharchelon opened his eyes slowly. The only illumination was a fire flickering just outside the opening of what looked like a lean-to of tree branches and skins. He was lying on a bed of pine boughs under the low ceiling. An old Rothkin woman he didn't recognize ladled soup at him. He suddenly realized he was famished and slurped it hungrily. He tried to prop himself up, but found that he was too weak.

"Where am I?" he asked in a shaky whisper, surprised by how frail and raspy his own voice sounded.

"Finish up some more soup, dear, and I'll fetch you some Bystle Mead to strengthen you up."

"Where am I?" he repeated more loudly this time.

"You are with friends now, dear... at the camp of the exiles.

That damnable traitor Nelcherath started rounding up anyone he suspected of being loyal to you, and kicked us out. Someone should teach him some manners. Hundreds of us there are now, and still more arrive every day. His mother should be ashamed."

"But where?" he asked again, through a spoonful of broth.

"We found you curled up, shivering and babbling under a tree. Almost dead you were. You've been asleep, awful fitful, ever since we got you here about a week ago. Old Thocka's been taking care of you ever since. Venison soup, Bystle Mead and dog's milk has brought you back from death's door, my King."

"Where?" he croaked again.

"I'm not good at judging distances, but I'd say we made our camp here about half a day's walk west of the vale. There's a stream here, and I suppose that this was the best place. I expect ol' Rathenel will want to talk to you, now that you're awake."

Before he could respond, she got up from her knees and shuffled out into the starlit night. Tharchelon could see the moon rising through the trees. It would be full in a few days.

Rathenel. He was still loyal! Many of his people were.

Things were suddenly looking up. Another thought occurred to him... nothing itched.

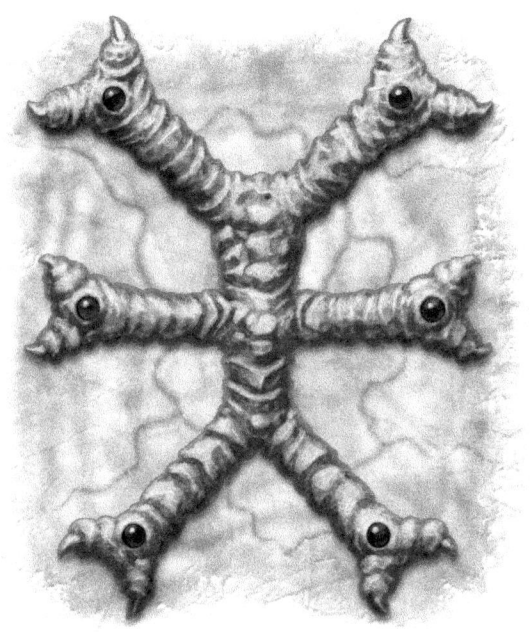

The story continues in:

BYSTLE VALE
Cult of Yex Saga: Part III

Acknowledgements

We have to thank everyone who read and commented on the novel, including: Randal Cox, Jennifer Stanchfield, Asher Smith, Riley Smith, Jessica Wilcox, Brittany Witt, Parker Webb, Matt Mecham, Raegan Garlitz, Mary Garlitz, Carol Archer, Gideon Larsen, Dave Reed, Sheriece Farr, Shane Farr, Megan Bangerter, Tyler Barnes, Kaitlin Jones, and Peter Jones.

A special thanks to Matt Mecham for going above and beyond as a beta reader.

Thanks to Jeremy McHugh for the art and Jennifer Leigh for the copy editing.

Authors' Note

So... Book Two! Glad you are coming along for the journey. We have quite an experience for you that we have discovered. It's only going to get better and better the deeper we go.

Prophecies of Old does not stand on its own. It was originally intended as the middle part of a much larger book entitled: *Bystle Vale.* Due to length considerations, the longer work was divided into three pieces. This then, *Prophecies of Old*, is the second movement of that much longer work. The third movement, closing the original arc, will be published shortly following this installment.

As I write this we are deep into working on the next arc, which will be two or three more books. In many ways, Cael, Brynn, Needle and Mallet's adventures are just beginning. Here's hoping you enjoy the ride.

As always, we love to hear from our readers.

ABOUT THE AUTHORS

Jason F. Smith

Jason F. Smith lives in the beautiful mountains of Utah with his wife, three children, and menagerie of furry family members. Jason finds a great deal of pleasure as well as a host of ideas on his daily walks through the winding mountain paths, and is an avid lover of the magical art that we call "life".

C. Parker Garlitz

Parker is a 14th Level Nerd / 9th Level Small Business Owner, who lives in the beautiful mountains of Utah with his amazing family. Parker's fondest wish is to not be multi-classed and focus on adding more levels exclusively to Nerd. If you liked what you have read, you can help him achieve that goal. Tell your friends about the Cult of Yex.

www.ingramcontent.com/pod-product-compliance
Lightning Source LLC
Chambersburg PA
CBHW060429180626
46817CB00007B/2731